THE

ANTARCTICA

INCIDENT

A James Acton Thriller

Also by J. Robert Kennedy

THE

ANTARCTICA

INCIDENT

A James Acton Thriller

J. ROBERT KENNEDY

ISBN: 9781990418419

First Edition

For the real Dr. Corkery, who has helped keep me alive all these years. Despite my best efforts.

THE
ANTARCTICA
INCIDENT

A James Acton Thriller

"Men Wanted: For hazardous journey. Small wages, bitter cold, long months of complete darkness, constant danger, safe return doubtful. Honour and recognition in case of success."

Advertisement placed for the 1914 Imperial Trans-Antarctic Expedition by Sir Ernest Shackleton

"A house divided against itself cannot stand."

Ancient Chinese Proverb

PREFACE

In traditional Chinese culture, family lineage is extremely important. Before the Communist dictatorship discouraged the practice, families kept track of their lineage in the *zupu*, the genealogy book. Many of these books go back thousands of years, recording every male member of the family, their male children, and significant accomplishments of the family. Some even include rules the family must abide by, and naming conventions for future generations.

Women born into the family, no matter how accomplished, were rarely recorded, and when they were, it was merely to record their existence rather than their deeds.

On extremely rare occasions, the wife of a male member of the family would be honored with an entry if, after his death, she continued his legacy with distinction.

This tradition held true for millennia.

And for one woman, born in 1775, her name known throughout Qing China and cursed by Western traders in the region, this was simply not acceptable.

She was determined to be remembered.

Tradition be damned.

Antarctica

Present Day

Archaeology Professor Laura Palmer peered into the billowing snow of the growing storm, pissed at what she was witnessing—people out of their shelters against orders. "Who the hell would be out in this? They were all given specific instructions to stay inside."

Her husband, Archaeology Professor James Acton, shook his head. "Those aren't our people. They're not near any of the safety wires, and they're out beyond the perimeter."

"Could they be from McMurdo? Maybe checking in on us?"

"Perhaps."

"Well, who else could it be?"

James shrugged. "No idea."

Her pulse pounded with a thought. "Could the Chinese be back?"

"That's a definite possibility. Come in during a storm when nobody can respond? I could see them doing that."

3

This was the type of situation she hadn't prepared for. She was in charge of the expedition on the frozen continent, but invading Chinese Special Forces were never part of the deal. For the first time since she had been here, she was uncertain. "What should we do?"

"Look!"

She spotted one of the McMurdo staff, Carl Ericksen, emerging from their shelter, striding toward the new arrivals. He waved at them, and it was clear he assumed they were a rescue team from McMurdo. He was much closer and had a better view. "We should go join him."

James gripped her arm tighter. "No, something's wrong here. There's no way McMurdo would've sent a rescue party that could have arrived here already. Our comms haven't been down that long. It has to be the Chinese."

One of the new arrivals, barely visible in the snow, suddenly moved. Muzzle flashes were followed by the report of gunfire, and she gasped as Ericksen cried out before collapsing to the ground.

James dragged her toward the Chinese shelter still attached to the safety line as more gunfire erupted. He disconnected them both from the line and she rushed for the door.

"No! We can't trust them!"

She turned. "Then where do we go?"

"They're not here to take prisoners. We have to get the hell out of here." He grabbed an axe mounted to the outside of the structure then took her hand. "Let's go!"

"But what about my team?"

"They're already dead if we can't get help."

She was in a daze and she let him lead her away from the gunfire erupting behind them, her heart breaking at the screams of her team as an unimaginable slaughter began.

All because of a ship found in the ice.

A ship lost for over two hundred years.

Lantau Island

Guangdong, Qing China

January 16, 1810

She was fed up. Fed up with her brother, fed up with her family, fed up with this life. It wasn't supposed to be this way, but she was a victim of her own success. She was a woman in a man's world, and she had never let that stop her. Years ago, she had been given a small piece of that world for herself, something almost unheard of, and that small piece had turned into an empire run by her, a woman surrounded by the petty jealousies and prejudices of men. She kept them at bay by being far more ruthless than any man would need to be. She tolerated no insolence, no disrespect, and absolutely no betrayal. She had slit more throats or had more throats slit than she could count.

But now the insolence, the disrespect, and the betrayal came from family.

Her own brother.

"You would deny me this honor?"

Her brother Bao glared at her. "You would disrespect the two-thousand-year tradition of our family?" He laid his palm atop the zupu, the meticulously kept genealogy maintained by most Chinese families of prominence, chronicling their clan's history. In their case, for almost one hundred generations the names of all males born into the family were recorded. But women like her were never listed unless they were a widow of distinction.

She had never married, and according to tradition, she deserved no mention in the zupu, and as a result, was to be forgotten by time. Yet she was the most prominent member of her family ever to have been born. She'd accomplished more than any man that had preceded her. She was Zheng Yi Sao, the most successful man or woman in her family's history. Her empire now consisted of over 400 vessels and she commanded 50,000 men. Her wealth was unfathomable to anybody except the emperor, her power so great, he had aligned himself with her, giving her free reign over the sea to attack any vessel not aligned with the empire.

Zheng Yi Sao was a name that brought terror into the hearts of even the strongest men, and it should be remembered not only by history, but in her family's zupu. "I deserve to be remembered."

"And you will be. No one will ever forget your name. You're too powerful. Your legacy will live on forever."

"My legacy be damned. I want my family to remember me. Over two-thousand years of our history are recorded in that genealogy. In two-thousand years, history will have forgotten who I am and what I've accomplished, but if I'm recorded in the zupu, then history will never forget. My family will never forget."

7

Her brother shrugged, a gesture that always made her blood boil, as it meant he was dismissing her words. "I'm sorry you feel that way, but tradition is tradition. You have no place in the record."

"Traditions are made to be broken. There was a time when no women were recorded, but then things changed and the first was. And now it is common practice for women of distinction to be recorded if their late husband was prominent and she carried on bringing honor to his name. Now I say the tradition has to evolve again. Women like me, who've done more than any man has before her, need to be recognized. We deserve to be remembered and we must be remembered. What I've accomplished for this family has done more for our name than any man ever recorded in the zupu. You know that, yet you who've been nothing but a thorn in my side since the day you were born will have an entry whereas I will not." She glared at him. "I will be remembered no matter what you say."

Bao picked up the massive tome recording millennia of the family lineage and held it against his chest protectively. "Sister, not even the emperor himself could force me to defile this sacred text with your name."

Zheng reached for her sword, the blade sliding from its sheath, when she stopped herself. There was still time. She shoved her sword back in its scabbard. "If you value your life, you'll leave my presence now. But mark my words, my name will be recorded in our family's history. This I swear to you."

West of McMurdo Station

Antarctica

Present Day, Three Weeks Earlier

Guillermo Ortega shivered. He couldn't help himself. It was warm enough inside the snowcat, and he was dressed for the conditions, but the ice outside that went on as far as the eye could see, and the fresh snow from last night's storm still whipped up by the wind restricting their visibility, caused his brain to insist he was cold. When he had arrived at McMurdo Station three weeks ago and complained about it, the more seasoned residents had assured him it would pass in time. It hadn't so far, and he wondered just how much time they had meant.

After his first week of constant shivering, he had been invited to join the 300 Club when paying a visit to Amundsen-Scott South Pole Station.

"What the hell is that?"

The woman who had extended the invitation, Dana McAlister, had grinned. "It's where you take all your clothes off, sit in a two-hundred degree sauna, then you run outside when it's minus-one-hundred

9

degrees, touch the south pole, then run back inside. The temperature differential between inside and outside is over three-hundred degrees. You'll never feel so cold again in your life. It just might cure your shivers."

He eyed the gorgeous woman. "Did you say you take all your clothes off?"

Her grin spread. "Yes."

"And you're going to do this with me."

She grinned even more. "Yes."

It had been a crazy night. They had got sauced up at Club 90 South, then stripped out of their clothes, spent ten minutes in an unbelievably hot sauna, then rushed outdoors, touched the ceremonial south pole, then headed back inside.

And she was right.

He had never been colder in his life, but the two of them had warmed each other up in her bunk, and for the first time since he had arrived, he was warm. He had been concerned the next morning that he was just fresh meat on the menu and that perhaps she did this with a lot of the new arrivals, but it had been weeks now and they spent every off-duty moment together. He was falling in love with this girl, something he never would have expected in the icy hell of Antarctica after years of romantic failure in Detroit.

He rubbed his hands together. "Man, I'm cold."

McAlister reached over and squeezed his thigh. "I know one way we can warm you up."

He gave her a look. "We're on duty."

She shrugged. "Nobody would know."

He eyed her as she shifted closer to him. "Are you serious?"

She said nothing as she unzipped her jacket.

"Holy shit, are we doing this?"

She nodded.

Then junior took over. He hurriedly stripped out of his clothes, his excitement growing as she revealed the naked body that had kept him warm on so many cold nights. Within moments, everything surrounding them was forgotten. The howling winds, the crackling ice, the chattering teeth, all that consumed his thoughts now was this woman, this insatiable woman. She straddled him and he groaned. He reached up and grabbed her hair, pulling her face closer to his. As she ground into him, a loud cracking sound like a steel cable snapping with a twang startled him, and the entire snowcat shifted slightly.

"What was that?" he asked.

"It was nothing," she gasped. "Don't stop."

He returned his attention to the bundle of lust in his lap and had almost forgotten the shocking sound when it was repeated. But he didn't care. She began to shake in ecstasy as he did the same, though something else was happening, and by the time they settled down it was too late. The entire snowcat was shuddering violently.

And sliding.

The ice they were making love upon was giving way. He held her tight as the vehicle dropped, the sensation of weightlessness momentarily flipping his stomach, and all he could think about was that if they ever found their bodies, the paperwork would make interesting reading.

11

They slammed to an abrupt halt. They sat there, saying nothing, neither of them daring to move lest they fall even farther. When they hadn't slipped any deeper after several moments, he finally let himself breathe and she stared down at him from their twisted angle and grinned.

"Did the earth move for you too?"

He groaned. "You're terrible."

"That's why you love me."

He stared in her eyes and smiled. "You're right, I do love you."

She dropped a kiss on him that had things firing up again when he pushed her away.

"We're naked and trapped in a hole in the ice. I think we better call for help."

She pouted for a moment then climbed off him, returning to her seat. Clothes were tossed back and forth before they were finally once again respectable. He flicked the switches activating the interior lights then gasped at what he saw outside the window.

"What the hell is that?"

Lantau Island

Guangdong, Qing China

January 17, 1810

Zheng Yi Sao groaned as she leaned back in her chair and closed her burning eyes. She preferred to be at sea. She had grown up on the water and it was where she felt most comfortable. Most of her youth had been spent on a junk, but when her father passed, she inherited the small family business and her new empire rapidly grew, and so did her responsibilities on land.

Paperwork.

She was a bureaucrat. She had become one of those she used to spit at with contempt, yet she had no choice. If she were a man, she could delegate much of what she did to other family members or trusted advisors. But as a woman, she had to assume every man surrounding her was consumed with jealousy, hoping she would fail in some way, searching for a way to somehow steal from her.

13

And that included her brother Bao, the most treacherous of them all. She was still steamed from yesterday's argument, and on several occasions through the evening she had almost issued a kill order for her brother. But she had stopped herself. She didn't want to be remembered for murdering the eldest son of her father. She wanted to be remembered for what she had accomplished in life. Her father had been special, had loved her unconditionally, and had given her every opportunity within the family to do what she wanted.

And that was to be at his side, learning everything she could, even if it meant she wasn't the little girl or the young woman her mother wanted. When he had been killed by rivals, she had sobbed for seven days and seven nights before the sorrow turned into rage and she declared war on those who had brought her so much pain.

It was when she had become so ruthless.

She sighed and turned her chair, facing the wall behind her where a portrait of her father hung. So handsome, so proud, and so respected. Respect. That's what she wanted. She had it in a fashion, though respect motivated by fear wasn't what she desired. She wanted respect for what she had accomplished, for what she had built, for how well she ran her empire—better than any man born not only to her family, but any in the empire.

The hundreds of ships, the tens of thousands of men, the goods and currency that flowed through her hands, that accomplishment deserved to be remembered. She closed her eyes again. There was nobody to leave it to except an ungrateful family. There was a time in her life when she did want to marry, but now, even should she desire it, any man she might be attracted to would be terrified of her. And a husband who was a coward was no husband at all.

She inhaled deeply through her nose.

If only I had a son.

She chastised herself for the thought. A daughter would be equally welcome. Someone she could raise and mold to be just like her, as strong, as tough, as unrelenting. Why wish for a male heir when a female one could do just as well, if not better?

There was a rapid knock at her door and she growled. "I said I was not to be disturbed."

"But it's urgent, mistress." It was Yingshi, her aide, a eunuch if there ever was one, though she did trust him—mostly because he was a fool who wasn't intelligent enough to attempt to steal from her.

"Come in!" The door opened as she turned her chair to face him. "What is it that has you disobeying my orders?"

"It's your brother, mistress."

"Please tell me he was hit by a runaway ox cart."

This appeared to rattle him and he stood frozen, as if searching for a suitable response. She frowned and flicked a wrist at him to get on with it.

"I'm sorry, mistress. Your brother, he's taken a ship and gone to sea."

Her eyes narrowed. "He's not due to leave for three days. Where is he going?"

"I don't know, mistress, however, he took one of the recently captured East India Company ships. The dock hand who reported it to me said it was being well provisioned as if for a long journey."

She growled as she sprung from her chair. "Call up my personal guard and send word. I want ten ships provisioned and ready to sail as soon as possible, and get one underway immediately to follow him. We'll at least need a bearing."

"Yes, mistress, at once." Yingshi receded backward through the doors then closed them as she headed into her chambers in the back, quickly donning the clothes she wore when at sea, where she was Zheng Yi Sao.

The greatest pirate the world had ever known.

Milton Residence

St. Paul, Maryland

Present Day

"I only see one way out of it. Somebody has to put a bullet in his head."

Professor James Acton's eyebrows shot up as all attention was focused on his best friend's wife, Sandra Milton. "So, to hell with the negotiation table?"

She gave a curt nod. "Of course. That man can't be trusted. The only way we can have peace is if he's dead."

Her husband Gregory Milton, the dean of Acton's university and best friend since their old college days, agreed. "He definitely has to die, though a bullet to the head is too good for him."

Acton's wife, Professor Laura Palmer, took a sip of her chardonnay. "While I agree he needs to die, it has to be one of his own people that does it. Otherwise, it could widen the conflict. I think the Ukrainians have shown remarkable restraint. How difficult would it be for them to

17

actually insert a team into Moscow and wreak havoc? Can you imagine what the Russian response would be if they did? They might nuke Kiev."

"I think it's Kyiv," said Acton.

Laura shrugged. "I don't know. You might be right, but my entire life it has been Kiev."

"Russian propaganda," said Milton in his best Russian accent.

Acton laughed. "Anybody who claims our mainstream media is fake news needs to take a look at countries like Russia. If you think things are bad here, it's nothing compared to what they are there."

Sandra sighed. "It's sad to see what's becoming of our country. They need to ban twenty-four-hour news channels and social media."

Milton chuckled. "Good luck with that. But you're right. There isn't twenty-four hours of news in the day, so they fill it with opinion disguised as news. And social media is just a squawk box for mental midgets to get out there with their idiotic theories." He waved a hand. "But enough of this. I want to talk about your trip."

Acton and Laura exchanged grins and he wrapped an arm around her shoulders. "I've been all over the world, but I don't think I've ever been more excited. It's a dream come true. How many people can actually say they've been there, let alone worked there?"

Sandra finished her glass of wine and her husband leaned over, refilling it then topping up Laura's. "Are you going to be the first archaeologists to ever work there?"

Laura shook her head. "No, there have been teams that have looked at old whaling sites and whatnot. And then of course they just found Shackleton's ship, so there's a team working on that."

Sandra shivered. "Antarctica. I would love to see it someday."

Milton grunted. "Just drive north far enough and it looks pretty much the same."

She giggled. "It might look the same, but it's not the same. The Eiffel Tower at the Paris Casino in Vegas might look like the one in Paris, but it's not the same thing."

Milton smirked. "You're right. They're both tourist traps, but only one of them has snooty Frenchmen looking down on the American tourists."

Sandra gave him a playful slap. "So, what time is your flight?"

"Nine tomorrow morning."

"How long does it take to fly to Antarctica?"

"Well, there are no direct flights, obviously, and we're coming in with a lot of gear, so we're heading to New Zealand first, and then a transport into McMurdo. It's going to be long, uncomfortable, and noisy."

Acton grunted. "That'll be nothing compared to the conditions on the ice. McMurdo has already set up portable buildings with heaters and generators, so we'll have a place to shelter and warm up, but nothing's going to help us when we're working."

"Have they begun any work?" asked Milton.

Acton shook his head. "No, they're leaving it to the National Science Foundation team led by my much better half."

Laura took his hand and gave it a squeeze. "Because of the nature of things in Antarctica, this expedition involves a lot of diplomacy. It was agreed that the NSF would head up the expedition, but the members of the team itself would be international. I obviously represent British interests and James the American interests, but there will be New Zealand, Australian, Chilean, and various others."

"It should be fun," said Acton. "As long as I don't freeze the boys off."

Laura patted his inner thigh. "Don't you worry about the boys, they'll make it. It's their friend that you have to worry about."

Sandra snorted. "That's one advantage to being a woman. We keep the plumbing on the inside."

Milton gave her a look. "Just wait until you have to pee."

Acton grinned. "One point for the men."

Laura shook her head. "Not so fast, Mister. When I'm on the ice, I'm packing Depends."

Acton's eyebrow shot up. "That's not a bad idea. Until it freezes."

Sandra's eyes narrowed. "That's a good point." She took a sip of her wine. "The more I hear you guys talk, the less I think I want to visit there."

Acton chuckled. "Yeah, it'll be tough, but it'll be nice to go someplace for a change where someone isn't trying to kill us."

Milton grunted. "Don't be so sure about that. I'm sure you'll figure out some way to get yourself in trouble."

Antarctica Quest

En route to Antarctica

Dr. Doug Corkery stared out the porthole of his quarters on the Chilean flagged Antarctica Quest, a boutique tourist vessel for the well-heeled. If you had asked him a month ago where he thought he would be today, never in a million years would he have said en route to Antarctica. He was a physician who had gained a bit of fame during the viral outbreak that originated in New Orleans, the city he had called home for much of his life.

But things had calmed down now, the pandemic that had threatened to wipe out half the planet pretty much forgotten, including his part in it. Like many in his city, it had changed his life. He had left the hospital and worked for the CDC for several years dealing with the aftermath and introducing new protocols that could prevent some of the idiocy that had made things worse.

But he had tired of it. He didn't want to spend his years behind a desk reading and writing reports. He wanted to be treating patients, helping people discover what was wrong with them, then either cure them or make their lives bearable. And when a friend had approached him about taking over his duties as ship's doctor on a trip to Antarctica, he had jumped at the opportunity provided by his friend's unfortunate appendicitis attack. It was a dream of his to visit all seven continents, and thanks to his work at the CDC, he had already ticked off six of them. Tomorrow, number seven would be checked off the bucket list.

It brought a smile to his face, almost enough to make him forget the chill. He checked himself in the mirror then headed for the infirmary. They had taken aboard their passengers at Tierra Del Fuego, the southernmost port in South America, and he was still familiarizing himself with the medical records of his passengers. Too many of them shouldn't be here at the bottom of the world where the nearest real medical facility was thousands of miles away. Many were senior citizens in the winter of their life looking to make headway on their own bucket list, most of them at least moderately wealthy—trips like these didn't come cheap.

If something truly egregious happened to any of them, there'd be little he could do beyond trying to keep them alive long enough to get them on a plane at McMurdo where they would quite likely die before they reached civilization. He was here to deal with sea sickness, food poisoning, and bumps and scrapes. Heart attacks, strokes, broken hips, and any number of things that afflicted the elderly and infirm were beyond his capabilities to deal with here. He had been assured that anything serious was rare, and that everyone on board had signed a medical waiver, indemnifying him of any responsibility should something go wrong. He wasn't overly concerned. That's what malpractice insurance was for—it wasn't there for when you screwed up, it was there for when you were accused of screwing up.

He unlocked the infirmary and stepped inside, closing the door behind him, but leaving it unlocked. He ran his eye over everything once again, continuing to familiarize himself with where everything was. In an emergency, seconds were precious and they couldn't be wasted yanking open drawers in an attempt to find a critical piece of equipment.

He sat at his desk and hauled out the stack of files from the bottom drawer. Yes, he had a computer with access to the Internet, but it was spotty at best, and in an emergency, power might be out, so he had insisted on paper copies of all records.

There was a rap on the door. "Come in."

It opened and the ship's nurse, Mercedes, stepped inside with a smile. "Good morning, Doctor. I'm sorry I'm late."

He glanced at the clock on the wall. "You're right on time. I'm just early. Did you sleep well?"

She nodded. "Like a baby. You?"

He groaned as he rolled his eyes. "Still trying to get my sea legs."

"We have the patches," she suggested, heading for one of the drawers in the supply cabinet.

He waved her off. "No, I've got to get a handle on this without medication. I'm a little better today than yesterday. I'm sure I'll be fine by the time we get there." He tapped the files. "Have you had a chance to look at these?"

She nodded.

"What do you think?"

She shrugged. "Not as bad as we normally have here."

His eyebrow shot up. "Oh?"

She giggled. "I forgot, this is your first time. This is my seventh. Normally, almost everyone has something wrong with them that should preclude them from coming here. This time, at least we have eight young healthy passengers that shouldn't cause us any medical problems."

"Is that unusual?"

"It is for this ship. Normally, they have their own charters, one-hundred percent Chinese, including Chinese staff and crew. This is actually a Russian charter, though maybe they've hired their own tour guides."

"Have you met any of our Chinese guests? Do they speak English?"

"I saw them sitting together in the galley speaking Chinese, but it's been my experience that most who have the money to do something like this speak English quite well."

"Well, if at least one of them speaks English, they can act as translator." Corkery leaned back and folded his arms. "So, how did you end up here?"

She giggled. "Complete accident. I was a personal care worker to a wealthy Hong Kong businessman, and he wanted to come to Antarctica. So, of course, because of his medical condition, he brought me with him. He had a medical emergency and the ship's doctor was impressed with how I handled it, and apparently wasn't impressed with his current nurse, so offered me a job."

"And what did your elderly employer say about that?"

"Not much. He died."

Corkery's eyebrows shot up. "Yet the ship's doctor was still impressed?"

She laughed. "There was no saving him. He should never have come here. The trip was just too hard on him, but some people are stubborn and don't listen to medical advice."

Corkery grunted. "Tell me about it. Have you ever lost a patient on board?"

She shook her head. "My former employer was the only one, though there have been some medical emergencies that we've had to send out by airplane who later died. The trip to Antarctica is for the young. Unfortunately, most of them can't afford it, but every berth is always full, and these trips go non-stop. There'd be more if there weren't international agreements in place to limit the numbers." She regarded him. "May I ask you a question?"

"Of course."

"How did *you* end up here?"

"Completely by accident, I assure you. A buddy of mine was supposed to be the doctor for this cruise but he had appendicitis, so asked if I wanted to take his place. I figured why not? I'm still young enough and healthy enough. And I've always wanted to see Antarctica." He shrugged. "A few phone calls and some paperwork and it was done. I'm just hoping I get a chance to play tourist."

She grimaced. "I hope that's not why you're here, because after what happened last time, I don't think the captain will let you off the ship."

"Why? What happened?"

She snickered. "Let's just say it involves a sea lion, a tourist's ass, and a doctor who couldn't be found because he was sightseeing."

Corkery chuckled. "A sea lion biting a man's ass. That's something I don't think I ever saw in the ER. This could be fun."

South China Sea

January 18, 1810

Zheng Yi Sao stood at the prow of the fastest ship in the fleet. They had already overtaken the vessel sent out after her brother, and its captain had confirmed the bearing of her brother's ship. It was heading due south, an unusual choice, though perhaps not. East, there was nothing but the vast Pacific, too far for him to travel. West was the interior, north and southwest the coastline where she had hundreds of vessels controlling the waters. But due south? She had no ships there because there was nothing there of value. Adjust his heading and he could land in Australia. Go far enough south and the waters would grow cold then turn to ice.

"He has to be hoping to land on one of the islands and hide out there. But to what end?" asked Yingshi. "Why is he doing this?"

She knew why, though it was a question she wasn't certain she wanted to answer. As soon as she had heard of what he had done, she had checked and confirmed that the zupu was gone, taken from its sacred

27

place of honor. Bao was clearly determined that her name should never appear in it, but was also fully aware of just who she was and how, when she was determined to have something, she always got it. He would know she would kill him to accomplish her goals.

Her name would be recorded if it was the last thing she ever did.

"He's stolen something from me," she finally replied. "Something important that we must get back at all costs. The family's honor depends on it."

"What has he stolen, mistress?"

"If I thought it was your business, I would tell you."

Yingshi bowed his head, staring at the deck. "I'm sorry for prying, mistress, it won't happen again."

"See that it doesn't." She peered at the horizon but still saw nothing. To starboard and port her fleet was spread out, each within sight of the next ship in the hopes they would spot her traitorous brother. A signal would be sent and they would all converge, and then the full sails of her vessel would be unleashed on the wind and they would quickly overtake her brother, leaving the others behind.

Her fear was how long this would take. It could be days, weeks, or perhaps months. She had already sent the scout vessel back with orders that ten ships with provisions should be sent every day for a week to catch up with the fleet. This could prove to be a massive undertaking, but it was nothing to her. She had hundreds of ships at her disposal and supply runs didn't need to be swift. They merely needed to be predictable.

They would catch him eventually. It was only a matter of time.

She shivered and glanced down at her outfit, form-fitting, and revealing as much skin as any man. In battle, she had found it proved distracting to her opponents unaccustomed to seeing a woman in such clothing, a moment's hesitation, a leering look, was enough for her to jab a dagger between someone's ribs, piercing his lusting heart.

But here she was, chasing her brother, possibly traveling to chilly climes.

Perhaps more appropriate attire would be needed.

"Mistress, we have a signal, port side."

She looked up to see the crewmember manning the crow's nest pointing. She turned but saw nothing. She rushed forward and jumped on the mast, scaling it rapidly to get a vantage point of her own. She peered to port, shielding her eyes with her hand and smiled at the bright flame on the horizon signaling they had spotted her brother's vessel. She jumped down to the deck.

"Signal the fleet! It's time for my brother to pay for his treachery!"

Phoenix Airfield, Antarctica

Present Day

Acton stepped off the C-17 Globemaster III transport aircraft and took Laura's hand as they headed for the strangest looking bus he had ever seen, "Ivan the Terra Bus" emblazoned on its side. Laura was the last to board as the leader of the expedition, and once they were loaded, the beast of a machine began its slow lumber toward the largest settlement on the frozen continent of Antarctica.

McMurdo Station.

He was already chilled to the bone, the C-17 that had brought them in not known for its insulation. The flight crew had made a joke of it, telling everyone on board that if they couldn't take this cold, they were doomed when they arrived. Acton didn't mind the cold so much, having experienced many a frigid winter during his lifetime. Laura, on the other hand, appeared to be in a perpetual state of shivering. London winters weren't known for being very cold, and her choice of dig sites mostly in

Northern Africa and the Middle East had not acclimated her for this frigid clime.

But the excitement was keeping everyone warm for now, and the length of the trip to McMurdo went unnoticed, the sights making time fly. They finally reached their destination and everyone rushed through the doors of the National Science Foundation Chalet, all sighing in relief at the toasty warmth. An American Air Force captain stood in the center of the room with a smile as he beckoned them all to move forward so everyone could get through the door.

"Hello, everybody. I'm Captain Blake Stanley. Welcome to McMurdo Station, Antarctica. If you ever made any promises in your life that would only take place if hell froze over, well, this is it, it's frozen over. Be prepared for people to start collecting."

Some chuckles rippled through the room though unfortunately for Captain Stanley, these were mostly scientists from around the world, too many of whom had no idea what he was talking about.

"Now, we have quite a few rules here, all of which were included in your orientation package, but I just want to go over a few that bear repeating. First, never go outside alone. Always go with a second person. And if visibility is at all reduced, always attach yourself to the lines. The building you're going to might only be a hundred feet away and visible, but if the wind picks up, you won't see two feet in front of your face, but that line will stay attached and you can either head back or continue forward." Stanley turned his focus to Laura. "Professor Palmer, this is your expedition. Do you have anything to say?"

Laura smiled and joined the captain, turning to face the others as Acton beamed with pride. "Hi, everyone. We've met individually on the plane, of course, but now that our feet are actually on the ground"—she rubbed her arms—"and the chill is actually in our bones, I'd just like to take this opportunity to say how honored I am to be leading this expedition to examine what has been found in the ice just south of here. The conditions will make this harsh, and for those of you who've done digs in the desert, many of the challenges will be similar. This is a frozen desert, resupply isn't guaranteed, the weather could prove uncooperative, and the cold will kill you as quickly as the heat of the Sahara. Everybody buddies up, nobody goes out alone, and every checklist is checked twice. We can't risk getting out there then discovering we don't have a critical piece of equipment."

She gestured at Stanley. "Our hosts here have already set up quarters for us at the site. They're rudimentary but will keep us out of the wind and keep off some of the chill. I've already drawn up a plan that you've all reviewed and have had a chance to comment on. I expect it to be adhered to, however, I recognize that circumstances can necessitate changes. You will find I'm quite flexible before the fact, not after. If you discover something that requires a change in what I've already approved, come see me and we'll discuss it, and most likely I'll approve the change. Do it afterward, hoping the old adage that it's better to beg for forgiveness than ask for permission, and I promised the powers that be not only here at McMurdo, but at the NSF and your respective institutions, that you will be cut and immediately sent home. It's far too dangerous here. If you get hurt, you could die because of where we are."

She clasped her hands in front of her, shaking them with a smile. "I think this is going to be one of the most exciting experiences of our careers, and if we follow the rules and stay safe, we'll be writing papers about this for years to come and telling our children and grandchildren what we did here for the rest of our lives."

She bowed her head slightly and Acton clapped heartily, the others joining in. Laura smiled at them then shook the captain's hand as the tour of the small station housing barely 1200 people began.

A young man with a head of fiery red hair strode up to Laura, his hand extended. "Professor Palmer, an inspiring speech."

She shook the man's hand. "Thank you. Dr. Llywelyn Evans, isn't it?"

His hand darted to his chest in mock humility. Acton already didn't like him. "You know who I am? I'm flattered."

She smiled. "I make it a point to know everybody on my team."

Ouch.

"You wound me, Professor. But I'd be willing to forgive you should you join me in one indulgence."

Acton hung back, curious to see where this was headed, and he could tell Laura was just as curious.

"And just what might that be?"

"There's a ritual called the Three-Hundred Club. It's where we both strip down naked, sit in a hot sauna for ten minutes, run outside, then come back inside after experiencing a three-hundred degree Fahrenheit differential. Then we warm each other up."

Laura regarded him for a moment. "That sounds like fun."

33

Evans grinned. "Wonderful!"

Laura extended a hand toward Acton. "Do you mind if my husband joins us?"

Evans flinched and he took an involuntary step back as Acton approached. "Do we have a problem here?"

Laura smiled. "No, Dr. Evans was merely extending an invitation to the Three-Hundred Club in which we're supposed to get naked together, run outside, then come back in and warm each other up."

Evans stared anywhere but at the married couple. "Yes. Well, I obviously didn't realize you were married, Professor Palmer. I, of course, apologize."

Acton suppressed a grin. "So then, the invitation was sexual in nature, not just friendly?"

"Uhm, uhm."

"We've been on the ground less than ten minutes and you're already trying to bang your boss?"

"Perhaps I should go."

Acton laughed and slapped the man on the shoulder. "I'm just messing with you. But next time"—Acton took Laura's left hand and held it up—"check the ring finger."

"Always good advice," stammered the man as he scampered off after the tour.

Acton gave Laura a peck. "That was fun."

"Yep, I've still got it."

"Ooh baby, you've got it in spades." His hand moved from her shoulders down her back.

She reached around and grabbed it, halting its descent. "I'm the boss here, remember."

"Ooh."

She giggled. "When we're alone, fine. But out in public, we have to be professional."

He clasped his hands behind his back and bowed his head slightly. "You're right, of course. Do you think our Scottish or Irish or whatever friend will behave himself?"

"I don't know about that, but our *Welsh* friend should. I think he nearly peed himself when you walked up to him."

"I would have paid good money to see that."

"Well, it just goes to show that sexism is alive and well in academia."

"It's unfortunate, but at least the powers that be saw fit to put you in charge." He extended a hand toward the group about to fall out of sight. "Perhaps we should rejoin the group so we can protect the other female scientists from the horny Welshman?"

Antarctica Quest

En route to Antarctica

Corkery entered the galley, having missed breakfast due to one of his patients having forgotten to take their beta-blocker the night before and waking up with a heart rate forty beats above normal. "With your heart condition, you shouldn't be on a trip like this, sir."

His patient had merely shrugged. "If I'm going to die, I'd rather die doing something like this than sitting in a chair in front of a television in my condo in New York."

Corkery hadn't bothered mentioning how he would have to live with the man's death, how much work it would cause the crew, or the trauma it would put the other passengers through. The selfishness of it all was galling. People these days seemed to only think of themselves, of what made them happy. Damn the consequences or anyone else. It was infuriating at times.

He spotted his nurse, Mercedes, standing by a table filled with their healthy Chinese passengers, speaking with them comfortably in either

Mandarin or Cantonese, he couldn't tell the difference, though he assumed Cantonese if she had learned the language in Hong Kong while she worked there. She spotted him and smiled before saying something to the passengers and walking away.

"Dr. Corkery, how's your patient?"

"Not healthy enough to be here, but that doesn't seem to stop anybody. The beta-blocker started to kick in so his heart rate's coming back down to normal. Half this boat is so excited that they're forgetting their meds. We should be treating this place like a mental institution where everybody has to line up for their meds then we check their mouths to make sure they actually took what's keeping them alive."

She giggled. "Something tells me our millionaire guests wouldn't be in favor of that."

"No, I doubt they would." He piled his tray with food, starving, and she nodded toward the unhealthy choices.

"It looks like not just our passengers are on vacation."

He laughed. "I figure a little bit of winter weight might actually help me on this trip. And besides"—he nodded toward what was on offer—"there's not exactly a lot of healthy food here."

"It's a Russian-run tour. They're not exactly known for healthy eating."

He sat down at a free table and he indicated a chair across from him. "Care to join me?"

Her eyes darted toward the captain standing in the doorway talking to the first officer. "I better not. Our captain might be upset that nobody's manning the infirmary during waking hours."

"He does realize the infirmary is only forty feet away."

She shrugged. "He's strict that way ever since the sea lion incident. He fired the last doctor for it."

Corkery snorted as he recalled her story. A man had broken off from the group to get a photo, and while laying prone, getting that perfect shot, a sea lion came up behind him, mistaking him for prey, probably a penguin, and took a healthy bite out of his ass, then, more critically, his arm as he tried to fight off the creature. The ship's doctor had been sightseeing with a separate tour and precious minutes were lost while they found him. By some miracle, one of the passengers was a retired vascular surgeon, and between him and the ship's doctor, they managed to save the man's life and get him onto a plane. The man survived and fully recovered, though had some interesting scars to explain.

And now the ship's captain was paranoid about their doctor being anywhere but on board.

Captain Shoigu spotted them together and Mercedes winced. "I'll be leaving now," she whispered before scurrying toward the door. The captain gave her a displeased look as she passed, then he strolled over and sat at Corkery's table.

"I thought the infirmary was to be manned at all times during waking hours."

"It is. I just finished with a patient and came to let my nurse know. I brought her up to date on the patient, and now she's left to man the infirmary until I've eaten my breakfast."

"Just remember, Doctor, you're not here on vacation. You're here to do a job and that's to keep these people alive until we offload them."

"Your odds would be much better if you screened your passengers better."

Shoigu grunted. "No doubt, but money talks, and these people have a lot of money. If they want to die here, who am I to deny them that as long as they paid in full and upfront." He stabbed a finger at him. "I'll expect you to remain on board the entire time."

Corkery firmly shook his head. "No. My contract specifically stipulates that I'll be allowed to disembark." Shoigu bristled and was about to say something when Corkery raised a hand. "Listen, I heard about what happened last time, and there are two things you need to remember about that. One is that your passenger did something he shouldn't have and your crew didn't catch it. And two, that man should be dead. The only reason he survived is not because there was a ship's doctor, but because there was a retired vascular surgeon on board. If your ship's doctor had been in the infirmary when the patient was first brought in, and that passenger wasn't on board, he'd have died regardless.

"All we can do is plan for the worst, but not be dominated by it. How about this as a compromise? I will only leave as any part of an organized tour that has the bulk of the passengers with it, and will never go on a tour that goes farther out than any other group. That way, if something happens in a more remote group, they'll have to go past us to get back to the ship, and they can collect me if they haven't already reached me by radio. I can even meet them and start working on saving the patient right away."

Shoigu pursed his lips, staring at him, his head slowly shaking. "I prefer Russian doctors."

Corkery smiled slightly. "And why is that?"

"They're more compliant."

"And that's a good thing?"

"I prefer a compliant crew. They follow orders."

Corkery regarded the man then the tattoos extending up both arms. "You're former Russian military, aren't you?"

"Yes."

"Well, Captain, I'm not military, and I'm definitely not Russian military. But I'll obey all your orders as laid out in my contract. I'm not here to put my patients' lives at risk. You've already done that by allowing them to be here. I just want to spend a short amount of time on the ice to say that I've set foot on the seventh continent. It's not like there's actually anything to see here. I'm sure you'll find me in my infirmary the vast majority of the time."

"Good," said Shoigu as he rose. "I'll let you finish your breakfast." He smirked. "So you can get back to the infirmary all the quicker."

Corkery laughed. "Thank you, Captain." He nodded toward the table of Chinese as they rose and left. "With so many young, healthy people on board, hopefully it will be an uneventful voyage."

"From your lips to God's ears, Doctor."

Shoigu walked past the guests, saying something in Chinese. They all responded in kind, whatever was said apparently a pleasantry. And it had him wondering why, if the Chinese normally took their own cruises, did everyone on this ship appear to speak the language?

McMurdo Station, Antarctica

Laura smiled at the two young staff members of McMurdo Station as they leaped from their chairs and snapped to attention. "At ease, cadets," she said with a laugh. She gestured for them to sit. "Make yourselves comfortable." She sat across from them and pulled out a file folder. "This shouldn't take long, but I thought I should talk to you two first since you're the ones who discovered the wreck."

"So, it is a ship." Dana McAlister leaned forward excitedly. "We only saw a little bit, so we weren't sure."

"It is a ship, or at least part of a ship. We have no idea at the moment how much there actually is." Laura held up a hand, cutting off any more questions. "Let's start from the beginning. In your own words, what happened? How did you find it?"

"We were out in the snowcat on a training run," started McAlister.

Guillermo Ortega held up a hand. "She was training me. I only got here a couple of months ago and they like to teach everybody the basics in case there's an emergency."

41

"Of course," said Laura. "So, you were driving?"

Ortega nodded. "Yes."

"And then what happened?"

Both shifted in their chairs and smirks were exchanged. "We stopped to take a break."

Laura smiled. "You mean to fool around." Both their jaws dropped but they didn't deny it, instead searching for words to say that continued to escape them. Laura laughed. "This wouldn't be the first archaeological find made during some hanky-panky. Just ask my husband about what happened in Peru." She frowned as she realized she had just slipped up. Two of James' students fooling around had discovered a secret entrance that led them to the crystal skull and events they didn't discuss with anyone not already in the know. She wagged her finger. "Actually, you better not. There are some bad memories there, but like I said, it wouldn't be the first time something was discovered by frisky people."

They both blushed, exchanging glances.

"Now, while you two were *resting*—"

Ortega snickered.

"—what happened?"

"The icesheet cracked and we fell below the surface. About thirty feet," explained McAlister. "Luckily there wasn't a lot of damage."

Ortega continued. "We radioed for help, and while we were waiting, I used my cellphone to take as many photos as I could of what we had wound up beside."

"And how would you describe it?"

He shrugged. "To be perfectly honest, it was just a lot of wood. Like, it was obviously man-made. It wasn't just trees stuck in the ice, but then I saw that lettering that looked like Chinese or Japanese or something. So, I got some good shots of that too."

Laura leaned back, folding her arms. "Then promptly shared them with the world."

Ortega stared at his hands clasped in front of him on the table. "Well, that was an accident, ma'am. My phone is set up to automatically upload everything to the cloud, and I had that folder shared with some friends and family. The photos were uploaded the moment we got back to base and then my brother uploaded them to his Insta account and the rest, well, the rest is history."

Laura flicked her wrist, dismissing the concerns. "You accidentally shared photos of an archaeological find, not the NOC list."

Two sets of eyes narrowed. "The what list?" asked McAlister.

Laura chuckled. "Watch Mission Impossible, the first one." Polite nods were returned, the expressions still blank.

I guess I'm getting old.

"So, all you saw is what was in the photos?"

"Yes, ma'am," they both replied.

"No bodies, no artifacts. You didn't take any trophies?"

Both vehemently shook their heads at the suggestion. "Absolutely not, ma'am," said Ortega. "That would have involved opening a window or a door, and we were pretty pinned in."

"Besides, we were too busy trying to find our clothes," added McAlister, immediately snapping her mouth shut. She pointed at Laura's tablet. "Can we make sure that's not part of the official record?"

Laura laughed. "Trust me. No one will know the truth unless you choose to tell them." She leaned forward, smirking. "You know, if they make a movie of this someday, telling the truth might be the only way you actually make the final cut."

Ortega grinned at McAlister. "I want Donald Glover playing me."

She gave him a look. "You have a mighty high opinion of yourself."

He shrugged. "Hey, the actors are always better looking than their real-life counterparts. If I'm going to be remembered, I want to be remembered for being the handsomest man on the base."

McAlister laughed. "And just who should play me?"

Laura bit her tongue, desperate to give the young man some advice.

"You should play yourself. There's not an actress out there who can hold a candle to you."

Laura laughed and clapped as McAlister leaned over and gave Ortega a kiss. "Thank you for that," said Laura.

"For what?" asked Ortega.

"For showing me what my husband must have been like when he was your age."

McAlister gave Ortega a gentle punch on the shoulder. "So, he's as smooth as him?"

"Smoothly awkward." Laura returned to business. "So, after they pulled you out, what happened?"

"We told the commander what we saw, filled out a bunch of paperwork, then we hit the sack, and that's about it."

"Anything else you think I should know about?"

Ortega shrugged. "I don't think so. Oh, the next day the CO sent out a team to go down into the crevasse and take a closer look. I don't know if they actually made it there before they were called off."

Laura stuffed her tablet inside her bag. "The report I read indicated they were called off en route once Washington realized what they might have and decided it was best to have it properly investigated." She rose and the other two jumped to their feet. "What are your assignments?"

"I'm a mechanic," replied Ortega.

"Comms specialist," said McAlister.

"And have you been assigned to the expedition?"

Both shook their heads. "No, ma'am." McAlister frowned. "I think the CO knows what we were doing."

"Why's that?"

McAlister blushed and looked away. "I couldn't find my bra, ma'am."

Laura roared with laughter. "I'll see what I can do. I think you two should be on the team. Even if you were no doubt breaking almost every regulation in the book when you discovered it, you still discovered it."

Both seemed excited by this. "Thank you, ma'am. We won't let you down," said McAlister.

Laura headed for the door then turned. "See that you don't, and make sure you keep your clothes on while you're on duty."

McMurdo Station, Antarctica

Acton stood with a tablet and stylus as each piece of equipment was called off before it was loaded into several trailers that would be towed by one of the snowcats. He and Dr. Manaaki Parata, a Māori scientist based out of New Zealand, were both checking the inventory, part of the redundancy ordered by Laura. There was no room for mistakes.

Colonel Richardson, the Joint Task Force-Support Forces Antarctica commander for the ongoing annual Operation Deep Freeze that resupplied McMurdo Station and other outposts, stood nearby conferring with several of his people when a young corporal ran up.

"Sorry to interrupt, sir."

"What is it, corporal?"

The corporal leaned closer and lowered his voice. Acton strained to hear what was being said but couldn't make it out. It had him wishing he could read lips. Yet he had no trouble reading facial expressions, and the colonel's told him something was up, and whatever it was, it wasn't good.

Acton handed his pad to one of the other expedition members. "Take over for me for a moment."

"Sure, Jim."

Acton intercepted Colonel Richardson as he rushed from the warehouse. "Colonel, I'm Professor Jim Acton. The expedition leader is my wife. Is there a problem?"

Richardson shook his head. "Nothing for you to be concerned with." He continued toward the door then stopped, turning to face Acton. "Wait a minute. You're the one I received the file on. Come with me."

Acton followed, saying nothing, though dying to know what file Richardson was referring to, and what it said that had him changing his mind. Acton had to assume it had to do with his recent past and his connections to not only the CIA, but American Special Forces. He assumed there was a similar file on Laura that had been sent to the senior military officer on the scene.

They went through a passageway leading to the administration building, and minutes later the rushed group entered a room with several large displays and about a dozen workstations, half of which were manned. Everyone in the room seemed focused on one large monitor showing a map of the region.

"Report!" snapped Richardson.

Captain Stanley pointed at the monitor. "Sir, a Chinese vessel, the Xue Long, is approaching the coastline."

Richardson's eyes narrowed. "She's not scheduled, is she?"

"Negative, sir. She's two weeks early." Stanley turned to one of the stations. "Bring up that satellite feed."

"Yes, sir."

Another monitor was brought up with a satellite image showing what Acton assumed was the Chinese vessel. A helicopter sat on its deck, its massive rotors slowly spinning up as a group of soldiers gathered. Richardson cursed. "Notify the Pentagon, let them know the situation and request instructions. If they launch, how quickly can they be here from their current position?"

"Thirty minutes."

Acton cleared his throat. "They're not coming here, Colonel."

Richardson spun toward him. "Explain."

"They're Chinese, sir, and what your people have discovered is an ancient Chinese pirate ship. They think it's theirs by right."

"How could you possibly know that?"

"When your people were trapped below the ice, they took photos, and one of those had Chinese lettering. It translated into Black Dragon. That was the flagship of the Blue Flag Fleet, part of the Guangdong Pirate Confederacy. The Chinese are aware of this. Not only did those photos go out on the Internet, the National Science Foundation invited the Chinese to participate, but they refused."

Stanley grunted. "Now we know why."

Acton agreed. "I believe they intend to take control of the site. If we don't get boots on the ground before they do, we could lose control of this find."

Richardson stared at him, slowly shaking his head. "Professor, just what do you think this place is? The United States military provides logistics support only. This isn't a military installation. It's not like I have a platoon of marines sitting in the barracks waiting to repel some attack."

Acton bowed his head slightly. "Of course, sir, that's not what I'm suggesting. What I'm saying is that if the Chinese get there first, we will be refused entry to the site. The few people we have there now will be handed over and that will be the end of it. If we leave now and put ten or fifteen people on the ground, including some US military personnel, we have a much better chance of negotiating a settlement that's acceptable to both parties. The Chinese aren't going to kill people over an archaeological find. There's no upside for them. But we have to act fast." He pointed at the satellite image showing the dozen heavily armed soldiers boarding the chopper. "We have to leave now if we have any hope of countering their move."

Richardson pursed his lips for a moment before giving a curt nod. "Very well, but this has to be seen as a civilian operation. I can give you six personnel, barely armed, and we have two choppers that can transport you there."

"Excellent." Acton headed for the door. "I'll let Professor Palmer know what's going on, and we'll put together a group of volunteers. When can we leave?"

"Ten minutes."

Acton left the command center and rushed down the corridor then came to a halt. He had no clue where the hell he was going.

McMurdo Station, Antarctica

Laura entered the warehouse being used as their staging area, and was surprised to find James wasn't there. She spotted Manaaki Parata, part of the New Zealand contingent, and waved at him.

The man smiled and walked over. "Professor Palmer, anything I can do for you?"

"Just checking on our status."

"We've triple-checked everything. Everything present and accounted for, and loaded. I was just about to come find you to get the okay to send it to the site." He handed her the tablet he was holding and she quickly scrolled through a long list of green check marks. She tapped on the approve button, pressed her thumb on the scanner, then handed back the tablet.

"Approved."

The door behind her opened and she turned to see James entering with one of the locals. "Thanks," he said to the woman as he rushed toward them.

"No problem," called the local as she disappeared back through the door.

Laura had been curious as to why he hadn't been here performing his assigned duty and was about to jokingly admonish him for abandoning his post, when the concern on his face had her re-thinking that. "What's wrong?" she asked as he joined her and Parata.

"The Chinese are moving on the expedition site."

"What?" exclaimed Parata. "What do you mean by moving?"

"They're launching a helicopter with what looked like a dozen armed Special Forces. If they get there before we do, they'll never relinquish the site."

Laura cursed, her mind racing. The Chinese had been given an opportunity to participate but they had refused, claiming they should be the ones in charge of any excavation since the vessel was potentially Chinese. But the territory it was found in was administered by New Zealand, and McMurdo was administered by the United States in a joint effort between the US military and the National Science Foundation.

The international community had agreed to a joint expedition with only the Chinese and Russians refusing. The Russians were of no concern, their participation wasn't welcome regardless, but the Chinese expertise could have proven useful. Unfortunately, politics almost always got in the way when it came to communist dictatorships, but this was a whole new level that she hadn't anticipated. She couldn't imagine the Chinese actually killing anyone over this, but if her team arrived after the Chinese soldiers, there was no way they would let them on the site.

She sighed. "I guess we will have to get the diplomats involved."

"Or…" James paused.

She regarded him. "Or?"

"Or we use the two helicopters I just arranged to bring six armed US military personnel and half a dozen or so volunteers to the site before the Chinese get there."

She shook her head. "Colonel Richardson will never agree to that."

"He already did. I was in the command center when they discovered the launch."

"What were you doing there?"

His eyes darted toward Parata before returning to her and she waved her hand, picking up on his unspoken answer—the colonel had likely been briefed on their past. "I just happened to be here when the colonel was notified and expressed an interest."

Parata chuckled. "It's cute how you two think that none of us know about your exploits."

Laura glanced at him. "Exploits?"

Parata gave her a look. "While I don't believe most of what I read on the Internet, there's enough smoke out there about you two that at least one has to have fire behind it. And if you're looking for volunteers, I'll go."

James grinned. "That's three. I say we invite your Welsh lover who won't dare say no to save face, and then we just need two more."

Laura chewed her cheek for a moment as Parata silently mouthed, "Welsh lover?" at James. Her entire team was physically fit and brilliant, and she had no doubt many of them were as brave as Parata and would readily volunteer. But this could still be dangerous. She turned to Parata.

"Are you sure about this? With the Chinese involved, you just never know."

"No, you don't, but even I don't think they're crazy enough to kill over something like this."

James agreed. "Listen, minutes count here. I say, we go, we get there before them, and then when they arrive, we make it clear we're not leaving. If it looks like things might turn violent, you order everyone to lower their weapons. We just surrender to them then let the diplomats take over. My guess is they'll just let us go. If we're lucky, cooler heads prevail and this turns into a joint operation, just like we always wanted."

Part of her wanted to damn the torpedoes. She was sick and tired of countries like China and Russia running roughshod over everything, thinking the rules didn't apply to them. And she had never backed away from a fight. But it would mean intentionally putting herself and her team in harm's way. It was different when it was just the two of them, yet she had to save the expedition and send a message.

She came to a decision and turned to James. "You go tell the others what's going on and ask for volunteers. Make sure they understand the danger. I'll coordinate the departure."

"You got it." James bolted for the doors at the far end of the hangar.

Parata grinned. "Looks like this thing is going to be a hell of a lot more exciting than we thought."

"Let's hope not." Laura turned to the station staff. "Who's in charge here?"

A woman raised her hand. "I am. Julie Pyne."

Laura gestured at the loaded equipment. "This is approved to go. We need it moving ASAP."

"Yes, ma'am."

"How long before it arrives?"

"Probably looking at three hours."

"Fine. Make sure you're monitoring communications the entire time. We might have a situation developing with the Chinese that could scupper the entire expedition. If it sounds like things are going south—"

"They don't get much more south than here," chuckled Parata.

"—I want you to turn around immediately. Under no circumstances are you to enter the camp without confirmation from myself or Professor Acton that the situation is under control. Understood?"

"Yes, ma'am." Pyne glanced around, lowering her voice. "Do you really think we're going to have a problem with the Chinese?"

Laura nodded. "Oh, we'll have a problem with them. The question is, does it get resolved peacefully?"

"That doesn't sound good."

"Nothing usually does when it comes to the Chinese." She shook Pyne's hand. "Good luck. Hopefully, we'll be seeing you in a few hours and everything will have been resolved."

"Let's hope."

Laura headed for the door with Parata on her heels.

"Aren't you scared?"

She glanced over her shoulder at the man. "About what?"

"We're about to face off with Chinese Special Forces. Doesn't that scare you?"

"No, not really. I'm concerned, of course."

"But you've been in worse."

She smiled. "You could say that."

"Well, if you're not worried then I'm not going to worry. I mean, what's the worst that could happen? We get taken prisoner, there's some negotiating, then we're released with an exciting story to tell our students."

Laura stepped through the door. "I'm afraid, Professor, that being taken prisoner is in no way the worst that could happen."

McMurdo Station, Antarctica

"So, that's the situation. Professor Palmer and I are heading out to the site by helicopter in the next few minutes with six armed military personnel. We're looking for volunteers to come with us to increase our numbers on the ground and to impress upon the Chinese that this is a civilian expedition. Professor Parata has already volunteered. Is anyone willing to join us?"

Most of the expedition members were in the room and no one said anything, though a lot of people shifted uncomfortably in their chairs. He wasn't surprised. These were academics. They had never seen any type of action.

The door burst open to his left and a young man and woman rushed inside. They came to an abrupt halt as all eyes turned to them. He recognized them from their file photos as the two that had discovered the wreckage.

"Can I help you?"

The young man stepped forward. "Yes, sir. Sorry to interrupt but we just received our approvals to join the expedition and we heard there was a meeting for all personnel, so…well, we're here."

"I'm afraid it's not that type of meeting. There's a situation with the Chinese, and we're looking for volunteers."

"Volunteers for what?" asked McAlister.

"A small contingent of armed personnel are going to the excavation site in the next few minutes, and I'm looking for civilian volunteers to join them."

The young man looked at his companion, who gave a quick nod. "We'll go."

Acton held out a hand toward them with a smile. "There we go. Two more volunteers. It would be nice though to have more academia there to lend credibility." He spotted the horny Welshman at the rear of the room, parked beside Isabella Baroni, one of the more attractive members of the expedition. "What about you, Dr. Evans? Chinese Special Forces sometimes include women. You might get lucky."

Snickers erupted around the room, especially among the women. Evans had evidently been busy.

Baroni turned. "I think you should go with them," she said in a thick Italian accent.

Evans uncrossed his legs then crossed them again, shifting himself away from the woman now offering up his services.

"If any of that Special Forces team are female, perhaps you can charm them to switch sides."

More snickers and some outright laughter.

Acton held up a hand, his little bit of fun with the man now going too far. "Okay, that's enough. Nobody's going to be forced to go. This is purely voluntary."

Evans, his cheeks burning, briefly raised his hand. "I'll go."

The subject of the Welshman's unwelcome attention held up her hand at the elbow. "I'll go too," she said. "Somebody has to protect those poor Chinese girls."

More outright laughter was the response, and Acton rose from his perch at the edge of the table. "Okay, good. That's enough. Everyone else keep prepping as if the expedition is a go. And as soon as we've straightened things out with the Chinese, we'll let you know."

The doors opened and Laura entered with Parata. She waved a hand at everyone. "Hi, all. I assume James has brought you up to speed?"

Heads bobbed around the room.

"Good." She turned to her husband. "Do we have volunteers?"

"Yes, ma'am. We're ready to go."

"Good. I've already sent the snowcat with the supply train. It should be arriving in three hours. Our group of volunteers along with a contingent of military personnel will be leaving in five minutes. So, anyone who's put their name forward, gear up immediately. The rest of you, keep prepping, however, nobody else will be leaving today. We'll straighten things out and send word for you to come tomorrow. If something goes wrong, it's a six-hour round trip by snowcat." She smiled at the team. "Good luck, everyone. Hopefully, this will just be another chapter to add to what I believe will be an academically interesting story. Now, if the volunteers will follow me, it's time to go."

Acton suppressed the proud smile that threatened to break out. He loved his wife, knew she was brilliant, and was relishing in the fact that she was getting to show off her skills in front of fellow scientists rather than just students. This was the biggest expedition either of them had been in charge of, and he was so delighted for her.

He joined her as they filed out of the room, Captain Stanley rushing up to them. "If we're going to beat the Chinese there, we've gotta go now."

Laura gave a curt nod. "We've got our volunteers. We're gearing up. Five minutes."

Stanley tapped his watch. "Not a minute more, otherwise it's too late. We can't land there after they're already on the ground. We have to be the first boots there."

Laura continued to march toward where their winter gear was stored. "What about the personnel already on the ground?"

"They're civilian and have a single rifle purely for defense against a deranged sea lion. They can't take on a dozen Chinese Special Forces."

Ortega rushed ahead and pushed open a door. Everyone filed in and Acton recognized the room where all their winter gear had been stored for their departure scheduled for later today. Ortega turned to them. "We have to get our equipment from a different spot. We'll join you in a couple of minutes."

Laura acknowledged him. "Just hurry up."

Ortega grinned. "Don't worry. I guarantee you we can gear up in half the time you can."

He and McAlister rushed from the room and Acton walked over to his bundle of equipment, his name emblazoned across his backpack, as Laura did the same beside him. He lowered his voice and leaned closer. "Do you think we should ask for guns?"

She shook her head. "No, I don't want any armed civilians. The Chinese have to understand that this is a civilian expedition. Besides, if things go to hell, I have a feeling you'll be able to pick up a weapon off a body."

He frowned but said nothing. An assumption was being made here that the Chinese wouldn't shoot, but that was one hell of an assumption. They had been in numerous situations where the Chinese hadn't hesitated to fire at them, and it had him wondering. If the Chinese knew the two of them were there, could that aggravate an already tense situation? He wasn't sure, but there was no way in hell he was sending other people into danger while he sat here, comfortably safe.

It just wasn't the way he was built.

South Pacific

January 19, 1810

This wasn't the plan, but it was reality. Zheng Bao had hoped to make his escape undiscovered, but unfortunately someone had talked and word had reached his sister almost immediately. They had provisions for two weeks and plenty of gold to purchase more. He had hoped to take aboard more before they departed, but they had been forced to launch early. This lack of supplies was a mixed blessing. It meant they were lighter than the fully provisioned ships pursuing them just on the horizon. They had been spotted late yesterday as flares from the closest ship signaled to the others they had been found.

He wasn't sure of the size of the fleet his sister had sent after him, but he had no doubt they were dead if they were caught. Yet she had left him no choice. The family's honor was at stake. Her name could not appear in the zupu. If she wanted her legacy to be remembered, she should marry then possibly be recorded in her husband's family genealogy.

That was what tradition dictated.

The record of the Zheng family couldn't be marred by a woman. While he couldn't deny her greatness—for she had accomplished much more than any man he knew next to the emperor—it didn't change the fact that the deities that controlled such things had put her on this earth as a woman, not a man, and two thousand years of tradition weren't about to be broken if he had any say in the matter.

Yet now he wasn't sure what to do. His intention had been to head south then west, to take refuge in one of the trading ports where they had allies that felt as he did—that no woman should wield such power. She would die eventually, perhaps quite soon for she had many rivals, and attempts were constantly made on her life. If he were lucky, she'd be dead early into his exile and he could return triumphant with the zupu unmarred, then take control of the empire his sister had built.

But all those plans were in disarray now. His sister had found out he was running and had given pursuit. Her fleet had found them and now they had no choice but to continue south—there was no stopping. All he could hope to do was wear them down and pray they would give up the pursuit.

Wishful thinking.

He knew his sister. She would never stop until she found him and punished him for his treachery. She was brutal, ruthless, unrelenting. It was what had made her who she was today, and he had admired her for it. But now it would be his undoing.

There was a knock at his cabin door.

"Come in."

It opened and his second-in-command, Qi, stepped inside, closing the door behind him. His expression had Bao concerned.

"What's wrong?"

Qi stepped closer, lowering his voice. "It's the men, sir."

"What about them?"

"I overheard some talk. They're afraid of your sister."

"As they should be. It should motivate them to work all the harder so that we are not captured."

"I'm afraid several of them have thought of an alternative."

Bao's fists clenched as he rose. "And just what is this alternative?"

"Mutiny, sir. I overheard three of them talking that if they took the ship, they could turn around and surrender to your sister and she would reward them rather than execute them."

Bao frowned. Qi was probably right. The only way any of his men were going to survive this were if they betrayed him, yet he couldn't let them know that. He needed them, though at the moment he had more crew than was required. He could see only one choice. Execute the potential mutineers, for if thoughts like this continued to spread, he could indeed have a full-blown mutiny on his hands. "Have them brought up on deck. I'll deal with this personally."

"At once, sir."

Qi disappeared as Bao readied himself for the unpleasant task ahead. He had killed before, countless times. It was part of the life of being a pirate. He had even killed his own men when they had committed an unforgivable sin, though he rarely took satisfaction in it.

Everyone on this ship was supposed to be a trusted man, one he could count on, and if three were already talking of betraying him, how many more were there? Was the fear of his sister so great that it overcame any loyalty to him? Could he, in fact, trust anyone on his own ship? Disloyalty, doubt, fear of his sister rather than him, had to be quashed now, for they were only in the second day of their journey, a journey he feared could extend far beyond their rations and far beyond their capabilities.

For to the south, if the stories he had heard were true, the ocean ended, surrendering to the unforgiving ice that would crush the hull of any ship.

Antarctica Quest

En route to Antarctica

Present Day

Corkery clipped the end of the final stitch, his patient having opened up his cheek after stumbling into an open cabinet during rough seas.

"Scar?"

Corkery nodded. "Probably."

He grunted. "Unbelievable. I made it through three tours in 'Nam without a scratch, and here I'm going to have a scar on my face for the rest of my life because of a medicine cabinet."

Corkery chuckled. "Well, Roy, nobody has to know the truth about the scar. For all they know, you got it in a bar brawl just before you boarded."

A smile spread as his patient's head slowly bobbed. "I like it." He slapped Corkery on the shoulder. "Good thinking, Doc, bar brawl it is." He stared at himself in the small mirror clipped to the procedure table. "You know, my wife didn't want me to come on this trip. She said if I

65

was going to have a mid-life crisis at my age, I should blow my money on a fancy British sportscar. I said if I was blowing that kind of money, I'd rather enjoy myself rather than suffer from the headaches one of those lemons would cause me."

Corkery chuckled. "When you come in tomorrow for a checkup, ask me about my lawyer's experience. You dodged a bullet." He stepped back and Mercedes moved in, placing a bandage over the now stitched-up cut.

"Mr.—"

"I said call me Roy."

She smiled. "Sorry, Roy. Come see us tomorrow and we'll—"

Roy bristled and held up a finger. "Do you hear that?"

Corkery cocked an ear, not hearing what his patient apparently was, then his eyes widened slightly. "Helicopter?"

"Damn right, it's a helicopter." Roy headed for the window. "I'm not seeing it. I think it's coming from the other side. Something's going on."

Corkery failed to see the significance. "What makes you say that? It's just a helicopter."

Roy gave him a look. "Son, this is Antarctica. That's not the traffic chopper going overhead like it does every morning during rush hour. Choppers only travel here with a purpose, and they never stray too far from home because there's not too many places where they can land around here. I'm going topside to see whose it is, because it sure doesn't sound American."

Mercedes stared at him. "You can tell?"

"I'm a bit of an aficionado. Let's go check it out."

Normally, Corkery couldn't care less about things like this, but his patient's concern had his curiosity piqued. Mercedes grinned at him, her questioning look indicating she was as eager to go see as anyone. Corkery acquiesced. "Okay, fine. Let's go."

The two of them followed their patient down the corridor and up the ladder to the main deck, reaching the frigid cold of the outside in time to hear Roy curse. "This can't be good."

Corkery joined him at the rail, staring at the helicopter as it passed by. "What makes you say that?" But his own question was answered when he caught sight of the Chinese flag on the tail assembly.

"What the hell is the Chinese military doing here?" asked Roy to nobody in particular.

"Maybe it's not military," suggested Corkery. "We use American military to move civilians around here."

"Perhaps, but there's no Chinese Antarctic outpost along this flight path, and that helicopter had to have come from a ship. Maybe I'm just being paranoid, but I have a funny feeling the shit's about to hit the fan right where we're heading."

Corkery shivered and noticed that Mercedes was as well, neither of them having time to get their winter jackets on. "Well, let's go back inside before we freeze to death. When I get a chance, I'll ask the captain if he knows of anything that's happening."

Roy grunted. "That Russian bastard won't tell you anything. They're always in cahoots with the Chinese." The old man headed back inside, Mercedes and Corkery following, and as they approached the hatch, Corkery noticed at the opposite end of the deck their eight Chinese passengers huddled together, concern on their faces. It had him wondering just what they had to fear, and whether the fact they were concerned meant he and the other passengers should be as well.

Was something going on that was about to put them all in danger?

McMurdo Station, Antarctica

Acton helped Laura into the back of the chopper then joined her as the lead helicopter carrying the military personnel lifted off. The door was slid shut and moments later they were in the air, heading toward their destination and a potential confrontation with the Chinese Special Forces team.

The horny Welshman sat pressed into a corner across from a calm Isabella Baroni, the balls he was so desperate to display to her apparently having tucked back in. Acton felt bad for the man, though only a little. If he was this scared, he shouldn't be here, though in all honesty, Acton had never expected him to be so terrified. It took a certain amount of bravado to hit on your team lead within ten minutes of an expedition beginning, but apparently ingratiating oneself on the ladies did not equate to courage in battle. He'd have to keep an eye on him.

Their Kiwi seemed almost giddy, every motion he made rapid. As he talked with Laura, the tense excitement mixed with fear could be heard, though based upon the content of the chatter, he had no regrets about volunteering. And neither did their young couple, Ortega and McAlister, sitting across from them, Ortega with his arm around McAlister, her head nestled in his shoulder, both wide-eyed and excited to be there, though Ortega's rapidly tapping heel betrayed his outward confidence.

Laura stepped forward and poked her head between the pilot and copilot. "What's our ETA?"

"Ten minutes," replied the pilot.

"Any word on the Chinese?"

"Last update I received was that they're about five minutes behind us."

"That's going to be cutting it close."

"No shit. My orders are to insert you and get the hell out. It's not too late to abort this."

Laura shook her head. "No. We are here legally under all the international accords. They have no right to insert a military unit and take control of a piece of Antarctic territory. The Chinese have to learn that they can't just run heavy-handed all over the world, doing whatever they want without being challenged."

"I admire your moxie, ma'am. Let's just hope you don't become martyrs for the cause."

Laura patted the man on the shoulder. "If we do die here today"— the Welshman yelped—"just make sure they spell all our names correctly."

"Especially mine," piped in Acton. "People keep spelling it with an I. While I like the idea of being an action hero. James Action just doesn't have the right ring to it."

Ortega chuckled. "The world of autocorrect gone mad."

Acton stabbed a finger at him. "That's exactly it. Nobody proofreads their text messages anymore. You wouldn't believe some of the shit I get. I spend more time deciphering what the hell they were trying to say to me than if I had just called them up and said, what the hell?"

McAlister elbowed Ortega, giggling. "He's terrible for that. Half my texts to him are just question marks because I have no clue what he's saying."

Laura sat back down beside Acton, jerking her thumb at him. "He's meticulous. Every text message he sends he rereads two or three times just to make sure."

Acton shrugged. "Just because the method is quick and convenient doesn't mean you should abandon protocol. A correctly typed message is a reflection of who you are, of what type of person you are." He leaned forward and tapped Ortega's knee. "No offense, man."

Ortega shrugged. "None taken. You're right. I should make a better effort." He turned to McAlister. "I'll try harder, at least with you."

Acton wrapped an arm around Laura and stared out at the harsh landscape below. In the distance, he could see Mount Lister, the highest peak in the region, but in all other directions it was desolation. There was little evidence of man beyond the occasional relay antenna or emergency hut. If they were to get trapped out here, it could mean death. And it had him wondering how he'd prefer to die. In the heat of the desert, desperately thirsty and hot, or in the frigid cold of the Antarctic, surrounded by frozen water that could quench his thirst, but at the same time hasten his death from hypothermia?

"There's the supply train," announced Ortega, pointing out the window on the other side.

Acton and Laura both peered out, just catching a piece of the driver's side of the large snowcat, a hand sticking out the window, waving up at them. Laura returned the wave, despite there being no chance of the driver seeing it. They settled back into their seats and Acton wrapped his arm back around Laura and she dug her chin into his shoulder a little harder than usual, her unspoken signal that she was troubled. As the leader, she had to put on the brave face to hide any fears so that the others could take comfort in her stoicism. Just like his calm demeanor was a mask for the world to see, so was hers, and she was as on edge as he was. While he was confident the Chinese wouldn't open fire, all it took was one itchy trigger finger, one misinterpreted gesture or movement, and they could all be on their way to hell in a hand basket, all over some ridiculous affront to Chinese honor as the increasingly belligerent nation attempted to establish itself as the new world's superpower while America faded.

Laura was right.

They had to make a stand.

The copilot turned in his seat to face them. "Okay people, we're five minutes out. Make sure you've got all your equipment that you're going to need. Don't forget anything. If you leave it behind on the chopper, you won't be getting it until tomorrow, and by then, you might have lost a foot or a hand or an ear. I want everybody off this chopper in sixty seconds, so that means get out and get clear. Last man out closes the door, got it?"

A round of acknowledgments satisfied him and he redirected his attention forward.

Acton grabbed his backpack at his feet and lifted it up, checking to make sure nothing had fallen out or that anything was loose as the others did the same. He leaned forward. "We'll all go out my side. I'll open the door and get out first, everyone else follows and gets clear. I'll close the door. Agreed?"

Another round of acknowledgments.

The copilot turned again. "Two minutes. Command says the Chinese are seven minutes out. So, you're going to have five minutes at most to do whatever it is you're going to do to convince them to back off."

Laura nodded. "Understood. You just get yourselves back to base safely."

"Don't you worry about us, ma'am. You guys just be careful. Don't provoke them and you'll be fine. You may not win the day, but you'll be alive tomorrow when we come to pick you up."

Laura glanced at Acton with a twinkle in her eye. "Sleep in, gentlemen. I don't plan on leaving my site for at least a week."

Antarctica Quest

En route to Antarctica

Corkery leaned back in his chair, stretching his arms high behind him. Other than the excitement of the Chinese helicopter earlier and the one minor laceration to a vet's cheek, it had been a boring day, which was fine by him. He had a sense that once the ground tours began, there'd be a lot of people slipping on ice, so he expected to be dealing with scrapes and bruises, sprained ankles, and broken bones for the full week they were there. It would keep him busy, though he preferred to be bored— it meant no one was hurting.

Mercedes entered the infirmary, returning from delivering several Dramamine patches. She plunked onto a stool. "I hate the smell of vomit."

Corkery chuckled. "It was that bad?"

"Ugh, two of those cabins are going to need to be hosed down. I don't understand why people make Antarctica their first sea voyage. At least take a cruise or two in the Caribbean. See if you actually have any sea legs."

"Well, at least they threw up in their cabins and not in here, otherwise we'd be the ones having to clean it up."

Mercedes's head bobbed. "True. I guess there's that." She sniffed her sleeve. "I swear I can still smell it on me, just from being in the room."

Corkery glanced at the clock. "It's almost lunch. Why don't you go change, have a shower, whatever you need to do, and I'll cover here?"

She smiled gratefully as she rose. "Thanks, Doctor." She headed for the door when Corkery stopped her.

"Before you go, did you notice our Chinese passengers on the deck?"

Mercedes faced him. "You mean when the helicopter passed?"

Corkery nodded.

"Yes, I saw them. What about them?"

"Did they seem nervous to you?"

She shrugged. "Not particularly, but I didn't really pay them much mind. I was freezing." Her eyes narrowed. "Why? Did they seem nervous to you?"

Corkery batted a hand. "Forget about it. It's probably just my suspicious nature. I just got the sense they weren't too happy to see a helicopter from their homeland."

Mercedes tilted her head to the side slightly and winced. "Well, I wouldn't necessarily assume that it's from their homeland."

"What do you mean?"

"While I was talking to them earlier it was in Cantonese, not Mandarin. And Cantonese is the language spoken in Hong Kong among other areas. And just because Hong Kong is controlled by China doesn't mean you think of China as your homeland."

Corkery folded his arms and scratched his chin. "Huh. Hadn't thought of that. Interesting." He flicked his fingers at her. "Go have that shower and change your clothes. I think I'm starting to smell Mrs. Arbuckle's vomit."

Mercedes giggled and headed out the door, leaving Corkery in his chair staring out the porthole. He was certain he was just making something out of nothing having read too many spy novels. Just because eight young men and women of Chinese descent was unusual on a tour like this and that they had expressed concern at the sight of a Chinese military chopper, didn't make them guilty of anything.

Yet for some reason he couldn't let it go. But even if they were guilty of something, what the hell could it be? This was Antarctica. There was nothing here. He pulled out his tablet and brought up his browser then searched for Antarctica in the news, just to see if there was anything that might explain what might be going on.

But his connection failed.

South Pacific

January 24, 1810

The nights were cold now, and Zheng's stomach grumbled. They had been unable to catch her brother. His ship was fast, though there was no doubt he was having troubles of his own. They were a week into this, and on the second day they had spotted bodies in the water. They had stopped to pull them aboard in case they contained any messages. They hadn't in any written form, but the fact their throats had been slit and they had been stripped of anything ceremonial, indicated they had been executed as mutineers. That meant things were falling apart discipline-wise on her brother's ship, his men, though loyal to him, more loyal to the organization, to her.

And while she would prefer that it be due to their respect for her, she was more than content to settle for the fear it undoubtedly was.

He had obviously taken action as she would have if the roles were reversed, and put an end to any potential sedition. It meant fewer mouths to feed and a slightly lighter ship, a ship far faster than she had expected.

77

They had taken it off the British East India Company several weeks ago, and he had been testing it, a crew of men loyal to him training on it since the day repairs had been completed. His reports had indicated it was quick, though not as swift as hers.

And now she was quite certain he was lying to her, for she just couldn't catch it.

She had spread her fleet out again in case they lost him on the horizon or at night so they could regain him in the morning. She had no idea how long this would go on. She had heard tale that the waters would turn to solid ice and then a continent would block the way at the bottom of the world, a land of nothing but ice and snow, nowhere to shelter, nothing to eat, just a barren wasteland that she had never heard tale of anyone returning from. It was still several weeks away, but if this were to continue for that long, she feared even she couldn't keep her men in line. Every day she had left one ship behind to be resupplied by one of the trailing supply ships, but she had left hers until last in the hope she might overtake her brother.

But it wasn't to be.

The men needed a break.

She stepped out onto the deck and her men came to attention. She waved them off and stared up at the crow's nest. "Any sign of our comrades?"

"Nothing, mistress."

"Send a green flare."

"Yes, mistress."

Her man launched a flare into the sky and it exploded in a brilliant display befitting any celebration. Green was reserved for her ship, reds were the other vessels in pursuit, and blues were the supply ships. Several reds shot into the air, far off in the distance, still well behind them and spread out as they should be.

"I see blue!" shouted her man at the top of the mast, pointing.

Everyone turned and she climbed up the mast as quickly as she could to catch a glimpse of it, and smiled. "That's our supply ship! Gentlemen, lower the sails. It's time for us to feast!"

Cheers erupted as the men sprang into action, lowering the sails and killing their speed. She returned below to her quarters, debating what to do. Her rage had subsided. Yes, she was still angry over what her brother had done, but was she following his impetuous action with one of her own? She was putting the lives of her men on scores of vessels at risk. That didn't bother her in the slightest, but she was also putting her own life at risk.

And risking her empire.

While she was away, her rivals could be taking advantage. She was already a week out, which meant a week to return, and this chase appeared to have no end in sight. Yet if she turned around now, what would be the consequences? Her brother would eventually notice she was no longer in pursuit then turn to take refuge wherever he had originally intended. She would set a reward on his head so high, thousands would be searching for him, and she would eventually capture him and retrieve the zupu and have her name added to the family history.

But if she gave up, if she quit, something she had never done in the past, would it harm her reputation if her brother and his men got away? Could it leave others thinking they too could do the same? Defy her and avoid her long enough that she might give up her pursuit of them? It was something she couldn't allow.

She sighed. This entire thing was ridiculous. Her father would tell her to continue on, her mother would beg her to stop and leave her brother alone. The woman had always protected him, had always been too soft on him, though had loved them all. She thought back to when they were children and how close they were. Her brother had been her best friend, had worked with her side by side on their father's ship. But when she had proven more adept with the blade than him, things had changed.

She was certain he felt emasculated by her, then betrayed when her father named her his successor when he had been injured in battle, the wound eventually taking him from them. She wondered sometimes if her father had done it to encourage Bao to step up and be more of a man. If he had, it hadn't worked. It had merely damaged their relationship even further, and left him hating their father on his death bed.

She had kept him as involved as much as she could, giving him command over vast fleets of vessels. He was, after all, family. And while a week ago she wanted him dead, his head sitting as a trophy on her desk, today she wasn't so sure. She stared at the far wall of her cabin, a portrait drawn years ago of her parents and all her siblings, commissioned by her father so that he'd always have them with him when he was at sea, now a distant memory of happier times.

She was tiring of this business, and perhaps it was time to rethink things. She had amassed a tremendous amount of wealth and could live a life as good as any of the emperor's daughters. Yet if she did leave this life behind, it would leave a vacuum that could lead to a tremendous amount of bloodshed as others attempted to fill the void. Yet was that her concern? As long as she protected her family and those who had shown her unwavering loyalty, were the tens of thousands of men that served her of any concern? Whoever won the battle to replace her in the end would earn their loyalty with the mere shaking of a purse. The vast majority of those who worked for her were loyal to her merely because she occupied the position she did. When someone else sat in her chair, they would command their loyalty.

No, the vast majority were of no concern to her. They would be fine in the end. Family and those closest to her, she would protect in her new life should she choose to venture in that direction. Her more immediate concern, however, was the zupu. If she were to leave this life behind, would she still merit entry? She had accomplished incredible things. Would retiring negate those accomplishments? Did she still deserve to be recorded so she could be remembered for all time?

As she thought about it, any doubts she had were removed. When a teacher retired after a long career, did his students still not exist? Did they still not retain the knowledge imparted to them? Did they still not contribute to the world they lived in? When a surgeon closed his doors for the last time, did the lives he saved still not go on?

Yet were her accomplishments the same? If she retired, the empire she had created would be carved up among the warring factions, and by the time the fighting was done, what she had created would be unrecognizable. She sighed. She had to be recorded in the zupu, and for that to happen, she had to die at her post with someone in charge of the family's record whom she could trust to document her legacy against tradition.

That obviously wasn't her brother, and if he would merely hand over their family's history, she would let him go unmolested. She no longer wanted his blood to stain her dagger. She merely wanted back that which had been stolen.

She lay in her bed and closed her eyes, allowing the now stopped ship to gently rock her to sleep, yet as always, it was restless, filled with torment and paranoia. She couldn't remember the last time she had enjoyed a good night's sleep. Certainly not since her father had died, leaving behind an eldest son far too weak to protect her and the family. Responsibility had been foisted upon her, and the damage it had done to her soul was incalculable.

She awoke with a start as someone rapped on her door. "Mistress, the supply vessel approaches."

She inhaled deeply as she steeled herself for another display that she had long grown tired of. "I'll be there shortly."

"Yes, Mistress."

She rose and straightened her clothing then stared at herself in the mirror. She was showing her age, but more critically, her eyes revealed how tired she was, and it had her debating her motivations. Did she want to be remembered as the incredibly powerful woman she was by the clan she had been born of, or did she merely want to be remembered? She could find a husband from a decent family, then perhaps be recorded according to tradition as part of his lineage, and history would never forget. Was that enough? Was everything they were doing here in vain, driven by her own pride?

She closed her eyes and her head slumped as excited shouts from topside indicated the supply ship was coming alongside. Soon they would have plenty of food and drink, and the men would be in good spirits again, but for how long? There was only one person who could know, and that was her jealous brother.

And unfortunately, at times, he was as stubborn as her.

Expedition Site, Antarctica

Present Day

Acton hauled open the door and jumped out, dragging his backpack behind him. He took Laura's then helped her down. He handed her pack back then pointed to an area where there was a cluster of shacks. "Fifty meters minimum!"

She nodded and slung her backpack, rushing away from the helicopter at a crouch as Acton helped down McAlister then Ortega, and finally Baroni, Evans, then Parata. He checked to see that everyone was heading toward the waving Laura then gave a thumbs-up to the pilot. He slid the door shut then slapped his hand against it before grabbing his backpack and slinging it over one shoulder. He trudged through the snow and ice, the brittle surface cracking under his feet, each step taken sinking him several inches below the surface. As soon as he reached the group the chopper lifted off and banked toward McMurdo, the first chopper already out of sight.

Captain Stanley hailed them, his team spreading out. The half-dozen civilians already at the site had gathered near the huts, all having volunteered to remain after being briefed about the situation. Stanley rushed over, joining them. "The Chinese are two minutes out. How do you want to play this, Professor?"

"This is a peaceful scientific expedition. I want everybody outside and in plain sight, preparing for the arrival of the supply train and the rest of my people. Just maintain a perimeter as if you're watching for wildlife pissed off that we're interfering with their daily lives. When the Chinese arrive, have your team converge between the Chinese and the civilians, but keep your guns down." She nodded at the .22 the captain was holding. "That peashooter won't do anything against their assault rifles."

"Agreed, Professor, however, if this turns into a firefight, you have to let my people deal with it."

Laura agreed. "If this does turn into a firefight, I highly recommend giving me and my husband weapons."

Stanley regarded her. "Oh?"

She smiled. "We're well trained."

"Well, let's hope it doesn't come to that."

"Here they come!" shouted somebody, pointing to the northwest. The thunder of the rotors echoed across the icy expanse, and after a moment Acton spotted a black speck, low to the ground, racing toward them.

Laura turned to the team. "This is it, people. Just remember, we belong here, they don't. This is a peaceful expedition, and we're not here to challenge them, we're here to explain to them the situation and talk our way out of this. At the first sign of trouble, I want everyone to just hit the ground and surrender. Captain, I'm not going to tell your people what to do, but I suggest the same. This is an archaeological find, and it's not worth dying over. If the Chinese truly want it, then they can have it. Understood?"

Head bobs were accompanied by a few verbal acknowledgments, but it was clear everyone was terrified now that the reality of the Chinese Special Forces team was almost upon them. Some were clearly regretting their decision to be here. Stanley's team sprinted to their positions surrounding the camp as Acton and the new arrivals carried their backpacks toward one of the buildings, leaning them against the insulated wall.

There was no ignoring the sound of the chopper now, and everyone who wasn't already facing it turned. A helicopter similar in size to a Black Hawk rushed toward them, its nose tipped forward, the massive rotors kicking up a windstorm of snow and ice. The pilot pulled up, leveling out the craft as it reached the edge of their camp. Stanley's team rushed from their positions, creating a line between the civilians and the new arrivals as the chopper bounced to the ground and a dozen Special Forces soldiers in winter gear poured out, their weapons raised and aimed directly at the peaceful expedition. They spread out to the left and right, but made no attempt to surround those that were there. Apparently, they were going to rely on intimidation and superior firepower to bring this to a swift conclusion.

A man stepped forward. "I am Major Chen of the Chinese People's Liberation Army. On behalf of the Chinese people, we claim jurisdiction over this archaeological find."

Laura gently pressed through the line of American soldiers, who for the moment were showing remarkable restraint, all aiming their inferior weapons at the ground, the Antarctic Treaty strictly prohibiting what type of arms could be kept on the frozen continent. "I am Professor Laura Palmer, and I'm in charge of this expedition." She patted her breast pocket. "I have paperwork from the New Zealand government that claims jurisdiction over this territory, and the National Science Foundation which is internationally recognized to hold jurisdiction over all scientific activity in this area, that shows that we are here legitimately under international law. Your presence here is a violation of several treaties that your government has signed."

Major Chen stepped forward and Acton clenched his fists in rage over the disrespect on the man's face. As an anthropologist, he understood most cultures had developed on this planet treating women as second-class citizens, but in the modern world, there was no place for that. It was appalling that societies that claimed to be advanced, like the Chinese, still treated their women like shit.

But he held his ground and bit his tongue.

His wife was in charge, and she didn't need a man to help her do her job.

"China doesn't recognize your authority here."

Laura stared at the man, clasping her hands behind her back, her legs spread slightly as she took a power stance. "Major, whether you recognize my authority here or not is irrelevant. It has been granted to me by international law. My team and I are here, and we intend to proceed with the expedition, an expedition your government chose not to participate in. Now, if you're here to tell us you've changed your mind and would like to participate in this international effort, you are more than welcome. I have been granted the authority under the expedition charter to bring on any new members I feel are necessary to the success of the expedition. The Chinese government and the Chinese people have exceptional scientists working for them." She made a show of scanning the dozen armed soldiers lined up in front of her. "I have a feeling none of those experts are here with us now, but the fact that you're here suggests to me you may have them on your ship. Is that correct?"

Chen glared at her. "Who and what we have brought with us is none of your concern. Rest assured, however, that we are fully capable of and prepared to assume control of this site and excavate this discovery, a discovery that belongs to the Chinese people."

"Actually, it doesn't belong to the Chinese people. We've identified the vessel as the Black Dragon, part of a pirate fleet from two centuries ago. And while that pirate fleet ultimately surrendered to Qing China, which eventually became China, what your government is conveniently forgetting to acknowledge is the fact that this ship was once the Admiral Gardner that belonged to the East India Company. It was stolen on the high seas, so if anyone has claim to it, it's the British, but they recognize international law that dictates no one has claim to this ship on this continent. Now, I'll ask you once again, Major, as a representative of the

Chinese government, are you requesting to join this lawful and internationally recognized expedition?"

"I'll only tolerate your insolence for so long, woman."

Acton took a step forward and Parata reached out, gripping his arm. "Easy, Jim, she's got this."

Laura stood her ground. "Well, I have good news for you, Major. Since your presence here is illegal, you won't have to tolerate my insolence for much longer. Unless you're joining this expedition, I expect you and your people to get back on that helicopter and return to your ship, and you can expect a formal protest, I'm certain, from the proper authorities."

Chen growled in rage and stepped forward, reaching out for Laura. She side-stepped him and grabbed his arm, hauling him forward as she extended a foot, tripping him up. He collapsed onto the snow and she released him, taking several steps to the side as the Chinese contingent surged toward her, their weapons now all focused on the one target. Stanley's team responded, raising their weapons and rushing forward to protect Laura.

Acton advanced, as did Parata and several of the others. Laura held up her hands, palm outward, one facing the Chinese, one facing the expedition. "Everybody calm down!" She pointed at Stanley. "Have your people lower their weapons."

Stanley gave her a look and Laura returned a firmer one. Stanley acquiesced with a frown. "Lower your weapons." His team warily complied while the Chinese continued to aim their assault rifles at them.

Laura extended a hand to the major, still on the ground. The major took it and she leaned back, using her weight to haul him to his feet, his previous anger now mixed with embarrassment. She picked up on it but continued to hold his hand. "There's no need to be embarrassed, Major, there's no way you could know I was Special Forces trained."

The man's eyes bulged briefly. "I'll keep that in mind for any further encounters."

She smiled and with her free hand patted their still clenched hands. "Major, I'm not your enemy. None of us are. And you're not our enemy, otherwise, your people would have opened fire on us the moment I put you on the ground. You have your orders, and I highly doubt they include killing a bunch of innocent scientists over an old shipwreck when we've already agreed that any items of archaeological or cultural significance to the Chinese people will be handed over as soon as we've had a chance to document them. We're not here to steal your history, we're here to properly preserve it. Have your people lower their weapons, then let's talk before anybody gets hurt." She released her grip on the major's hand and he regarded her for a moment. An order was snapped in Chinese and the assault rifles lowered.

Acton exhaled loudly and Parata patted his arm. "Told you she had this. That's one hell of a woman you've got there."

Acton marveled at her. "You can say that again."

Laura had bought them a reprieve. The question now was how long would that reprieve last?

St. Paul's University

St. Paul, Maryland

Dean Gregory Milton leaned back in his ridiculously expensive office chair, his wealthy best friends having bought the vibrating massaging bit of luxury to help minister to his tender back. As it worked its wonders on him, he closed his eyes and moaned.

There was a knock at the door that he recognized as his secretary's, Rita Perdok. "Go away," he groaned.

But the door opened nonetheless. "Back bothering you?"

He nodded. "I'd love to shoot the bastard who shot me, but now he's one of Jim's best friends."

Rita didn't say anything and Milton opened his eyes to see she was staring at him, puzzled.

"One of Professor Acton's best friends tried to kill you?"

Oh, shit!

He scrambled for an explanation then batted his hand. "Forget about it. I don't know what I was saying, it was just a poorly worded joke about

91

his love for guns." He turned off the nearly erotic experience and sat upright. "What can I do for you?"

"Well, you know how you had me set up those alerts on Professor Acton and Professor Palmer, and anywhere they happened to be going?"

Milton groaned, grabbing at his temples as his elbows hit his desk. "How can they possibly get in trouble in Antarctica?"

"Well, I don't know if they're in trouble, but a bunch of hits started showing up on social media over the past half hour. Looks like something to do with the Chinese." She nodded toward his computer. "I forwarded you some of the hits and flagged one of them."

He brought up his email and opened the flagged message, clicking on the link. A YouTube video of a military helicopter flying over icy waters played. He read the caption underneath: "Chinese military helicopter heading toward Antarctica. I hope they're not going where we're going." He cursed as he brought up more of the messages, some of them posts from McMurdo staff, one showing a video of a chopper being loaded with armed military personnel. He sat back, pinching the bridge of his nose as he closed his eyes. "Something's definitely going on."

"What should we do?" asked Rita.

He sighed and looked at her. "There's not much we can do. I'll reach out through official channels and see what I can find out. You keep monitoring."

She nodded and headed out of his office, closing the door behind her as his back spasmed and he suppressed a yelp. If something was going on, he needed to act, but if something weren't, pushing the panic button wouldn't be wise.

He pulled out his cellphone and dialed the only person he could think of that would know what to do.

Acton/Palmer Residence

St. Paul, Maryland

Interpol Agent Hugh Reading leaned back and patted his stomach with a satisfied sigh. "That was delicious, Rose. Thank you."

"It was my pleasure, Mr. Reading," replied Rose, his best friends' new domestic, as she cleared his dishes.

"Please, call me Hugh."

She rapidly shook her head. "Oh no, sir. I could never call my employer by their first name."

He laughed. "Rose, I am by no means your employer. That's Jim and Laura's domain. I'm just an old copper who can barely afford to bring someone in to clean his flat every fortnight."

"Still, you are the professors' guest. It wouldn't be proper."

Reading smiled at her. "You're a good woman."

"Thank you, sir." Rose put the dishes in the sink. "Is there anything else I can do for you?"

Reading shook his head as he pushed to his feet, his chest still protesting, the wounds from his ordeal in Thailand healed but the scars still fresh. He was up to half an hour a day on the elliptical, and was confident the stent inserted into his artery was doing its job and his heart was now recovering. He was starting to feel his old self again, though still old.

If he were to repeat the events in Thailand now, he might not be as much of a liability as he was then, and might have been able to keep up with the others. Though he had no interest in testing that hypothesis.

"I'm just going to go to my room and read the news."

"What time would you like lunch?"

"Midday, but I can take care of myself."

Rose shook her head. "No, sir. The professors made me promise I would take care of you. Now you go relax with your newspaper and I'll take care of everything."

He chuckled. "Careful, Rose, I have a weakness for women who cook for me."

She giggled and batted a hand at him. "You're terrible, Mr. Reading."

Reading grinned then headed up the stairs to the suite his friends had given him in their new and very large home. They were filthy rich thanks to the inheritance left to Laura by her brother, a tech entrepreneur who sold his company for hundreds of millions then died in a tragic accident at one of her dig sites years ago. They had offered him the choice of retiring here and living with them in the fully equipped suite, or to split his time between here and his home in London. He hadn't decided what to do yet.

He was feeling more like his old self physically, so his thoughts of retirement were slowly being pushed back again. It was his mental condition that was failing him. Nightmares of what he had gone through haunted him, and he found he was a little jumpy and easily startled. He recognized the symptoms. He was suffering from PTSD. He had kept this self-diagnosis to himself, and had used his lack of sleep as an excuse to get out of the dinner at the Milton's the other night. He wasn't good company.

He was supposed to have returned to London several days ago just before his friends headed out to Antarctica, but with the chaos at the airports and with flights being constantly canceled, everyone agreed it was best for him to stay here rather than suffer through the unpredictable travel nightmare. It also gave him some time to himself so he could try to come to grips with what had happened to him.

So far, he hadn't been successful.

Rose was taking care of him during the day and had agreed to come in on the weekends as well. He still had daily visits from a nurse, and five days a week, a physical trainer would come in to put him through his paces.

He loved his friends. They were the best of people even without their money, but they were extremely generous with their wealth, and he had no doubt if he were recovering on his own at home, he wouldn't have made the progress he had so far thanks to his friends.

And he might need to ask them for one more favor if he ever hoped to truly recover.

His cellphone rang as he walked down the hallway and he picked up his pace, reaching the phone just in time. "Hello?"

"Hello, Hugh? Greg Milton."

Reading smiled as he dropped into the ridiculously expensive and comfortable chair his friends had bought him, one definitely not made by lazy boys who didn't answer their phones, return voicemails, or service their products in a timely manner. "Hi, Greg, what can I do for you?" He was already concerned. Milton was Acton's best friend, and while Reading and Milton were on friendly terms, they weren't close enough to be calling each other up to chit-chat.

"Something is happening in Antarctica."

Reading groaned as he flipped open his laptop and grabbed a pad of paper and pen. "If we ever have a colony on the moon or Mars, they're going to have to pass a law that says those two aren't allowed to visit. How in the hell do you get in trouble in Antarctica?"

Milton chuckled. "Well, in their defense, I don't know if they're actually in trouble. All I know is that alerts are starting to show up about a Chinese military helicopter heading into Antarctic airspace, and about two choppers from McMurdo with armed personnel leaving in a hurry. I have no idea if the two events are connected, but the timestamps overlap. I have no idea where they're going or if Jim and Laura are involved. Nothing."

"Have you tried calling them?"

"I didn't want to risk it. If they're in a situation and they have access to their satphone, I would think they would use it if it was safe to do so.

Calling it might reveal their position or reveal the fact they have that phone."

Reading's head bobbed. Milton was right. With their track record, his friends could be in the middle of a situation where a ringing phone could be problematic. They had to be involved in whatever was going on. The shipwreck they were investigating was Chinese, the Chinese had apparently raised a stink about the National Science Foundation running the expedition, and obviously things were happening near McMurdo if the Americans were sending soldiers somewhere in a hurry.

"No, you're right, calling them could put them at risk. Besides, if they're already in danger, there's no point in calling them, and if they're safe, then there's no need."

"What should we do? I was thinking that we could reach out to Dylan, but I hate to play that card too often, especially when we're not sure."

"No, I think it's a little too early for that. Let me make a couple of phone calls and see what my colleagues in London have to say. I'll get back to you when I hear something."

"Okay, thanks, Hugh. Hopefully, this is much ado about nothing."

Reading ended the call, concerned. His friends' history had him convinced they were either involved or were about to be, in something concerning the Chinese.

And past experience with that country told him to expect the worst.

Trinh/Granger Residence
St. Paul, Maryland

"So remember, be good to each other because there might be a mental midget out there who thinks you should be canceled. If you aren't canceled before then, we'll talk to you next time. TG, out."

Tommy Granger removed his headset and carefully hung it in its cradle, the equipment for his podcast not cheap. He leaned back in his chair and stretched, groaning as he worked the kinks out. His show had exploded in popularity since the events in the Philippines, and it appeared he might actually make a living out of it.

And he loved it.

He flicked the switch he had rigged to his desk that turned off a red light installed over the bedroom door. His little studio was in the corner of the bedroom in the one-bedroom apartment he shared with the love of his life, Mai Trinh. The light was visible from the living room where she normally set up camp while he was doing his work, and he smiled as the door opened seconds later.

She poked her head inside. "Good show?"

"I think so. Still getting used to doing live shows. Who would've ever thought that an introvert like me would be doing live podcasts with hundreds of people listening?"

Mai came up from behind and wrapped her arms around him, squeezing him tight. "I'm so proud of you."

He smiled and patted her hand. "Thanks." He pointed at the screen as scores of comments continued to flood in. "Looks like they liked it."

She leaned closer, her breath hot on his ear. "What do you want to do today?" Her hands slid down his chest, past his belly button and toward Tommy Jr.

"Sometimes I think you have a one-track mind."

"I've never heard you complain."

He grabbed her hand and dragged it the rest of the way. "God, I love you." Her tongue swirled on his neck and he jerked away. "No hickeys. We're not teenagers."

"Aww, but I like to mark my territory."

Something scrolled past on his screen and his hand darted forward, grabbing his mouse. He brought the comment back up.

What do you think the Chinese are up to in Antarctica?

Mai continued her downtown exploration.

"Wait a minute."

"I've waited long enough."

"No, there's something going on in Antarctica."

Mai immediately stopped. They both owed their lives to the professors. Mai thought of them as her surrogate parents since her exile to the United States, and with he and Mai now talking marriage, he thought of them like his in-laws. They were extremely friendly people who treated the two of them like gold, and were uncommonly generous, recently offering them the down payment for their first home. "What is it?"

"I don't know. Let me check." He clicked on the user and fired them a private message.

First I'm hearing of it. Links?

Moments later, half a dozen links were sent and he began clicking on them. Some of them showed a video of a Chinese helicopter, others of American. He thanked the listener then outsourced some of the research as his concern grew. He posted the video of the Chinese chopper.

Deep-dive time, people. What can you tell me about this video?

He posted the link then brought up the video purporting to be from McMurdo.

"What are we looking at?" asked Mai as she squatted beside him.

"I'm not sure. The first video looked like Chinese military and claims to be from the Antarctic. And this video claims to be from McMurdo, which is the staging area for where Jim and Laura are."

Mai pointed at the screen. "That looks like Laura, doesn't it?"

He agreed, tapping the screen. "And I think that's Jim."

"What does it mean?"

He brought up another video showing a helicopter being loaded with American military personnel, all carrying guns, though none appeared impressive. "Something's going on down there. Remember what they said. There's not supposed to be any military activity there except to support the science. If the Chinese truly are sending in a military chopper and we're responding like this"—he flicked his wrist at the video—"then something is going on."

Mai rose. "Didn't Laura say the Chinese weren't happy about the expedition?"

"Yeah, apparently they refused to participate." He brought up his forum and found scores of responses about the video. His listeners had identified the type of chopper and what it was typically used for, and somebody had even posted a freeze-frame where whoever was taking the video had stumbled for a split second and the camera panned down, catching the name of the boat on a life preserver. They had also posted a link showing the current location of that ship. He brought up the mapping software and cursed.

"What?"

"The video of the Chinese chopper, which my listeners have confirmed is military, shows it was taken from the deck of a ship that's approaching McMurdo."

"So then, it's legit?"

He shrugged. "I don't see why anyone would fake it. It could have been taken out of context, perhaps from years ago, perhaps in the north instead of the south. But my guys are telling me that the time codes match for it having just been taken in the past hour, and it was geo-tagged in the same location the ship was at that time."

"Should we do something?"

Tommy scratched his chin. "I don't know. It's not like we can warn anybody. This was taken an hour ago. Wherever the Chinese were going, they're already there. So whatever is going down is already going down."

"True, but maybe nobody else knows it's actually going down."

He turned in his chair to face her. "What do you mean?"

"I mean, if the Chinese surprised them, then maybe nobody got word out. We might be the only people who know something is going on."

A burst of air escaped his lips. "You're right. I'm ninety-nine percent sure that everybody who needs to know probably knows since that first chopper had American troops with guns, but we can't take the risk." He grabbed his phone.

"Who are you gonna call?"

He grinned at her. "Ghostbusters."

She gave him the stink-eye. "Not funny."

He shrugged. "I thought so."

"Seriously? Who are you going to call?"

"Chris. He'll know what to do, if anything."

Mai smiled. "Good idea. I just hope whatever is going on down there doesn't involve the professors. They were so looking forward to this. I'd hate for it to be ruined on them."

"I'm not so much worried about their expedition being ruined as I am their lives being ended. They don't have a lot of luck with the Chinese."

Mai's smile faded. "Do you really think it could get that bad?"

Tommy shrugged. "With them, anything is possible."

Mai hopped up and down. "Then call him, call him! Seconds could count!"

Tommy brought up Chris Leroux's number, his contact at the CIA whom he had met through Professor Acton's former student, Dylan Kane, a CIA operative that Leroux had gone to high school with. Both Kane and Leroux had brought him in on several occasions to help man Kane's secret off-the-books operation center. Leroux had given him his number with strict instructions to only ever call it in an emergency. He had to think that a possible conflict between the Chinese and Americans in Antarctica would constitute just that. And at a minimum, even if they were aware of what was going on, they needed to know that James Acton and Laura Palmer could be in the middle of the action, two valuable assets they might make use of.

At least that was the excuse he would use.

Leroux/White Residence, Fairfax Towers
Falls Church, Virginia

CIA Analyst Supervisor Chris Leroux lay on his back, exhausted. But it was the best kind of exhaustion. His girlfriend, CIA Operations Officer Sherrie White, had just returned from a mission and whenever she did, she was as horny as hell and would abuse him and use him for hours on end.

It was awesome.

Years ago, if someone had told him he'd be suffering from too much sex, he would have laughed. He had been a loner and introvert doomed to be a bachelor for the rest of his life until he had met her. She had forced him at least partway out of his shell. He was still a loner, though enjoyed the company of his close circle of friends, and was definitely still an introvert, though not the painfully awkward one he once had been. He could honestly say he was happier than he'd ever been in his life. He lived with a woman he loved deeply and who was good for him, he had a few very good, very close friends, a job he loved and was good at, and a team and managers that respected him. There wasn't much more he wanted out of life.

Sherrie emerged from the bathroom. "Ding, ding, ready for round six?"

He stared at her and groaned, then gently patted Little Chris. "I think he needs more recovery time."

She grinned and skipped across the bedroom then leaped onto the bed. "There are things we can do without him."

Leroux chuckled. "I suppose there are. You know that old Monty Python skit?"

Her eyes narrowed. "No."

He grinned. "It goes something like this. Sit on—" His phone rang and he reached over and grabbed it. "Tommy Granger."

Sherrie frowned. "That can't be good."

Leroux agreed. "No, it can't." He took the call. "Hello?"

"Hello, Mr. Leroux, it's Tommy Granger. I'm sorry to interrupt on the weekend, but there's something going on in Antarctica that I think you should be made aware of."

"Antarctica?"

Sherrie's eyebrows rose and she turned on the TV, putting it on mute and switching it to the news. All she found was a talking head spouting off about something 90% of Americans didn't give a shit about.

"Some of my listeners sent me links to some videos that were taken in the past hour or so in Antarctica, one showing a Chinese military helicopter heading into Antarctic airspace, and several others showing two American helicopters leaving McMurdo, one with military personnel carrying guns."

"Just a second. I'm going to put you on speaker so Sherrie can listen in."

"Okay."

He tapped at the screen then placed the phone on the bed. "You said there's video of American soldiers with weapons leaving McMurdo?"

"Yes, sir."

"Well, that's illegal. There's not supposed to be any military weaponry on the continent." Sherrie sat on the edge of the bed. "They're allowed to have weapons for defense against wildlife, but that's it. Could you tell what kind of weapons they had?"

"No, ma'am, but I'll send you guys the links if you want."

"Do that."

"Just a sec."

Leroux's phone vibrated with several quick messages.

"The first one is the Chinese helicopter, the second is the first American chopper with the soldiers, and the third one shows the second American one with civilians boarding it, two of which we believe are Professors Acton and Palmer."

Leroux and Sherrie both cursed, hers far more colorful than his. "What the hell are those two doing down there?" he asked.

"Professor Palmer is leading the expedition into exploring an old shipwreck they just found."

"Shackleton's?" asked Sherrie.

"No, I think it was something Chinese."

"Chinese? And you're talking about a Chinese military helicopter? Just a second. Let us look at the footage that you sent." He forwarded the three messages to Sherrie's phone and she pulled them up in order.

She pointed at the Chinese chopper. "That's a Z-20. Definitely military. Sort of like our Black Hawk." She pointed at the American soldiers. "Those are pea shooters. Those weapons would be legal on the continent but there's no way they can compete with the fully automatic assault rifles the Chinese will have." She zoomed in on the third, pointing at two of the people. "I guess those could be the professors. Hard to tell in all that gear."

"It's definitely them," replied Tommy. "Mai agrees."

Leroux asked the $64,000 question. "Why are you bringing this to our attention?"

There was a pause. "Well, I thought it was sort of obvious."

"What do you mean?"

"Well, you've got the Chinese military going in. You've got the American military responding, and you've got the two biggest magnets for trouble in the world heading there as well. You know something bad is going to happen."

"Oh, I agree there. But what do you expect me to do about it?"

"I don't know, help them? Let whoever's in charge know that they're there. You know what they're capable of. They're not normal civilians."

Leroux could hear the desperation in the young man's voice. Tommy and his girlfriend Mai were very close with the professors, but Antarctica was an entirely different ball of wax. There were countless international treaties involving the continent, many of them prohibiting military activity, but he had to give the kid a bone. "I'll tell you what I'm going to do. I'm going to notify my boss about what you found and the fact that the professors are there, and I'll keep an eye on the situation. Other than that, there's not much I can do. Deal?"

"Yes, sir. Anything is better than nothing. Thank you."

"No problem," replied Leroux. "If I hear anything I can share, I'll let you know."

"Thank you."

Sherrie leaned closer to the floor. "And Tommy?"

"Yes, ma'am."

"If you call me ma'am again, I'll slit your throat."

Acton/Palmer Residence

St. Paul, Maryland

Reading sat fully reclined in his chair, the remote control clenched in his hand as the expensive chair vibrated the hell out of him like a cheap motel bed. He loved it. The first time he had used it, he had felt dirty, especially with his friends in the room sporting wide grins. But once he had tried it alone and forced himself to relax, he found he thoroughly enjoyed it, especially when combined with the massage function slowly kneading his back. This chair had done more for his physical recovery than any physiotherapist had, at least in his mind. He would have to look into how much it cost so he could have one at his flat back home.

He sighed as he ran his hands over the plush fabric. There was no way he could afford one of these. And the sad thing was, all he'd have to do is say the word and his friends would buy him another one and have it shipped to London, and their generosity would affect their pocketbook no more than him buying them a bottle of wine. He always felt guilty whenever they offered him something or simply did something, like this suite in their new home. He sighed.

Can friends be too good?

His phone rang and he leaned over, grabbing it as he turned off the dirty functions of his chair,. The call display showed it was Milton again. He took the call. "Hello, Greg, any more news?"

"Yes, as a matter of fact. I just heard from Tommy Granger. Apparently, he's seen the same videos we have, but he has one that shows Jim and Laura getting on a helicopter around the same time, apparently heading toward where the chopper with the American soldiers is going."

Reading cursed. "Well, that settles that, they are in the thick of it, whatever *it* is."

"Have you heard from your people?"

"I've spoken to Michelle and she said she'll look into it, but I doubt she'll be able to find out much. If Tommy has found footage of Jim and Laura being involved in this, it might be time to pull that trigger."

Milton chuckled. "The young man already pulled it."

Reading's eyebrow shot up. "What?"

"He already called Leroux as soon as he saw the footage. Apparently, Leroux said there's not much he can do, but that he'll pass it on to his superiors so they're aware Jim and Laura may be on site."

"That doesn't sound too promising. I would've expected more."

"So would I. All I can hope is that they were just being sparing with the details. I can't see Leroux not informing Kane, but really there's not much more we can do."

Reading frowned. He had an entry for Kraft Dinner in his contacts list that would connect him to Kane's secure network where he could leave the man a message. But until they knew more, he was still hesitant. He thought about it for a moment and came to a decision. "I'm going to send Kane a message just telling him what's going on. He would want to know. He can decide if he's going to do anything further."

"I think that's a good idea. I know I'll sleep a little easier knowing that someone like him is on the case."

"All right, I'll send that message now and I'll let you know if I hear anything more."

"Sounds good. Thanks, Hugh."

Reading ended the call and quickly crafted a message with everything he knew, and sent it to Kane, the one man who could and would break any and all rules to help his friends. He leaned back in his chair again, restarting the massage functions, but they had lost their appeal. While he had no evidence his friends were in danger, he was certain they were.

And once again, he was helpless to do anything about it.

South Pacific

February 1, 1810

Bao had done the deed himself, slitting the throats of the three traitors and tossing their bodies overboard. It had brought to a halt any talk of mutiny, at least any overheard since. But they were now two weeks into their journey, and supplies were running low. The men were scared, tired, and he had no doubt any one of them could turn against him at the slightest provocation.

Normally, on a ship like this, he would keep his distance. The men should respect the position. But these weren't normal times. He wouldn't do anything which had him on deck participating in the menial work—he left those tasks for the men, but he didn't hesitate to haul a line, crack jokes with them, make certain they saw he ate the same rations as they did, and when visible, always portrayed confidence that they would make it out of this alive.

"Master, you have to see this!"

He stared up at the crow's nest, the lookout pointing ahead to starboard. Bao peered into the distance but saw nothing. He climbed halfway up the mast then gasped at the sight of what he had only ever heard of. Icebergs. Frozen chunks of water only partially floating on the surface. Incredible. And terrifying.

"Adjust course five degrees to port!" he shouted. The orders were acknowledged, and he pointed at his second-in-command, Qi. "I want a second lookout. We can't risk hitting one of these things. Have them watch the surface because my understanding is the vast majority is underwater. We could tear open our hull before we even knew it was there."

"Yes, Master."

He scrambled back to the deck and forced a smile, burying the foreboding he now felt. "This is good news, men. All we need to do is press on, and those who pursue us, who lack the courage we have, will turn back in fear."

His speech didn't have the rousing effect he had hoped, his men merely returning to their tasks. He headed back to his cabin as the second man scrambled up the mast to the crow's nest. Bao sat on the edge of his bunk and stared at the case holding the 2000 years of history that was his clan. He wondered if the British captain who had once occupied this cabin had been so fixated on family business.

He highly doubted it.

His sister was a force of nature, unique perhaps the world over. He highly doubted there were brothers like him forced to deal with sisters like her anywhere else. He stared at an ink drawing of the family, one his father had commissioned years ago. His sister, upon their father's death, had gifted it to him, perhaps as a reminder of how close they were in their youth.

He sighed.

Why did she have to be so stubborn?

He shook his head as he stared at his hands, far too soft for those of a sailor.

Why did you have to be so weak?

"More icebergs ahead!" shouted one of the lookouts.

"What bearing?" asked Qi.

"The entire horizon!"

Bao cursed. A decision had to be made, and it would have to be made soon. Continue forward, or give up and surrender to the mercies of his notoriously unforgiving sister.

Expedition Site, Antarctica

Present Day

Acton stood with a cluster of the scientific team and the McMurdo staff already here prepping the camp for their arrival. The military personnel were in their own group, keeping a wary eye on the Chinese standing near their chopper. Everyone was cold, but no one dared go inside and miss the moment of truth. Laura, Captain Stanley, and Major Chen were inside one of the shelters negotiating, and he had to think progress was being made, otherwise the Chinese would have certainly called it off. Chen had emerged twice in the past several hours, boarding his chopper to use the radio then returning. Laura had the full authority of the National Science Foundation and the expedition charter to negotiate, so she didn't have to consult anyone, and Stanley, as US military, could merely act as an observer and advisor.

What he would give to be a fly on the wall.

The door to the building hosting the negotiations opened and everyone turned. Laura emerged then the major followed by the captain.

Laura and Stanley were all smiles, the major's expression neutral, though handshakes were exchanged all around. The major indicated with a swirl of his finger for the pilot to power up the chopper and he barked an order in Chinese, his men quickly scrambling on board. Nobody said anything as the massive helicopter slowly rose in the air then banked back toward where it had come from.

Stanley and Laura talked for a moment, then he broke off toward his men and she joined the civilians, everyone clustering around, eager to find out what had happened.

"We've come to an agreement. The Chinese will be sending in a team of scientists tomorrow. No armed personnel. They will be under my direction. All our American military personnel will withdraw as soon as we can get a chopper in for them, and then things will proceed pretty much as already planned. For the moment, it appears we've averted a crisis."

Claps and cheers erupted from the small group and hugs were exchanged. As congratulations were given to Laura, Acton stood back, smiling broadly, enjoying his wife's moment in the sun. She was incredible. She had just single-handedly negotiated a truce between the international community and the Chinese military and government. How long it would last, who knew, but if it held for twenty-four hours, it would give the powers that be enough time to position assets should it become necessary.

Stanley approached and again shook Laura's hand. "Excellent job, Professor Palmer."

"Thank you, Captain. Your counsel was appreciated and contributed greatly to the successful outcome."

Stanley laughed. "You flatter me, ma'am, but that was all you." He tapped his radio. "I called in the chopper to take out my team. It should be here in fifteen minutes."

"Good. I have no doubt the Chinese will deploy a drone at some point, if they haven't already, to make certain we honor the agreement." She indicated his radio. "I think it's safe to call in the supply train."

"Yes, ma'am." Stanley stepped away, calling in the snowcat with their supplies that had been holding position several miles out while the negotiations were underway. Smiles spread among the civilians, for its arrival meant a much more comfortable night than they had been facing. The backpacks they had brought had their emergency gear only. The supply train was bringing their heavy sleeping bags, changes of clothes, and many more creature comforts. Stanley gave a thumbs-up. "Thirty minutes."

Laura acknowledged him then joined Acton.

"So, you saved the day."

She chuckled. "I wouldn't say that. It was more Captain Stanley's men being here than anything else. It was quite obvious the Chinese had expected to get in here unchallenged and then just bully us out. Once they were challenged militarily, even though they could have easily won the fight, they had to negotiate. My concern is how long will they honor the agreement? You know how they are."

Acton frowned. "They'll honor it for as long as it's in their best interests, especially since this is, I assume, a verbal agreement."

"Everything on a handshake."

"Now what?"

"Captain Stanley is going to brief Colonel Richardson, then we'll wait for instructions from the NSF and see if somebody wants to send troops to counter any Chinese move."

Acton pursed his lips as he stared in the direction the Chinese helicopter had headed. "Whose troops would they be?"

She shrugged. "New Zealand?"

Acton shrugged as well. "Your guess is as good as mine. New Zealand administers this area, but McMurdo is American, and I doubt New Zealand wants to challenge China alone."

Stanley approached. "Professor Palmer, McMurdo is asking if you want the second supply train launched?"

Laura nodded. "Yes, let's proceed as if we're on schedule. Nothing's changed. Also, find out if it's possible to send another sleeping structure that'll hold the six Chinese scientists that are supposed to be coming here."

"Wouldn't they be bringing their own equipment?"

"I'd rather not assume that they'll come properly equipped. I'd rather be prepared for the worst. I don't want my people inconvenienced because of a lack of preparation."

Stanley smiled slightly. "They definitely picked the right person for the job."

Acton grinned. "I'll second that."

119

"I'll pass on the instructions to send a shelter plus a heating unit and generator and additional provisions for six people. It'll delay the train probably by an hour."

"That's fine," said Laura. "The primary train has everything we'll need for tonight, and the Chinese aren't supposed to arrive until late tomorrow morning."

"We've got company!" shouted someone, and Acton turned to see several fingers pointed at the sky. They all turned and looked up to see a drone circling overhead.

Acton frowned. "It would appear the Chinese don't trust us."

Antarctica Quest

Winter Quarters Bay, Antarctica

Corkery stood at the rail, as did most of the passengers as they pulled into port. To call it a port was a stretch. Winter Quarters Bay was only open during the Antarctic summer for a brief period after a US Coast Guard icebreaker cleared the harbor so the supply ships could come in along with a few tourist vessels. This was frontier living if there ever was any, and if he squinted as he stared out at the barren land and the sparse signs of humanity, he could imagine what the first settlement on the moon would be like, or Mars.

He followed Elon Musk avidly, praying the man achieved his goal of putting humanity on Mars within his lifetime. Now, that would be the life. They would need healthy, experienced doctors, and if it happened soon enough, he'd definitely consider escaping the madness quickly taking over the planet.

"This is the part I never get tired of," said Mercedes beside him. "It's so unlike any other place."

He had to agree. "An entire massive continent with less than five thousand people on it, even less during the winter, so many of its secrets yet to be discovered. I don't see how anyone could tire of this. I can't wait to get off this ship and plant my feet where hardly anybody has ever stood before. It's too bad we won't get to see McMurdo. That would be fascinating."

Captain Shoigu stepped up beside him as his crew tossed the ropes to be tied off to the temporary pier. "McMurdo isn't for tourists. If you want to see that, you either have to get yourself badly injured, or get a job there."

"Have you ever been?"

"A few times, and never under pleasant circumstances." He jerked a thumb toward the hatch behind them that led to the infirmary. "As soon as the passengers start to disembark, I suggest you get back to your station, Doctor. Someone always slips on the first day."

Corkery decided not to bother arguing with the man. There would be plenty of opportunities to venture out onto the frozen wasteland over the coming week. Beyond experiencing walking on the most mysterious continent on the planet, there wasn't a lot to see that couldn't be seen from the deck of the ship. He just wanted to tell people he had actually set foot on all seven continents.

"Don't worry, Captain, I'll be manning my post."

"Good." Shoigu slapped him on the back. "And don't go sneaking off at night just because the sun's still up. We have a strict curfew, remember."

Corkery held up his hands in mock surrender. "The prisoner shall behave."

Shoigu roared with laughter. "You're a funny one, Doctor. Much better sense of humor than the last one I fired." He jerked a thumb at Mercedes as he walked away. "Remember what she told you about the sea lion, and you'll understand why I'm so hard on you."

Corkery took one last look then turned to Mercedes. "Shall we?"

She smiled up at him then gestured toward the passengers eagerly gathering around the gangplank about to be extended. "Which one do you think will slip first?"

He chuckled. "Is it true that someone always does?"

"Not always, but most of the time. They usually just end up bruising something. Give them some painkillers and they keep going. Most of them know they'll never get a second chance here, so they tough out the pain."

Corkery indicated a millionaire's plaything in a coordinated pink outfit. "My money is on Bubbles. She's been bumping into everything since she got on board."

Mercedes snickered. "Well, as long as she falls forward, those Hollywood boobs should act as airbags and save her from getting hurt."

Corkery snorted as he patted Mercedes on the back. "Thank God you're on board, otherwise, this could be one hell of a boring trip." They headed for the hatch and Corkery paused and slowly spun, confirming what he had just noticed. None of their fit healthy Chinese passengers were on deck.

And that just made no sense.

Spokane, Washington

CIA Operations Officer Dylan Kane sat down the street in an unmarked SUV with tinted windows as he watched the final stage of his recent operation in North Korea wrap up. There had been a brief firefight lasting only seconds, and now a woman carrying her daughter was helped outside and into the back of an ambulance to be checked over. The FBI Special Agent in Charge turned toward him and gave a thumbs-up, and Kane flashed his lights at him.

She had come through. She had held up her end of the deal, and now he just hoped his government lived up to their end and let the woman who had more of an effect on him than he had expected lead a life free from the tyranny of the North Korean dictatorship that had subjugated her for her entire life.

He just prayed she hadn't fooled them all.

His CIA-customized TAG Heuer watch pulsed an electrical signal into his wrist in a pattern indicating his secure network had received a message. He pulled out his phone and brought up the encrypted email from Interpol Agent Hugh Reading. He groaned. There was only one reason the man would be contacting him, and it was if the professors were in trouble yet again. He read the message, sparse on details, then watched the videos. There wasn't much to go on, and there wasn't much he could do regardless. Antarctica might as well be as far out of his jurisdiction as the moon, but if there was something happening on the frozen continent, then the powers that be needed to know that the professors were there. He forwarded the message to Leroux, about all he could do at the moment.

Then decided there was one more thing he could do.

He pushed a copy to his former brother-in-arms, Command Sergeant Major Burt "Big Dog" Dawson of the Delta Force. If the Chinese had indeed sent military personnel into Antarctica, then Washington would respond. If Dawson knew their friends were in trouble, then he just might agitate to get Colonel Clancy to assign the mission to them, though that depended on where in the world they were versus other qualified assets.

A black car slowly approached, the rear window down, and he gasped as she leaned out, smiling up at him. He pressed the button, lowering his window as the car came to a halt.

"Thank you for keeping your word," she said, her eyes glistening.

He extended a hand and she clasped it, squeezing hard. "Thank you for saving my life."

Somebody inside the car said something he couldn't hear, and she let go of his hand, blowing him a kiss as they pulled away.

125

And his heart broke slightly as he realized he had developed feelings for this woman, despite being totally committed to his girlfriend Lee Fang.

Sometimes he hated this job.

Manila, Philippines

"I would have punched the guy's teeth out," rumbled Sergeant Leon "Atlas" James. His best friend, Sergeant Carl "Niner" Sung, agreed.

"You have to give my man Chris Rock props for reacting the way he did. That scene could have got a whole lot worse."

Atlas chuckled. "Can you imagine if he had hauled off on him?"

Sergeant Will "Spock" Lightman cocked an eyebrow. "I wonder who would have won."

Niner shrugged. "There's no way it would have lasted long. Security would have been in there pretty damn quick."

Sergeant Gerry "Jimmy Olsen" Hudson dropped in a seat beside Atlas. "Do you think his career will ever recover?"

Atlas shrugged. "Who knows? The way Hollywood was fêting him an hour later for winning the Oscar just goes to show the average celebrity is a hypocrite and a moron. But I like a lot of his movies so I'll still watch them."

Niner gave him a look. "Really? You're not going to boycott him for what he did?"

Atlas shook his head. "Like that little message at the end of a lot of those movies says, over fourteen-thousand people were involved in the production of this movie. When you go and boycott a movie because of what one star did, you're actually punishing thousands upon thousands of innocent people. If you truly feel strongly about a certain person, boycott anything that they do after the fact because then, all those people who work on the project made a choice to ignore what they had done. If I refuse to watch Men in Black, am I really punishing him, or am I hurting Tommy Lee Jones and everyone else in that movie?"

Command Sergeant Major Burt Dawson, the commander of Bravo Team, a group of elite Special Forces operators from 1st Special Forces Operational Detachment—Delta, commonly known to the public as the Delta Force, looked up from his draft after-action report as the C-17 Globemaster III they were in rumbled down the runway, a small church group they had just rescued from their captors holding hands in the back, their eyes closed as they prayed.

After what they had been through in the jungles of the Philippines for the past two months, he would hope they had learned their lesson, but he doubted they had. Too many of these groups headed into dangerous regions thinking God would protect them, but when God decided he had enough stupidity for one day, it was people like him and his team that had to go in and extract these morons.

He understood their motivation. They thought they were doing good, and in many cases they were, but sometimes the facts had to get in the way. Heading into Mindanao, a majority Muslim area with thousands of active militants, then preaching the Bible, was not a smart move. Philippine Special Forces had rescued six of the group a week ago then identified the location of the remaining four. Delta had been brought in for a joint operation and the remaining four had been rescued.

Ten lives saved, but five lost in the initial attack.

He would love to ask their leader who had survived the ordeal whether he felt those five deaths were worth it, but he already knew the answer. The man would say yes it was, and that those people were now with God. And while that very well might be true, and God might embrace them, He might also be a little pissed that they wasted His greatest gift.

Life.

It drove him crazy because he saw it all the time around the world, and it didn't matter the religion. The old refrain, "God will save me," had people rejecting medicine, doctors, science, vaccines, surgery, because God would save them. What about the old adage, "God helps those who help themselves," and then of course the elephant in the room, if God had meant to personally save all of His children, why would He have allowed for doctors to be born, for scientists, for His creations to invent medicines and vaccines and surgical procedures to save His flock? Those highly trained people, those brilliant scientists, those amazing medicines? If you believe God is all-powerful then those are His creations, put on earth by Him to save the sick and infirm, to prevent disease, to cure disease, to prolong life on this incredible creation. Unfortunately for too many people, they didn't think things through and instead let people with agendas do the thinking for them.

He wondered how long it would be before someone would have to rescue these people again.

The plane leveled out, the rattling of the airframe settling down, and the Oscars conversation resumed. He tuned it out. He had never understood the fascination with celebrities. He enjoyed a good movie as much as the next guy, but couldn't care less who was dating whom, who was feuding with who, and he certainly didn't care about people only famous for being famous. To him, the real heroes of society were those who served. Doctors, nurses, paramedics, firemen, policemen, and of course soldiers, who never received any recognition unless they screwed up, and then all were tainted with the same brush.

His phone vibrated with a message. It was an encrypted email from his old comrade-in-arms, Dylan Kane. He read the message, slowly shaking his head. Somehow the professors had managed to get into trouble in the unlikeliest place on the planet.

"What's up, BD?" asked Niner.

Dawson wagged his phone. "Just got a message from Dylan. Apparently, the professors might be getting into trouble again."

"Again?" Atlas groaned. "What the hell did they do this time?"

"Oh, you're not going to believe it, but they might be about to get mixed up with the Chinese in Antarctica of all places."

Spock's eyebrow shot up as high as Dawson had ever seen it. "Antarctica, as in the land of penguins and ice?"

"None other."

Jimmy shook his head. "I hope they never decide to try space tourism."

Sergeant Zach "Wings" Hauser laughed. "Oh man, I hope they do. I'd like to go up in one of those Moonraker shuttles and do some laser battles in space."

Spock shook his head. "I think we've lost the technology to do that type of stuff, or the movie was way ahead of its time."

Dawson smirked. "You're forgetting, gentlemen, that they wouldn't be sending us."

"Who would they be sending?" asked Niner.

"The Space Force."

Everyone roared with laughter.

He held up his phone. "So, what do we do about this?"

Niner eyed him. "What, we've got a choice?"

"Well, we haven't been assigned to any mission, and according to this, Dylan is not even sure if anybody in charge knows the professors are there. And from what I can tell, this has all been going down over the past couple of hours, so there hasn't been much time for Washington to react."

"React to what?" Atlas had his own phone out, scrolling through the news. "I'm not seeing anything here, so it hasn't hit the major outlets yet."

"That's just it. I have no idea if anything's actually happening. However, if there is, we're probably as close as any unit. I know we're all tired, but if we're willing, I can contact the colonel and see if we can get assigned the mission."

Niner leaned forward. "You know me, I'll do anything for my girl."

Atlas grunted. "And I'm sure Angela appreciates that."

Niner swatted him. "Just because I'm hopelessly infatuated with a woman way out of my league doesn't mean I don't love my girlfriend." Everyone stared at him and Niner shrugged. "Hey, I'm complex."

"You're something," agreed Atlas.

Dawson addressed the team. "Show of hands, who's up for a side mission if I can convince the colonel?"

Everyone's hand shot up, just as he had expected. They owed the professors big, not just for what his team had done to them in their first encounter, but for what the professors had done for them in the years since. They had fought side by side, all of their lives, at one point, saved by these two academics. And whenever they needed them, they were there, including funding the revenge mission in Moscow recently. There was nothing he wouldn't do for them, and the entirety of Bravo Team felt the same way. "Well then, gentlemen, I hope you packed your winter gear, because we might be heading to Antarctica."

Niner groaned. "We deployed for the jungle. You're lucky I brought underwear."

Antarctic Ocean

February 15, 1810

Four weeks. The fourth supply ship would soon rendezvous with them, and it would be the last until they turned around—the waters were too crowded with ice. Zheng's brother's ship was in sight, and from where she stood on the prow, she could see them furiously shoving ice out of the way with long poles. If the waters were open, she could reach them in minutes, but they weren't, her own men contending with the same problem.

The fleet was converging behind them as everyone caught up, but she had signaled for them to remain behind. This chase was coming to an end. Her brother was going to lose, and the fewer that witnessed her eldest sibling's humiliation, the better, for if he begged her to be merciful, she would be. Her rage was now merely concern. She wanted to save her brother for the sake of their parents.

They were family and family should trump all ambitions. And it meant most sins could be forgiven.

She left her cabin and headed out onto the deck. The crew was excited and rightfully so. Nothing was fresh anymore, for the supply vessel they were rendezvousing with was four weeks out of port. It would only be dried goods and fresh water, but simply knowing that one wouldn't go hungry or thirsty for another week was enough to put anyone in good spirits.

She let the men tend to the resupply efforts as she hopped on board the newly arrived vessel, its captain bowing deeply.

"Mistress, it is a relief to see you are well."

"An uncooperative sea and a chill in the air will never be enough to stop me. I want you to return to port and signal any ships along the way to hold their positions."

"You don't want to be resupplied after this?"

"No, not until we're out of the ice. This will be over soon, and if it isn't, we'll all be dead."

"I understand, Mistress."

She leaned in and tapped his chest. "And when you return, make certain that everyone knows I'm still in charge. And should I find anyone has attempted to challenge my position while I've been gone, they will die heinous deaths."

The man paled slightly. "Yes, Mistress."

She stepped back aboard her vessel, the flagship of the Red Flag Fleet, the largest and most powerful of all the fleets that made up the Pirate Confederation she led. A chain gang transferred crates of food, work that would take at least a couple of hours. She headed for the prow, staring into the distance, her brother's ship still visible, and she wondered how hungry they must be. There was no way he could have anticipated he would be at sea this long. And even if he had gone to half rations, he would have run out long ago.

She shook her head. All of this nonsense due to tradition and jealousy.

A stray shout carried across the icy waters and she held a hand to her mouth, calling out as loud as she could. "Brother! I forgive you! End this now!"

The crew behind her came to a halt and she held up a hand, signaling them to remain so as she cocked an ear, listening for a response. But none came and her heart sank.

He was determined to see this through until the end.

Expedition Site, Antarctica

Present Day

Acton stared at the sun on the horizon, the sun that wouldn't set for months. It was fascinating, and a little disorienting. With it still fairly bright out, his mind demanded he keep working, but he had to shut it down, which was difficult with everyone still fueled by adrenaline from the Chinese encounter. The military personnel were gone, leaving only two guns behind to protect against wildlife. They were defenseless should the Chinese return. The drone monitoring things was gone, or at least hadn't been spotted in several hours, and he suspected if anything untoward were to happen, it wouldn't be until the next day.

The second supply train had arrived and they had just finished unloading it. Laura had driven them hard but had recognized when to stop. The original intention had been to set up the quarters for the Chinese arriving tomorrow, but she had scrapped that idea. "Let them take care of themselves," she said. "If they need help, we'll provide it tomorrow. Tonight, get your bunks set up the way you want them and get comfortable. Make note of anything you think we should have that we missed on the master list, then I want everybody to get a good sleep."

Self-congratulatory applause spread through the team and Laura headed for her shelter that housed a bed for the two of them plus the office to run the expedition. He joined her inside, closing the door behind them as she flicked on the LED lighting, the energy-efficient bulbs casting a sickly white glow over everything. He shoved his hood back then removed his goggles and facemask.

And he could see his breath.

Laura flicked the switch to start the generator. It roared to life on the other side of the wall. The electric heater quickly glowed orange as they continued to strip out of their layers. Acton dropped on the bed as Laura sat in her office chair.

"Well, that day certainly didn't go as planned."

Acton chuckled. "No, it certainly did not, though I'd consider it a great success. Not only did we accomplish everything we set out to get done today, but my brilliant wife also negotiated a peace treaty with one of the most belligerent countries on the face of this earth."

She laughed. "I'd hardly call it a peace treaty. At best an informal detente."

Acton shrugged. "I'll take that over gunplay any day."

"Me too." She shivered. "I'm exhausted."

Acton propped up on his elbows. "Me too. Does that mean we're not joining the Three-Hundred Club tonight?"

She rolled her eyes at him. "Remember what I said, you wouldn't want that tallywhacker to freeze and drop off."

Acton instinctively cupped the tallywhacker in question. "Don't even joke about things like that. You know men have nightmares about that type of stuff."

Laura grinned. "Another advantage of being a woman."

Acton stood and stripped out of the rest of his clothes, wagging the whacker before wincing. "Holy shit, it's cold in here!"

Laura agreed, indicating his junk. "You've definitely got some shrinkage going on."

Acton flushed. "Never joke about stuff like that either."

"Seems to be a long list of things I'm not allowed to joke about when it comes to your genitalia."

"You're right. I'll send you the PDF." He grinned. "There has to be some sort of ritual about getting laid in Antarctica."

She grinned at him. "If there isn't, there is now."

Antarctica Quest

Winter Quarters Bay, Antarctica

Corkery lay in his bunk, light from the midnight sun shining through his porthole, a bed lamp lighting the screen of his e-reader. He had always thought he would hate reading an eBook, but with all the traveling he had done with the CDC, he quickly discovered the advantage of not lugging fifty pounds of books. He now loved it, and hadn't read a paper book in years. He closed his tired eyes and rested the device on his chest for a moment.

Jack Reacher would have to wait.

He slowly drifted off, fantasizing about what it would be like to have those skills, to be the hero, to save people from the bad guys. It was a common fantasy, he was sure. He had saved lives, countless lives, but always in the safety of an operating room. What was it like to have nothing but your fists and wits, battling criminals rather than a torn artery? He could only imagine. And if life were to treat him right, that's all he would ever do. Imagine.

139

For real people should never be put in such a situation.

A sound had him jerking awake and he listened for what had woken him. Something creaked and his heart leaped. It was the gangplank. His eyes narrowed. They were long past curfew and all the passengers had been accounted for. He turned out his light then pressed his face against the porthole. His heart picked up a few beats as he saw several of the crew carrying large duffel bags off the ship. He checked his clock. It was after midnight. Most if not all the passengers would be asleep—there were no parties today. Everyone wanted to be in tip-top shape for tomorrow when the tours really got underway.

Why the crew was unloading gear at this hour was beyond him. What were they unloading? Was it for the tours tomorrow? And if it was, why do it at this hour? It was frigid outside, and though it was still fairly bright, the shadows were long and the conditions difficult. This was not the time to prep for tomorrow, but who was he to know what was best? And he also was thinking of things in Western terms. While American safety standards might have relegated such work between normal hours, the Russians had an entirely different mindset. What he was witnessing might be perfectly innocent.

He slid the blackout curtain over the porthole and lay back in bed, setting his e-reader aside and fitting his eye mask in place.

And was out within minutes, playing the hero.

Antarctic Ocean

February 15, 1810

Bao froze, quickly turning his head toward his sister's ship, now uncomfortably close. Someone was shouting and he had no doubt it was his sister—he would recognize her voice anywhere. He couldn't make out the words, and when her voice fell silent, he turned to the others. "Did anyone hear what she said?"

Heads shook. She was too far away, though knowing her, it was a threat. He leaned hard on the pole he had been manning, shoving ice away from the prow. They were all weak. He had cut them to half rations quickly into the journey, then quarter. The men had taken to sucking the icicles clinging to their rigging to quench their thirst, but the water was contaminated with salt and it only made their suffering worse. He couldn't order them to stop doing what they already knew was wrong.

They were all suffering. It wouldn't last much longer, though. If only his sister weren't the heartless creature she was, he would surrender to her if she would spare his crew. He was prepared to face any punishment including death for himself, but his men were only following orders, and the moment he died, would fiercely pledge their loyalty to her.

Somebody cried out behind him and he spun toward the sickening sound of a splash. Everyone rushed to the starboard side, leaning over the railing. Bao pushed through them and extended the pole he still gripped down to the floundering man below. "Grab on to it! We'll pull you up!"

But it was too late. The man was already weak from hunger and thirst, and he sank below the waves within seconds.

One of the men turned. "Master, we can't go on like this!"

Qi smacked the man with the back of his hand. "You dare question your master's orders?"

Bao held up a hand, halting a second blow. This was over. There was no escape. They were trapped in the ice and it was only getting worse. His sister and her crew faced the same fate, but they were well-supplied, her men strong. They would survive. He stared back at her vessel and wondered what she had shouted. Was it a taunt? Was it a threat? Or was it an offer? Was she as heartless as he thought?

He came to a decision. His men deserved the right to choose their own fate.

"Everyone listen! The loyalty you have demonstrated to me over the past month has warmed my heart. You are by far the bravest and most courageous crew I have ever had the privilege to command, but this is over. We cannot win, so I offer you all a choice, and it is each man's decision on what choice to make. No one pressures anyone and everyone honors the other man, even if his decision doesn't match yours. I intend to continue forward as best I can, and on my own if necessary, but I give you this choice: continue with me, with no provisions, or get on the life rafts and paddle to my sister's ship and beg for her mercy. I will send a letter with you to indicate that I ordered you to leave to prolong our supplies, and that no dishonor should be implied by your surrender. Now, I will be honest with you. My sister's reputation is notorious for a reason. She may slit your throats the moment she sees you, she may leave you in the water to freeze to death, or she may welcome you and provide you with refuge should you swear your loyalty to her."

He pointed to the two small boats lashed near the bow of the ship. "I will go below. Make your decision swiftly. When I return to the deck in fifteen minutes, I expect anybody who has decided to leave to be gone with my blessing and my thanks." He pointed at Qi. "Come with me. I have a letter to write."

He disappeared below decks, his heart heavy though happy with his decision. He silently prayed that when he returned, he would find the deck empty, his entire crew choosing to save themselves from his folly. "Wait out here," he said as he stepped inside his cabin and closed the door. He sat at his desk and pulled out a piece of parchment then cursed. The ink was frozen. There would be no letter.

He pinched the bridge of his nose as he squeezed his eyes shut. He couldn't send them without a message. He smiled. He grabbed the portrait of his family and placed it in the center of the paper. He folded the edges around the portrait, then sealed it with the wax from the candle. He pressed his family ring into the hot wax then rose. "Qi!"

The door opened and his second-in-command entered. "Yes, Master."

Bao handed him the letter. "Have them give this to my sister, and have them tell her that I ordered them to surrender so as to save myself due to lack of supplies."

"Yes, Master." Qi took the letter and rushed topside. Bao closed the door then sat on his bunk, instinctively turning to stare at the portrait no longer there.

It truly was over.

Expedition Site, Antarctica

Present Day

Acton woke toasty warm. He and Laura had either joined a club or formed one last night, and it had been exciting. When they were finished, they had zipped up their double sleeping bag, leaving just a small air hole for the humidity to escape, then fallen asleep in each other's arms, their naked bodies sharing their heat. He reached over and disabled the alarm on his phone that had woken him, and Laura groaned beside him. She squirmed with delight as he wrapped his arms around her, squeezing her tight and giving her a kiss. "Good morning."

She buried her head in his chest. "Good morning. Last night was fun."

He grinned. "You're telling me." He ground his pelvis into hers. "Care for a little hair of the dog?"

She giggled and pushed him away. "Absolutely not. I can't be late on our first full day. I'm supposed to be setting an example."

He sighed. "Fine." He extricated himself from her and unzipped the sleeping bag. "I've got to pee anyway." He shivered as his naked skin was exposed to the chill of the shelter, the heater doing only so much with these temporary structures. "Man alive, I don't envy anyone who slept alone last night." He quickly pulled on his long johns, part of the mandated winter wear required to be worn by anyone going outside.

"You're going out?" said Laura, still in the sleeping bag.

"How much trouble would I get in if I just hang ten and squirt out the door?"

She eyed him. "Well, first, I'd assume you're referring to metric measurements, and second, you could get kicked off the expedition. You know the rules. Everything including our waste leaves the continent."

Acton sighed. "So, not only do I have to get all geared up, I have to live with that horrible insult from my wife, whom I completely satisfied last night?" He held up two fingers. "Twice."

She whipped the sleeping bag aside, giving him a glimpse of the goods before she rapidly closed it back up. He quickly pulled on the rest of his gear then pointed at her. "I'll be back in two minutes. Don't you dare put on a thing."

He stepped outside, the camp still asleep, the hum of generators the only sound. He headed for the outhouse and did his business, and by the time he was done, he swore he had an icicle where it shouldn't be. He zipped everything back up and returned to their building. He stepped inside, groaning at the sight of Laura, fully dressed. "Hey, you promised."

She gave him a look. "I did no such thing."

He frowned. "And I thought sleeping with the boss would be a whole lot more fun."

She walked over and gave him a peck and a gentle tap on Mr. Happy. "Don't you worry, Sweet Cheeks, I'll have use for you tonight."

Acton grinned and a shiver swept through him. He wasn't sure if it was from the cold or excitement. "I look forward to being inappropriately propositioned tonight."

She patted his cheek. "You better behave. We wouldn't want to make our horny Welshman too jealous." She checked her watch. "All right, I'm going to take care of my morning ablutions and you do the same, then we'll get this camp up and running." She opened the door and looked out then turned back. "Check the weather. I'm not liking what I'm seeing on the horizon."

"Will do."

She disappeared and Acton connected to the Wi-Fi set up by the earlier crew, a relay connecting them to McMurdo's Internet providing them with fairly decent access. Nobody was streaming any Netflix here, but email could be checked and websites browsed. He pulled up the weather report first. Yesterday's cold but clear day looked like it was to be the exception. A storm was coming that might prevent them from making any progress.

The door opened and Laura entered. "Brrr!" She rubbed her arms with her hands then removed her goggles and facemask. "I don't know about you, but I'm not sure how the hell we're going to work in these conditions."

"They say we'll get used to it." He tapped his phone. "Bad news on the weather front. We could have a storm hitting as early as noon."

"Oh no, really? Yesterday they said it was going to go south of us."

Acton scratched his chin. "Isn't like everything south of us? We're almost as south as south can get."

"Well, then, wouldn't that mean that almost everything is north of us?"

Acton shrugged. "I'm an archaeologist, not a cartographer. All I know is the weather radar is projecting it's going right over us."

"How long?"

"I don't know. The projection is only for the next twelve hours, and I have no idea how accurate weather forecasting is down here."

"All right, I'm about due for my morning check-in with McMurdo, regardless. They'll have a better grasp of what to expect. We'll try to get as much done as we can before the storm hits, and then I guess we hunker down."

"Our Chinese guests better get here soon," said Acton. "Or they could be literally left out in the cold."

RNZAF Air Movements Harewood

Christchurch, New Zealand

Dawson stepped off the C-17 and into the warmth of a New Zealand summer, the opposite of what was happening in the northern hemisphere his team called home. It wasn't that much different—Fort Bragg wasn't known for its winters.

A Kiwi flight sergeant walked up to him with a broad smile. No salutes were exchanged. They were all NCOs. "Welcome to New Zealand, gentlemen. I'm Flight Sergeant Langdon Johns. I've been assigned as liaison while you're here."

Dawson shook the man's hand. "Sergeant Major John White," he said, using his cover name. "I understand you have a secure comms facility for us?"

"Yes, Sergeant Major." He pointed at two nearby vehicles with drivers standing next to them. "These will take you to your temporary quarters. We've set aside some space where you can operate independently. There'll also be a joint briefing on the situation with our own boys."

Dawson jerked a thumb at the plane. "And the civilians?"

"Our people are coordinating with the local Red Cross. They'll all be taken to a nearby hotel where they can clean up. There'll be fresh clothes for them and they'll be fed. Transport will be arranged for them to continue back to the United States tomorrow."

"Excellent. Then I formally hand responsibility for them over to you." Dawson headed back to the plane. "Come with me and I'll make the introductions." He climbed back on board then headed down the aisle to where the civilians were still huddled. He addressed their leader. "Mr. Stewart, this is Flight Sergeant Johns of the New Zealand Army. He and his government will be taking over responsibility for you for the moment. The local Red Cross has arranged a hotel for you where you can clean up and get fresh clothes and food, and then tomorrow you'll continue back home."

"God bless you, sir. You and all your men."

Dawson gave him a curt nod and smile, then left them in the hands of Johns. Dawson stepped onto the tarmac and climbed in the passenger seat of one of the two vehicles provided for them. Within minutes, he was receiving his classified briefing from his commanding officer, Colonel Thomas Clancy.

"At the moment, Sergeant Major, it appears Professor Palmer was able to negotiate a temporary truce with the Chinese. The Special Forces unit they sent in has withdrawn and today the scientific team is supposed to join hers. If everything remains peaceful, then you might not be needed."

"And what do we think the chances are of that?"

"It's the Chinese, Sergeant Major, you never know with them. For the moment, we're going to move your team into position to respond should it become necessary."

"Understood, sir. Will we be deployed to McMurdo or the expedition site?"

Clancy shook his head. "McMurdo for now. Your team deploying with weaponry violates the Antarctic Treaty, so we're already treading on thin ice here. Pardon the pun."

Dawson frowned. "Permission to speak freely, sir?"

"Of course."

"Sir, travel time from McMurdo to the expedition site could take some time, and the Chinese are just off the coast. They could go in, wipe out everybody and leave before we even get there. We should deploy to the expedition site."

"I realize that, Sergeant Major, but the situation is very delicate. And at the moment, nobody believes that's the Chinese intention, especially based on the accounts I've read of what happened yesterday. I believe, worst-case scenario, they come in and force everyone to leave and then simply hold the position. If that's the case, Washington isn't willing to shed blood over a two-hundred-year-old shipwreck."

Dawson's head slowly bobbed. "I see. I assume the after-action reports have been sent to me?"

"They have."

"Then I'll review them and prep the men. We're going to need proper equipment, and everything we have is meant for fighting in the jungle."

"Red is already putting together a list of everything you should need. Coordinate with him to make sure you're both on the same wavelength."

"Yes, sir."

"Make that your top priority, Sergeant Major. I've already talked with our New Zealand allies and they're prepared to equip you. Also, you didn't hear this from me, but we have a weapons cache set aside just for this eventuality. I want you properly equipped and in the air ASAP. Your SAS liaison should already be on site to coordinate with you. They'll be joining you on this op."

"I look forward to meeting with him."

"Good luck, Sergeant Major. Hopefully this turns out to be nothing." He held up a finger. "Stand by one moment. There's someone here who wants to speak to you."

Dawson's eyes narrowed as Clancy stepped away from the camera, replaced moments later by Dawson's fiancée and Clancy's personal assistant, Maggie Harris. She smiled broadly at him and waved. "Hi, sweetheart!"

He leaned back and laughed. "Hi, babe! I didn't expect to get to talk to you."

"I was just bringing the colonel his coffee and he told me to wait."

"You've got two minutes," called Clancy from off-camera, followed by a door closing.

Dawson leaned closer to the camera. "Are we alone?"

"Yes."

He grinned. "Talk dirty to me, baby."

She laughed. "In two minutes?"

He grinned. "I'm not proud to say it wouldn't be the first time."

She snickered. "I like to think it's because I turn you on so much." She became slightly more serious. "So, when do you think you'll be back?"

He shrugged. "No idea. Could be in a couple of days, could be a couple of weeks. If I had to hazard a guess, I suspect whatever's going to happen is going to happen in the next two days, three tops. From the brief description the colonel gave me, it sounds like the Chinese expected to get there first so as not to encounter a large number of personnel, including armed soldiers. Now they've retreated until they can get new instructions from Beijing. We'll have to see if cooler heads continue to prevail."

She shivered. "Antarctica. Just the name gives me the chills."

Dawson agreed. "We've got jungle fatigues, and there's some question as to whether Niner even brought underwear."

She chuckled. "That guy always makes me laugh. Well, be safe and stay warm. I'll tell Red to provision you an insulated cup."

Dawson roared with laughter. "Fur-lined, baby. Fur-lined."

Antarctica Quest

Winter Quarters Bay, Antarctica

Corkery watched as the passengers disembarked, heading out for their first full-day excursion on the icy continent. His headcount was eight short and he knew exactly who was missing from the group—their eight Chinese passengers. And it made absolutely no sense. This was the only organized tour of the day, and no one was allowed off the ship without a guide. Did these eight people in the prime of their lives intend to stay on board rather than take advantage of this once-in-a-lifetime opportunity? He couldn't see it. It made no sense, but the fact they hadn't joined the group meant he was stranded here. As long as there were passengers on board, he couldn't leave. Not if he wanted to keep the commitment he made to Captain Shoigu.

Mercedes joined him at the railing. "Something wrong?"

"Our Chinese friends didn't join the group."

She said something he assumed was a curse in Tagalog. "Well, there goes our plans for the day."

Corkery agreed. "I'd tell you to go join the others, but I'm afraid it might get you in trouble with the captain."

"You're probably right, but I don't want to leave you alone either. You'd be bored to death."

He chuckled. "Don't you worry about me. I'll just lose myself in a good book."

She waved an arm at the view. "With all this to explore?"

He sighed. "We're the help, my dear, not the passengers."

"I wonder what it's like to have that kind of money."

He shrugged, hesitating to answer as he was quite certain he made substantially more than she did, yet he had to respond. "Perhaps we should start buying lottery tickets."

She grinned up at him. "And we'll split it, if either of us wins."

He put a hand on her shoulder and gave it a gentle squeeze. "Deal."

"Doctor!" she hissed, her voice low. He saw where her eyes were directed and he casually glanced behind him. Their eight Chinese passengers were filing out the hatch, heading for the gangplank. Neither of them said anything as the eight men and women disembarked alone with no guide. Several crewmen were in sight but nobody challenged the unaccompanied group.

"Something is going on," muttered Corkery. "There's something not right about this."

"What do you mean?"

"I mean, eight passengers come on board, an uncharacteristic bunch, stick to themselves, then don't join the group and are allowed to leave unaccompanied, against the rules? That's not right."

"Maybe they're just going to catch up with the group."

"Perhaps, but there's something I haven't told you."

"What's that?" she asked, her voice filled with trepidation.

"Last night, after midnight, I saw the crew offloading duffel bags. This is your seventh cruise. Have you ever seen anything like that before?"

She shook her head. "No, I haven't. The curfew is there for a reason. It's just not safe at night, even with the sun still partially up."

Corkery pushed off the rail and headed back toward the hatch, Mercedes on his heels. They said nothing until they reached the infirmary and he closed the door behind them. "I'm going to follow them," he said as he started to properly suit up.

"Are you insane? What if they are up to something and they catch you?"

"Then I'll have to just make sure I'm not caught."

She grabbed her own gear. "Then I'm coming with you."

"Absolutely not."

She continued to dress. "We stand a better chance if there are two of us, that way if something happens, one of us can go for help."

"Are you sure about this? It might be dangerous."

She fit her goggles around her neck. "I think you're going to find that eight young, fit, healthy people bribed the captain so that they could go exploring on their own rather than with a bunch of infirm old fogies."

Corkery laughed. "You know, when you put it that way, it does sound kind of ridiculous, doesn't it? You're probably right. I'm seeing things that aren't there." He jerked his chin toward his e-reader sitting on his desk. "Too many nights lost in a spy novel." He shrugged. "Let's go anyway and play spy."

She grinned. "You are definitely way more fun than the last doctor."

RNZAF Air Movements Harewood
Christchurch, New Zealand

Dawson entered the hangar and removed his sunglasses, his eyes surveying the scene. It turned out that somebody in Washington had indeed foreseen the possibility of a military incursion into Antarctica, so had pre-positioned a healthy stash of equipment. His team was currently going through the inventory and matching it to their projected requirements.

"How's it looking?" he asked.

Atlas turned to him, holding up a clipboard. "Pretty good. Everything we requested is here, and if not, there's an acceptable substitute. Just one problem though."

"What's that?"

Atlas jerked a thumb at Niner. "We haven't been able to find winter camo in boy's large."

Snickers and outright laughter tore through the hangar, even the Kiwis joining in.

Niner flipped him the bird. "I can wear loose camo, but you'll always be the bigger target. That's why you keep getting shot, especially in that fat ass of yours."

Atlas jabbed a finger at his friend. "Hey, you and I both know there isn't an ounce of fat on this ass."

Niner reached over and smacked it then turned to the others. "He's right. There's no junk in that trunk."

Spock cocked an eyebrow. "You know, there's no one in the barracks right now if you two need a little alone time."

Niner flashed his pearly whites at Atlas. "You want to prove there's no junk in that trunk?"

Atlas' open palm darted out and Niner flew five feet as if he had just been Hulk-smashed. "This trunk is the exclusive domain of Vanessa."

Niner picked himself up and brushed off. "So you keep saying."

Dawson cleared his throat. "Gentlemen, we've received an update from HQ. We're being sent in immediately just in case the Chinese decide to take advantage of the storm."

"Are we landing or jumping?" asked Niner.

"It depends on the situation when we get there. A jump is possible though very dangerous. We'll only be doing that if we need to insert near the expedition site because something has gone wrong. Depending on visibility, we could be relying completely on altimeters and you could end up landing in a crevasse and we'd never find you."

"I'm willing to take the risk," said Niner. "The Docs have done a lot for us."

Spock stepped forward. "Me too. I owe them big."

159

"We all do," agreed Atlas. "I say, we get our asses in there then deal with the consequences once we're on the ground. If we go in with the right equipment, we should be fine. Even if we get injured, we can hole up with our emergency gear and wait for McMurdo to come get us while the rest of the team deploys."

Dawson held up a hand. "Let's not get ahead of ourselves yet, gentlemen. This is a staging operation. As far as we know at the moment, nothing has actually happened that merits a risky jump."

Squadron Leader Jingo Dunn, their New Zealand SAS liaison, entered the hangar, ending the conversation. "Did you find everything you need, Sergeant Major?"

"Yes, sir. And my men have all indicated a willingness to jump despite the weather conditions."

Dunn smiled. "Why am I not surprised at that? I just got off the horn with my CO and yours. It's been agreed it'll be your six men and six of mine. Joint operation."

"Who's in command?"

Dunn regarded him with a smirk. "Well, you're an NCO and I'm an officer, but it comes down to the fact it's a New Zealand-administered zone. It's been agreed that I'll be in command of the operation. Is that going to be a problem?"

Dawson smiled slightly. "Not at all, sir. It'll be a pleasure to watch an officer's back for a change."

Niner snickered in the background. "He means it'll be nice for an officer to take the first bullet."

Antarctic Ocean

February 15, 1810

Zheng stared from the prow of her ship, slowly shaking her head as her heart ached for her brother's humiliation. From what she could tell, his entire crew had abandoned him, had mutinied against his command, proving they were cowards. She would slit the throats of every single one of them for abandoning her brother, for leaving their master to die. No quarter would be shown for betraying her family.

The first of the two boats pulled alongside and one man stood, holding something high. "I have a letter from my master to his sister, that is accompanied by a verbal message."

She nodded curtly at her second-in-command and Yingshi gave the order for the man to be brought aboard. The emaciated figure could barely walk, and part of her took pity on him, for she imagined her brother, who was honorable enough to limit his own rations just as the men's were, would be suffering just as these men.

"What is your message?"

161

"My master instructed me to tell you that we were ordered off his ship in order to save him due to a lack of supplies."

The words the man spoke were meaningless. She had no way of knowing whether they were her brother's words or words these men had made up in the hopes she would spare their lives. She flicked her fingers at the man and he handed over the folded paper, sealed with wax, the impression of her brother's ring embedded in it.

This would tell the truth. What had her brother written to her? Was it more defiant words, or was it a plea for mercy? She snapped the wax, brittle from the freezing cold, and unfolded what turned out to be a blank page. Tucked inside was the drawing she had gifted him after their father's death. It meant as much to her brother as it did to her, and the fact that this was the message he had sent with these men told her everything.

He regretted his actions and was sorry for what he had done.

A lump formed in her throat and tears threatened to reveal to those surrounding her that she indeed had a heart. She folded the drawing back inside the paper and stuffed it under her coat. She drew a deep breath, steadying herself, then gulped. She couldn't risk her voice cracking. She clenched her fists, her nails digging into her palms, then addressed the man standing before her.

"You have all served your master well, and remaining with him for so long under such arduous conditions proves to me that you were loyal to him until the end when he released you from your oath. I now give you the opportunity to swear your allegiance to your new master."

"You have it, Mistress. Our oath is now sworn to you and you alone."

She leaned over the railing and stared down at the two boats below. "Do you men now swear your oath of loyalty to me and to me alone?"

A chorus of, "Yes, Mistress," responded and she turned to her men.

"Bring them aboard, give them food and water and whatever else they may need. They are now your brothers and should be treated as such."

The response was not as enthusiastic as she would have hoped, though it wasn't unexpected. This many men would cut through their supplies all the quicker. She was about to admonish them, to strike fear back in their hearts, when an awful cracking sound startled them all, interrupting the tirade she was about to deliver.

"Mistress, look!"

She spun toward the sound and spotted one of her crewmen pointing at her brother's ship. She rushed forward and stared in horror. The prow of his ship had snapped off and the vessel was leaning heavily forward as it took on water.

This time, there was no holding back the tears.

Expedition Site, Antarctica

Present Day

Acton shoveled in his lunch, the first break he had had since the arrival of the rest of the team with the remainder of their supplies, just ahead of the storm that threatened to sock them in. When McMurdo had confirmed the snowcat would arrive well ahead of the storm, Laura had ordered them to proceed. The storm was scheduled to last for two to three days, but their shelters had been set up and they had plenty of food and supplies to ride it out. "It will be a good way for us all to get acclimatized quickly," she had said.

He and the others had agreed, and those back at McMurdo were eager to get started now that the threat from the Chinese was apparently over. The question was, was it? The clapping of rotors in the distance had him questioning that once again as the entire camp came to a halt, staring in the direction from which the Chinese had arrived yesterday. Acton spotted the small black dot rapidly growing and tensed as he recognized it as the same military chopper from yesterday. Though of course it was.

Whatever ship they had come from likely only had room for one helicopter.

"They're carrying cargo!" shouted somebody, pointing, and Acton dropped his gaze slightly to see the large pallet that he had missed swinging under the chopper.

"Light the flares!" ordered Laura, and two people at the designated landing area lit half a dozen flares and jammed them in the ground. The camp was already mapped out for optimal efficiency, and the Chinese hadn't been part of the plan. They had to set up at the edge of the camp, otherwise it could disrupt their workflow and their safety line setup between buildings in case of whiteout conditions.

Acton cursed as it was clear the Chinese pilot was ignoring the landing area and heading straight for the center of the camp. If he placed the cargo there, it would put the entire camp in danger, and no amount of negotiation would likely get them to move—they would probably set up their structure right where they landed.

"To hell with this," he cursed and motioned to the others. "Let's block the center of the camp so they can't land!" Most of the people stared at him bewildered as he ran into position. Parata and Baroni joined him and when Laura realized what he was doing, she too rushed over, waving to the others.

"Let's go! Spread out all over this area so they can't land!"

Within moments, the entire center of the camp was filled, everyone waving their arms toward the lit-up LZ. At the last minute, the chopper banked then hovered over the flares, lowering until the large pallet hit the snow. Two of the McMurdo staff rushed in and unhooked the cable

165

then ran back, signaling the all-clear to the chopper that then landed nearby. Laura trudged over to greet the new arrivals, and Acton joined her. He counted six in what he would consider semi-civilian gear, the uniform bright red of their outfits taking away any of the individuality communism despised.

Major Chen stepped out with them in his winter combat gear, but this time sporting nothing but a holstered sidearm—still a violation of international law, however minimal. "You should not have done that!" he snapped.

Laura ignored the tone. "Sorry, Major, but you were about to set down in the middle of our camp. We have a very specific site plan that was designed for these conditions. Where you tried to land must be kept clear for safety reasons. Now, who's in charge of your team?"

A man stepped forward at least twenty years her senior. "I am. Professor Liu Haitao. National Natural Science Foundation. You must be Professor Palmer."

Laura extended a hand. "Pleasure to meet you, Professor, I've read some of your work."

"Good. Then you'll understand why my government feels I should be in charge and not you."

Laura smiled pleasantly at the immediate challenge to her authority. "Well, Professor, we are all entitled to our own feelings, but not our own facts, and the fact is, I am in charge. You have been invited to participate in the expedition as regular team members under my direction, as per the agreement negotiated with Major Chen yesterday. If that's not acceptable, then I suggest you return to your ship and have your government contact the National Science Foundation to begin negotiations for your participation."

The man's jaw clenched then relaxed. He smiled broadly, and it appeared genuine. "You are everything the major described. It will be a pleasure to work under your direction."

Acton calmed slightly, as did the others.

"I'm happy to hear that, Professor." Laura indicated the large pallet. "Is this all your equipment or will you be bringing more?"

"We have two more shipments due to arrive, however, I'm not sure the weather's going to cooperate."

Laura agreed. "I suggest your helicopter leave now to stay ahead of the storm, and I highly recommend they don't attempt another delivery until it clears."

Major Chen turned to Liu. "I'm afraid the professor's right. There's no time for another shipment."

"Do you have a shelter in there?" asked Laura, gesturing toward the pallet.

"We have emergency tents. The second pallet was going to bring our shelter."

Chen cursed and a brief, terse discussion occurred in Chinese that grew in intensity.

Laura held up a hand. "Gentlemen, I'm sorry to interrupt, however, I planned for this contingency yesterday and had our second supply train bring another temporary structure for your team as well as extra food, fuel, and supplies. I assume you all have your proper winter weather gear."

Liu nodded. "Yes, that's what's in the first shipment. Everything to keep us alive for the rest of the day." He smiled. "Very forward-thinking, Professor."

"I've learned to always expect the unexpected." Laura turned to Chen. "Major, your people are in good hands. I suggest you get back to your ship before that storm hits. We will get the shelter up immediately. It has a heater and a generator with fuel. Your people will be as safe as any other member of my team."

Chen snapped out a curt nod. "Very well, Professor, as expedition lead, you will be held accountable should anything go wrong."

"You're a very glass-half-empty person, aren't you, Major?"

His eyes narrowed. "What do you mean?"

Laura smiled. "Look it up when you get back to your ship." She shook the man's hand then waved everybody back. "Let's make some space!"

The major climbed back onto his chopper and the door was closed by a crewman. The helicopter lifted off, giving everyone a taste of what might be to come, as snow and ice whipped at them before settling down as the chopper put some distance between it and them.

Laura faced the group as a whole. "All right, everybody, we've got a storm coming in, which means we're going to be cut off so we don't have much time to make sure we are prepared." She turned to the rest of her expedition that had arrived earlier. "I want everybody who wasn't here yesterday to focus on getting your own situation dealt with. Make sure you know which shelter you're bunking in and get it set up. It's going to get cold and harsh. And remember, as soon as visibility is reduced, everybody travels in pairs, everybody uses the safety lines. When the storm hits, you won't be able to see your hand in front of your face." She indicated the Chinese arrivals. "The rest of you who were here yesterday, let's help our new friends set up their structure and make sure they're prepped for the storm ahead. If we don't get it done in time, then they're bunking with you, so let that be your motivation."

Chuckles replaced the annoyance at the situation. The Chinese had come unprepared, exactly as Laura had feared they might. A sane regime would have waited until after the storm before inserting their team unprepared, but that wasn't the Chinese way. But it didn't matter. Now they were all in this together and there was no way in hell they were letting six people freeze to death just because their government were a bunch of morons.

South of Winter Quarters Bay, Antarctica

Corkery trudged along the path blazed by their Chinese passengers with Mercedes directly behind him, chattering away about all the family she supported back home in the Philippines. It was nice to turn off the clinical brain, to forget about medicine for a while and just enjoy the company of an intelligent, beautiful woman in a purely platonic way. They had already been slogging it for almost fifteen minutes and hadn't yet caught sight of those they were pursuing. They were making good time, their pace as brisk as one could make it on this surface, but it was clear to him that their mysterious passengers weren't sightseeing but instead heading to a destination.

"So, you're sure there's nothing in this direction?"

"Nothing specific, but then there's nothing really anywhere except for where we were and McMurdo. Especially not by foot."

They came over a rise and he spotted something below. He immediately dropped to his knees then his belly, Mercedes doing the same beside him. He retrieved the binoculars he had packed in the hopes of enjoying some sightseeing during his assignment, and peered below. Their eight Chinese passengers were pulling large black duffel bags out of the snow, and he cursed.

"What is it?"

He handed the binoculars over to Mercedes. "That's definitely them."

She leaned slightly closer. "They didn't have those bags with them when they left, did they?" She handed the glasses back as Corkery shook his head.

"No. Those look like the same bags I saw the crew offloading last night. This is very odd. What do you think they're up to?" He peered through the glasses and caught his breath. He wasn't a gun expert, but he was quite certain what he was looking at were machine guns of some sort. "They've got guns," he hissed.

Mercedes gasped. "Guns? Why would they need guns here?" She turned toward him. "Wait, do you mean like hunting rifles?"

Corkery shook his head, handing the glasses back. "No, these look like machine guns. Military."

She pressed the glasses to her eyes and gasped again. "Oh my God. What could they possibly need those for?"

Corkery shrugged. "I have no idea."

Mercedes continued to peer through the glasses. "What should we do?"

"I don't know what we can do."

"Should we tell the captain?"

"Definitely not. Remember, it was his crew that unloaded that equipment last night and brought it here. There's no way he's not involved."

"We have to tell somebody." She handed the glasses back to Corkery and he watched as the now armed Chinese geared up in preparation for continuing their journey. Then a thought occurred to him.

"Maybe they intend to take the ship. Hold everybody hostage, demand ransom."

Mercedes' jaw dropped. "Oh my God, what are we going to do? If the captain is in on it, then we can't warn him."

"Do you know if anybody has a satellite phone?"

Mercedes squinted. "Didn't Roy say he had one? His wife insisted he bring it?"

Corkery smiled slightly. "You're right, he did say he had one. I wonder if he took it with him or if it's in his cabin."

She shrugged. "I don't know. I would think he'd take it with him."

"Okay, let's get back to the ship and see if we can find that phone."

"Wouldn't it be better if one of us went to the ship and the other tried to find the tour group?"

She was right. By splitting up, it pretty much guaranteed they would find the phone, but he was hesitant to have her go off on her own. "You're right. You go back to the ship and I'll go find the tour group."

She shook her head. "No. You don't know where they've gone. I do." She pointed to their right. "They're just over there, maybe a fifteen-minute hike."

He peered through the glasses then excitedly put a hand on Mercedes' shoulder. "Look!" he said as he handed her the glasses. "They're not going back to the ship."

Her jaw dropped again. "Then where are they going?"

"I don't know, but wherever it is, it isn't to make friends. We have a decision to make."

Expedition Site, Antarctica

It was like an Amish barn-raising in the Antarctic. Everyone was working together to unload the Chinese supplies and erect their sleeping quarters. The wind was picking up and everyone was freezing. The Chinese scientists seemed quite pleasant and all spoke near-perfect English. If the goodwill kept up, cooperation shouldn't be a problem. Unfortunately, the horny Welshman was already extending his olive branch to one of the attractive scientists on the Chinese team. If anything disrupted the detente on this first day, it would be that man's inappropriate flirtations.

Someone fired up the generator and another member of the team leaned out of the shelter extending a thumbs-up. "We've got heat!"

A cheer erupted from the group and a chain gang was formed to get all their personal supplies inside. Laura turned to Professor Liu. "Professor, I suggest all your people get inside and get your sleeping areas prepped." She pointed at one of the McMurdo staff. "Get safety lines out to here right away. One to the latrines and one to the main storage building."

"Yes, ma'am."

She faced the Chinese contingent. "Remember, never go out alone, and always attach to the safety lines when visibility is down. It just might save your life."

The entire team bowed slightly, acknowledging the instructions. Acton just hoped they would obey them.

A fierce gust blasted them, strong enough to knock a few people off their feet. Acton helped up Baroni, her slight frame not standing much of a chance against Antarctica's bluster. "You all right?"

She nodded, brushing off. "Only my ego was bruised."

He laughed and slapped her gently on the back. "Don't worry about it. By the time this expedition is over, all of us will have fallen on our asses at some point."

Laura turned to the team. "All right, anybody who doesn't need to be outside get to your assigned emergency stations or inside your shelters. Use your waste bottles if you can, but if you absolutely have to go, go in pairs. And double-check your fuel. Don't assume there's fuel by your generator just because there's a can there. It could be half full, it could be empty. The last thing we need is somebody having to go out in white-out conditions to get fuel that should have already been there to keep everyone from freezing to death." She smacked her hands together. "Let's go people!"

Everyone scattered, most heading to their quarters, some heading to their assigned stations. Acton rushed over to the newly constructed Chinese shelter and confirmed they were good for fuel and that the generator was running smoothly, then waited for Laura as she checked on their guests inside their structure. She reemerged, closing the door. They could still see fairly clearly, though the gusts were getting brutal and the temperature was dropping despite the midday sun.

As they headed back to their own shelter, he shivered. "I have a feeling this is going to be pretty nasty."

Laura pointed at the communications mast swaying in the wind. "I just hope we don't lose comms in case of an emergency."

Acton frowned. "Should we secure it better?"

Laura shook her head as they reached their shelter. "No, I already had it double-checked. It's as secure as it's going to get. There's only so much you can do in these conditions on something that's mounted on ice. We're just going to have to pray nothing goes wrong."

South of Winter Quarters Bay, Antarctica

Mercedes pushed across the ice, moving as quickly as she could. It was times like these that she cursed her five-foot-nothing frame. It was decided she should join the group and find Roy to see if he had the satellite phone on him, and if he did, to ask him if they could borrow it while making sure nobody heard their conversation. They didn't know who they could trust. The eight Chinese were obviously in on it, and at least some of the crew were too, which meant it was possible the tour guides were as well.

If he didn't have the phone with him, but agreed to let them borrow it, she was to return to the ship and get it and make the call. There had been a brief debate over who to call, and Corkery had decided their best bet was an old colleague of his.

"You have access to my file?"

"Yes."

"She's my emergency contact. Call her, tell her what we saw, and she'll be like a dog on a bone. She won't stop until somebody pays attention."

"Is she your wife?"

Corkery laughed. "No, definitely not."

"Girlfriend?"

"No. Just a friend."

She was surprised at how happy she had been to hear that. She found this man intriguing. The chances of there being anything between them were next to nothing. Once this cruise was over, they would go their separate ways. It was just nice to fantasize about being with someone attractive, intelligent, and funny.

She spotted something ahead and sighed in relief as she caught sight of a cluster of people, one of the outfits a bright pink, the Antarctic bunny with the big boobs standing out among the group. Mercedes attempted to run toward them but failed miserably, the brittle ground swallowing her feet. She continued her trudge, repeatedly praying that they didn't leave before she reached them.

Someone spotted her and waved. She waved back and several of the group broke away toward her. She had no doubt they had no idea who she was from this distance, especially considering her entire face was covered. She reached the group and thanked God that Roy was one of those who had broken off to investigate the newcomer.

"Hello," said Roy, removing his facemask and goggles so she could see his face. "Lost?"

She laughed, removing her own face coverings. "No, I just came to make sure everybody was all right."

He chuckled. "We've had a few people fall on their asses, but nothing broken yet."

"Dr. Corkery will be relieved to hear that." She pointed at his bandage. "Let me check that for you before you cover your face again."

"Sure."

She glanced at the others. "You might as well go rejoin your group. I'd hate for you to miss your tour. There's a storm coming in so I think they'll be cutting it short."

Pleasantries were exchanged and the rest of the group headed back to join the others. She leaned closer to Roy. "I'm going to be honest with you, sir, and take you into our confidence."

Roy eyed her. "What do you mean?"

"Dr. Corkery and I saw something we shouldn't have. And I'll be honest with you, sir, we don't know who we can trust."

"Well, I can assure you that you can trust me, young lady."

"I hope so, but the less you know, perhaps the better. I have a favor, or rather *we* have a favor to ask of you."

"Anything."

"Do you have your satellite phone with you?"

His eyes widened. "My satellite phone? No, actually, I left it in my cabin. It's just one more infernal thing to have to carry around. Like I told you and the Doc, that was my wife's idea, not mine."

"So, it's in your cabin?"

"Yes."

"I'm going to be heading back to the ship now. Do I have your permission to get it?"

"Absolutely, but I'll come with you."

She shook her head. "No, that could raise suspicions. You stick with the group, and if anyone asks, I was just checking your stitches."

"What are you going to do?"

"I need to go back to the ship, get the phone, and make a call."

"And the Doc?"

"He's elsewhere for the moment," she said, not wanting to reveal too much. "Hopefully, he'll be returning to the ship shortly."

"Okay, you go get that phone. The pin number is my birth year. You'll have that on my records, I assume?"

"Yes."

"Make as many calls as you need. When I get back, I'll come see you in the infirmary. I'll tell people my stitches are hurting."

She smiled. "They probably will be from the cold. I'll leave the infirmary unlocked, and if something goes wrong, I'll try to leave a letter in the top right drawer of Dr. Corkery's desk explaining what we saw."

Roy eyed her. "You're not intending to go out in this, are you? To go find him?"

"Let's hope it doesn't come to that." She leaned closer, despite the fact no one was around them. "Trust no one, especially the crew."

He took her by both shoulders, staring into her eyes. "You be careful. You hear me?"

She forced a smile. "I'll do my best." She fit her goggles back in place then raised her facemask. She pointed at his bare face. "You better cover up or you really will need to see me when you get back."

She turned toward the ship as Roy headed to rejoin the group. So far, the plan was coming together, but she feared what Corkery might be getting himself into by following the heavily armed Chinese.

And she still, for the life of her, couldn't figure out what they might possibly be after.

South of Winter Quarters Bay, Antarctica

This is stupid.

Corkery should have turned back after the first wind gust, but he had to know what these Chinese, now heavily armed, were doing. They were still moving at a brisk pace, all of them clearly in peak physical condition. He always kept himself in shape, eating right, working out, getting in a kayak any chance he got, but his preferred form of physical exercise hadn't prepared his legs for this, and they burned. He wasn't sure how much farther he could go regardless, and if they were to abort and turn back to the ship, he doubted there was any way he could keep ahead of them. He would have to find someplace to hide.

This is really stupid.

He stopped for a breather and pulled out his binoculars, scanning the horizon ahead, again seeing nothing. Wherever they were going couldn't be much farther. They didn't appear to have enough gear with them to survive the night, and it was certainly not enough for a multi-day excursion.

He took a risk and stood high on his toes, once again scanning ahead. "There you are!" he exclaimed, spotting something in the distance. He squinted then refocused the binoculars. He wasn't sure exactly what he was seeing, but if he wasn't mistaken, it appeared to be the top of a communications mast. It had to be their destination. It was the only thing within sight, and even it was still a good distance away.

Now the question was what to do? If that indeed was their destination, then he had achieved his goal and should return to the ship. But he had to know what they were there for, and against his better judgment, he pressed on.

This is ridiculously stupid.

Expedition Site, Antarctica

Acton peered out the window then checked the thermometer. It had dropped another five degrees. He glanced at the others in the shelter. "If we had a sauna, we could join the Three-Hundred Club."

The two McMurdo staffers in the room snickered.

Carl Ericksen, manning their radio, laughed. "If you're interested, Professor, I'm sure arrangements can be made."

Acton grinned at Laura. "I'll need a partner."

She rolled her eyes. "I'm sure Evans is available."

Blank stares from the McMurdo staff told him they hadn't yet been exposed to the Welshman's legend. Acton waved a hand. "Stay here long enough and you guys will figure it out." He nodded toward Ericksen. "Any luck with that?"

"Keeps breaking up. It could be atmospheric conditions, but I think we've got a loose connection."

Acton cursed. "Do we risk fixing it?"

Laura wagged her phone. "Internet is useless. All we've got now is the satphone and that radio."

Acton grabbed their personal satellite phone off the table. "It's fully charged, but the signal strength is shit."

"And it's only going to get worse, sir," said Ericksen. "You'll learn pretty quickly down here that things don't work as well as the advertisement claims. If you want, I'll go outside and take a look. If we're lucky, it's something at the base, but if we're not, it could be fifty feet in the air, and the only way to fix it would be to lower the mast and check the entire length."

Laura sighed and Acton didn't envy her the decision. He knew she was hesitating because she didn't want to put lives at risk, so he solved one of the variables.

"I'm fairly handy. I'll go with him and you two can tell us if we've fixed the problem."

Laura's eyes conveyed her thanks. "Good. You two gear up, go out there, but no more than ten minutes. It's getting too cold and too windy. Just do it methodically, front to back, so that if need be, you can tell us where you left off and we can take turns."

Ericksen left first and Acton gave Laura a thumbs-up. "Be back in ten."

She tapped her watch. "Not a minute longer."

He laughed and fit his goggles in place then raised his facemask. He stepped outside and the wind and cold immediately hit him. The visibility was still fairly decent. He could see all the other structures, and for the moment, everybody seemed to be keeping inside—the two of them were

185

the only people stupid enough to be out in this. As a McMurdo staffer, Ericksen had far more experience in these conditions, so Acton planned to simply follow the man's lead.

"Don't bother clipping on. Those don't lead to where we're going." Ericksen patted the wall of the structure. "Just always keep this in sight."

Acton gave a thumbs-up. "Gotcha."

They set to work, checking the cables, starting at the connection point to the structure and working their way to the nearby mast that swung violently by design. As everything at the structure checked out, Acton peered up at the mast, shielding his eyes with his hand as he searched for the source of a pinging sound. When he found it, he cursed and pointed. "Look!"

Ericksen stared up and shook his head at the loose cable near the top of the structure. "There's no fixing that now, not in this."

"How *do* we fix it?"

"We'd have to lower the entire assembly to the ground and reattach it. There's no way you can climb up there in this."

"What's involved in lowering it?"

Ericksen pointed at the connectors driven deep into the ice in four directions. "We'd have to unhook two of those, lower this thing, reattach the cable, then raise it again and re-hook the lines. Even in perfect conditions it's a hell of a lot more than a two-man job. And with the way the wind is whipping here, somebody could get seriously injured or killed." He shook his head. "I'm sorry, Professor, but we don't have comms and we won't until this storm is over."

Acton cursed again. "Let's get back inside before I freeze my boys off. We're just going to have to hope nothing goes wrong before this storm lifts."

South of Winter Quarters Bay, Antarctica

Corkery pushed forward against the wind, thanking God that goggles and a full face-covering were required equipment. He was cold, but none of his skin was exposed. He was already convinced it was too late to turn back. This was officially the dumbest thing he had ever done, and it could very well be the death of him. The distances involved weren't great, it was simply that they took a long time to cover on foot.

As he continued to follow the Chinese, the mast he could only see the top of had turned into a cluster of buildings. There was shelter there, perhaps supplies, perhaps even heaters and generators. It was obvious this was the Chinese group's destination, and the fact they had weapons meant they likely intended a hostile takeover. But unless they intended to kill everyone, his best bet at survival might simply be to surrender and offer his services as a doctor, services the present occupants of the encampment might desperately need in the next few minutes.

He stopped and again peered through his binoculars. The Chinese had spread out now and were approaching the edge of the cluster of buildings. He prayed they were unmanned, but he could swear he heard a generator chugging away, perhaps more than one. His heart stopped when he saw two people battling with the communications mast before giving up and heading back inside.

The camp was manned.

People's lives were at risk.

God, I hope Mercedes was able to make that call.

Winter Quarters Bay, Antarctica

Mercedes cried with relief at the sight of the ship. She sprinted down the well-trodden path along the shore, the workers milling about taking notice, but she ignored them. She reached the gangplank and rushed onto the ship, running headlong into Captain Shoigu.

"Where have you been?"

It was clear from his tone that he was outraged, but she had already planned for this on her trek here. She had come up with every possible scenario for what could go wrong, and an answer for it. "One of our patients forgot to pick up his medication this morning so I brought it out to him."

This caught Shoigu off guard. "You mean you trekked all the way out to the tour group to give a man his medicine?"

"Shouldn't I have?"

Shoigu regarded her for a moment before shaking his head. "No, I suppose it was the right thing to do. Where's that bloody doctor?"

"I'm sure he's about somewhere. Now, can I go inside, I'm freezing?"

Shoigu grunted and stepped aside. "Go ahead, but tell Corkery I want to see him."

"I will." She rushed inside and headed directly for Roy's quarters. She used her staff passkey to gain entry then closed the door gently behind her. The phone was sitting in the top drawer of his nightstand exactly as he had described. She grabbed it and stuffed it in an inside pocket then slowly opened the door, peeking out to make sure the corridor was empty.

It was.

She stepped outside, gently closed the door, then rushed down the corridor and through several hatches before reaching the infirmary. She unlocked it and her shoulders slumped in disappointment when she didn't find Corkery waiting for her. It meant he was still out on the ice in the worsening conditions. But for the moment, there was no second guessing what to do. She knew exactly what her assignment was.

She locked the door so no one would walk in on her, then retrieved Roy's medical file and Corkery's personnel file. She entered Roy's birth year, unlocking the phone, then dialed the emergency contact number and suppressed an excited yelp when a woman answered the phone.

"Dr. Best speaking."

Expedition Site, Antarctica

Acton yanked off his gloves and stomped his boots as Ericksen delivered the bad news.

"Sorry, Professor, but there's no way we're getting comms up until this storm is over."

Laura frowned. "That's not good."

"No, it isn't," agreed Acton. "But we should be fine. We're well equipped. We have shelter, food, water, generators, heaters including some backups. A whole lot would have to go wrong for us to actually need help. You planned this trip well."

Laura batted away the compliment. "I had a lot of help. But you're right, we should be fine." She turned to Ericksen. "If there were a break in the storm, how long would it take to fix?"

Ericksen shrugged. "If enough people chipped in with muscle power, twenty minutes. It's not really a repair, it's just reattaching a cable. It's just that the connector is up at the top. Like I told your husband, we just have to unhook two of the support cables, gently lower the mast to the ground, reconnect the loose cable, then raise the mast again and resecure. Obviously, we'll do a test of it while it's on the ground to make sure something else didn't go wrong, but assuming nothing else did, twenty minutes should do it, if that."

Laura pinched her chin, her head slowly bobbing. "We'll have to pay attention for a break."

Ericksen jerked a thumb at the weather outside. "The only problem with that idea, Professor, is that there's no way to know if we've got a twenty-minute break in the storm. I've seen these things raging and then suddenly it's as calm as can be for five or ten minutes and then it's a rager again. There's just no way to know without radar. And with all our comms down, we can't get that report."

Acton cursed. "We need to get those comms up. If somebody gets hurt, we have no way of getting help."

Laura shook her head. "Even if we could call for help, there's no way it could arrive. Nothing's flying in this."

"A snowcat could still get here."

Ericksen dismissed the idea. "They're not going to put a snowcat out in zero visibility. You could have a fifty-foot crevasse open in front of you and not even see it coming. So even if we needed help, we're screwed. It's part of life out on the frozen continent, ma'am. You have to accept the fact that you might die from something as simple as a nosebleed."

Acton sighed then an idea occurred to him. He started gearing up again and Laura looked at him. "Where are you going?"

"To visit our new Chinese neighbors."

"Why?"

"Because they might have comms. We don't know what they brought with them. Just because we can't get through doesn't mean they can't."

Laura geared up as well. "I never thought of that. I'll go with you. Besides, checking in on them might help maintain the current detente."

Acton grinned. "And it'll give us a chance to make sure Dr. Evans hasn't ingratiated himself on that young Chinese scientist."

Laura growled. "He's going to be the death of me."

Antarctica Quest

Winter Quarters Bay, Antarctica

Mercedes ended the call with Corkery's colleague. She had the impression the woman believed her and would indeed take action, though what that action might be and whether it would come in time, neither of them could say. But at least someone on the outside, someone who could be trusted, was doing something.

She committed Roy's birth year to memory then put his file away along with Corkery's. She stared at the porthole as the wind continued to pick up. The first group would likely be back on board shortly, then the ship would be buttoned up to ride out the storm. The question was, where was Corkery? How far had the Chinese gone, and had he followed them to their ultimate destination? He might be back in ten minutes, he might be back in two hours.

She logged into the computer and brought up a map of the area. She traced with her finger where she was, where the tourist group had been, then the slight deviation to where she had left Corkery. She continued to trace the route, finding nothing. There was nowhere the Chinese could possibly be going unless it was something new that hadn't yet made the map, and that was quite rare in Antarctica.

Her eyes widened slightly at an idea, and she popped over to Google, quickly entering the search, "Recent discoveries in Antarctica," and she gasped. A ship had been discovered a few weeks ago buried in the ice, and an expedition was being sent to investigate. As she pored over the articles, she hit upon the key element.

It was believed to be an old Chinese pirate ship.

She leaned back, biting her finger. "A Chinese ship, eight Chinese passengers. *Heavily armed* Chinese passengers," she corrected herself. "There has to be a connection."

She clicked on the link that brought up a map showing the exact location of the discovery, and her heart hammered. It was in the direction the Chinese had been heading. In fact, it wasn't much farther past where they had already been when she left. This was obviously the destination. There was obviously something on that wreck that they wanted, and if it was a pirate ship, it was likely gold or some other valuables.

She closed the open tabs and cleared the browser history then leaned back, folding her arms as she debated what to do. Corkery was out there alone, in a growing storm, and he only had his emergency supplies. She rose then dropped back down. She grabbed the phone and dialed Dr. Best again. She had to get this vital new piece of information into her hands, because if the expedition had already begun, the number of lives at risk was now far beyond one foolhardy doctor who had marched into the frozen wasteland merely to satisfy his curiosity.

Expedition Site, Antarctica

It was tempting to ignore the rules and just make a beeline directly for the Chinese building still visible in the blowing snow, but that could change in a heartbeat. Instead, they followed the guidewire to the largest structure that held most of the supplies, then connected to the newly set up line leading to the Chinese.

It was a biting cold, unlike anything Acton had ever experienced, and every little gap in his clothing where the wind could reach had him regretting not being more careful.

Lesson learned.

"How are you doing?" he asked Laura.

"Regretting taking this job. I think my tatas are getting frostbitten."

Acton laughed and held up his hands, wiggling his fingers. "I can offer you free tata warmers."

She pushed his hands away. "Save those for tonight. I think we'll both need warming up."

"You got it, boss."

As they approached the structure, Acton looked about to make sure everybody was still inside and no horny Welshmen were hiding in a snowbank. He spotted something and stopped, grabbing Laura by the arm, his wife not having noticed his abrupt halt.

"What is it?"

"I don't know, look." He wiped his goggles clear and squinted. "Does that look like people to you?"

Laura stepped closer. "It does. Who the hell would be out in this? They were all given specific instructions to stay inside."

Acton shook his head. "Those aren't our people. They're not near any of the safety wires, and they're out beyond the perimeter."

"Could they be from McMurdo? Maybe checking in on us?"

"Perhaps."

"Well, who else could it be?"

Acton shrugged. "No idea."

"Could the Chinese be back?"

Acton tensed. "That's a definite possibility. Come in during a storm when nobody could respond. I could see them doing that."

"What should we do?" asked Laura, sounding uncertain for the first time since they had arrived.

"Look!" Acton turned and spotted Ericksen emerging from their shelter. He strode toward the new arrivals, waving at them, obviously assuming they were a rescue crew from McMurdo.

"We should go join him."

Acton gripped Laura's arm tighter. "No, something's wrong here. There's no way McMurdo would've sent a rescue party that could have arrived here already. Our comms haven't been down that long. It has to be the Chinese."

One of the shadowy forms suddenly moved and muzzle flashes sent Acton's heart racing. Ericksen cried out, hitting the ground as the gunshots rang out over the roar of the storm. Laura gasped and Acton acted. He dragged her toward the Chinese shelter, still attached to the line as more gunfire erupted behind them. He disconnected them both from the safety wire and Laura headed for the door.

"No! We can't trust them."

She stopped and turned. "Then where do we go?"

"They're not here to take prisoners. We have to get the hell out of here." He grabbed an axe mounted to the outside of the structure then took her hand. "Let's go!"

"But what about my team?"

"They're either already dead or they will be if we can't get help." He led her away from camp as quickly as he could, taking his bearing from the sun still dimly visible behind the cloud cover. Their best bet was the harbor to the north, but it was several hours' walk on a good day.

More gunfire erupted behind them followed by screams, and his heart ached with the knowledge their colleagues were being slaughtered, all because of politics and a ship no one had thought about twice for almost two centuries.

Outside the Expedition Site, Antarctica

Corkery watched in horror from his vantage point as the Chinese passengers entered the camp, any doubt as to their intent eliminated the moment they shot the first person they encountered. He had seen death in his career, an unbelievable amount of death, especially during the New Orleans pandemic, though he had never seen murder, not in front of him. The aftermath, of course, he had. You couldn't avoid it in an American ER, but to see it upfront was horrifying. He would have thought movies and TV would have desensitized him, but they hadn't.

This was real.

This was a real life taken for no plausibly valid reason, and what made things worse was that he was helpless. There was nothing he could do. If he made his presence known, they would surely kill him too. And he was a few hours away from the ship where the crew couldn't be trusted to do the right thing.

All hope lay with Mercedes.

Had she been able to get the phone to make the call? Would Best believe her and be able to reach the proper authorities?

More gunfire erupted and he breathed a sigh of relief as it appeared they were shooting into the air. The occupants of the structures were being ordered outside, and he bit his glove praying it wasn't for a mass execution.

Antarctic Ocean

February 15, 1810

Bao gripped some netting as the only two remaining aboard clung on for dear life while their ship shifted violently in the troubled seas, the ice surrounding them slamming into the hull, wood splintering around them. They were already taking on water from a shattered prow. All was now lost, but his men were safe. When he had come on deck and found the entire crew had abandoned him, it had been heartbreaking. Only Qi remained, one lone man willing to sacrifice his life to honor the oath he had made years before.

"I guess I know where I stand and where I probably always stood," he had muttered.

Qi faced him. "You don't understand, sir."

"What?"

"Not one of them would leave."

Bao's eyes narrowed. "What do you mean?"

"When I came on deck with your letter, they had all chosen to stay."

202

"I don't understand. Then why did they leave?"

"Because I ordered them to. You wanted them to leave to save themselves, but out of loyalty to you—"

"Or fear of my sister," interjected Bao.

Qi conceded the possibility with a bow of his head. "They were willing to see this through to the end at your side. I told them it was your wish that they live, so they agreed. Don't be disheartened by the fact your crew is gone. They are only gone because they believed you wished it. And despite knowing this, they remained hesitant until I told them I would remain behind so that you would not face the end alone."

Bao stared back at his sister's ship and smiled as his crew was hauled aboard, his sister obviously accepting his heartfelt message. He turned to Qi and clasped the man's shoulders. "You have been a faithful, capable, and trustworthy servant for most of my adult life. But now we are equals, we are brothers."

Qi clasped Bao's shoulders, gripping him tight. "I am honored to be your brother, and together we will face what comes with honor." He smirked. "And hope our sister doesn't kill us."

Bao laughed. "I doubt my sister will have that honor. Today, the sea and the ice are the greater enemy."

The ship shook again and he cursed himself for not having given the zupu to his crew to take back to his sister. Now it would be lost forever and the family would be forced to attempt to recreate it through previous compendiums, and when his name was recorded, as it would be required through tradition, his dishonor would be set in ink and passed down another hundred generations, his hubris never to be forgotten.

"What do we do now?" asked Qi as the ship shuddered once again.

"There's nothing we can do with the ship, so I suggest we get comfortable."

Qi gave him a look. "Comfortably numb?"

Bao eyed him. "What do you mean?"

"I've hidden away some spirits in the hopes that we would be able to celebrate our victory. They're in my cabin."

Bao smiled. "Then go get it, brother, and we will drink to our past glories and to our newfound brotherhood."

Qi disappeared below deck and Bao sat on a crate that had once been filled with dried fish, awaiting his return. He closed his eyes when he heard a shout.

"Brother, are you still with us?"

Leroux/White Residence, Fairfax Towers

Falls Church, Virginia

Present Day

Leroux jerked awake, lying sprawled on the bed, Sherrie's naked body draped over him. He forgot at what round she finally declared herself satisfied, but it had to be some sort of new record. His phone vibrated again on the nightstand, revealing what had woken him.

And he groaned.

Can't a guy just have a weekend off?

He grabbed it and checked to see that it was Sonya Tong, his second-in-command. He pictured their recent kiss and a little bit of life sprang up down below. He took the call, pushing away the guilt-laden memory. "Hey, Sonya, what's up?"

"Sorry to interrupt your weekend, but you know how we've got alerts set up on the professors?"

This piqued his curiosity and he extricated himself from his partner's entanglement. "Let me guess, Antarctica?"

There was a pause. "Now, how the hell could you possibly know that? Of all the places on earth, Antarctica is your guess?"

Leroux chuckled. "Tommy Granger put me on to it. I passed it on to the Chief then had you put on the alert list in case something came up."

"Me? What did I ever do to deserve that?"

Leroux laughed. "Sometimes it's good to be the King."

She snickered. "I guess so."

"So, what's happened?"

"We just got an alert. Apparently, a Doctor Katherine Best was contacted by a nurse on a ship currently docked in Antarctica. She said that she and the ship's doctor spotted eight Chinese passengers collecting what looked like military-grade weapons from a stash they believe was put there by the Russian crew. Apparently, they were last seen heading toward a National Science Foundation expedition site where a Chinese pirate ship has been located. The expedition is being run by Professor Palmer, and of course Professor Acton is there with her."

Leroux cursed. "Okay, this changes things. I'll let the Chief know that I'm coming in right away. Can you make it?"

"Let me check my calendar. Oh look, nothing."

Leroux laughed. "I'll see you in a few minutes then."

"Okay."

He ended the call and found Sherrie sitting beside him. "So, the professors are in shit?"

"Could be deep shit. Eight Chinese passengers from a cruise ship have been spotted heading toward the expedition site with military-grade weaponry, possibly provided them by the Russian crew."

"Holy shit! They really can find trouble anywhere in the world."

"Yeah. I have to go in."

"Of course. Anything I can do?"

"I don't think so." He paused. "Actually, contact Tommy Granger. Tell him that there have been developments you can't talk about, however we are getting actively involved now. That'll keep him off my back for a while. And send an update to Dylan. He'll want to know."

"I'm on it."

Leroux headed for the showers to wash hours upon hours of debauchery off himself. And smiled.

I love my life.

Winter Quarters Bay, Antarctica

Mercedes peered through the snow billowing about her. This was just the front edge of the storm and it would get far worse. She wasn't foolish enough to attempt to reach Corkery on foot—she'd merely get herself killed. On her way back to the ship, she had spotted something that could save both their lives—a snowmobile. In fact, several of them. If she could get her hands on one, she could reach Corkery in no time.

That of course assumed she could find him in the storm.

That's why she had brought emergency supplies with her including flares. If she could get in the general vicinity of where she thought he was then fire off a flare, and if he could reach her first, they could easily escape the Chinese passengers since they would still be on foot. It was risky, but it was a risk she was willing to take. This was her chance to do something good, to pay back everything that had ever been done for her, and to perhaps even pay it forward some.

She headed toward one of the storage units where she had seen the snowmobiles parked along the outside earlier. She rounded the corner and saw them sitting there unattended. Keys were always kept with the vehicles here. There was no theft in Antarctica.

Until today.

She smiled as she found the key in the ignition as expected. She loaded her backpack filled with all the supplies she thought they might need, then straddled the vehicle she had only ever ridden on and never driven. She started it up, confirmed a full tank, then took off before anyone could stop her. She'd figure out the niceties of operating the machine en route.

Someone shouted behind her but she ignored it. Nobody would give chase—it was a government-owned machine and only taxpayers were losing money here. And that assumed she wasn't successful. If she were, the vehicle could be returned within an hour or two.

As she left the harbor, she took her bearing based on the map she had memorized and the faint sun in the sky. If she could maintain her speed, it would barely move by the time she should reach the expedition camp, and if she were lucky, she just might encounter Corkery already returning.

An outcome she prayed for.

Outside the Expedition Site, Antarctica

Acton could still hear gunshots behind them but they had lost sight of the camp in the snow and he couldn't see what was happening. He stopped and faced Laura. "How are you doing?"

"I'm all right. Cold, but it's tolerable." She glanced up at the sky. "This is only going to get worse. We need to find shelter."

Acton pointed up the coastline. "There's a harbor to the north. It's a few hours' walk."

"Winter Quarters Bay."

"Yeah, that's the one. If we make it there, we can get help."

"There's no way we can make it there in this. It's too far."

"Then what should we do?"

Laura shook her head. "I know what I'd like to do. I'd like to go back to the camp and kill every one of those bastards."

Acton chuckled. "I'd like nothing better, but we both know that's not an option."

"No, it isn't." She pointed in the direction of the harbor. "If we're going to try to make it there, we're going to have to get around the camp. I suggest we at least attempt that and see how we make out."

"Agreed." Acton checked their bearing against the rapidly fading sun then pointed. "Let's head in this direction then we'll hang a left and head directly north. We should be able to bypass the camp with no problem then we can decide if we want to do three hours in this or not."

"Sounds good."

They started walking once again and Acton cocked an ear. "I haven't heard any more gunfire, have you?"

"No, I haven't."

Acton thought back on what he had heard after the initial murder. Everything was in short bursts.

Laura beat him to the punch. "There weren't enough shots to kill everybody."

He agreed. "So then, what do you think is going on?"

"Maybe they weren't there to kill everybody. Maybe it was an itchy trigger finger that killed Ericksen."

He pursed his lips as they continued forward. "That begs the question then, if they're not there to kill everybody, should we go back and surrender. At least then we'd have shelter and would be shipped back to McMurdo probably as soon as the storm broke."

Laura remained silent for a moment as she no doubt debated the idea. "If we assume you're right, then it definitely is the safest bet. But if we're wrong, then it could be certain death, not only for us, but the team. Right now, we're their only hope."

Acton cursed. "Okay, here's what I think. We stick to the current plan. We're going to keep heading in this direction then we're going to bear left. That'll have us crossing past the camp. We'll see if we can spot what's going on and if it looks peaceful and it's merely the Chinese coming in and taking the location, then maybe Ericksen's death wasn't supposed to happen so we hand ourselves over. But if it looks like they killed a bunch of people or worse everyone, then we head north to the harbor."

Laura agreed. "Sounds like as good a plan as any."

They crunched through the snow in silence, and when he felt they had gone far enough, he made an abrupt turn and took another bearing based on the sun. They continued on in silence and Acton took the opportunity to adjust some of his clothing to block the biting wind from reaching tiny slivers of his body.

"There's the camp," said Laura, pointing.

Acton turned and could make out some of the structures, though barely. It appeared that the entire encampment had been forced out of their shelters and was now standing in the center of the compound, the Chinese Special Forces team aiming their weapons at them. He glanced slightly to the right and could see Ericksen's body still lying in the snow. Thankfully, everyone else appeared to be fine.

He scanned the area, his hands raised to shield his eyes and did a slow 360, searching for options. If there were someplace they could shelter, it would give them more time to make a reasoned decision rather than a rash one forced upon them by the frigid temperature. He spotted something not too far from them and he tapped Laura on the shoulder, pointing. "Do you see that?"

She turned and looked. "See what? Oh, wait. That patch of yellow?"

"Yeah. What do you think that is?"

"I don't know. Is it a person?"

"It can't be a person. Not out here, but if it is, they're not dressed in camo. Maybe someone else from our team escaped."

"Well, if they did, then we should join up with them."

Acton agreed but gripped his axe a little tighter. "Let's go."

Outside the Expedition Site, Antarctica

Corkery peered through the binoculars, staring at the camp. So far, the expected massacre hadn't occurred, and it had him wondering just what the hell was going on. What was this encampment? There were a couple of dozen people at least, and they were in the middle of nowhere. The entire situation begged quite a few questions. Why were these people here? How did the Chinese passengers know they would be? And what was here worth killing over? And why just kill one and not all of them? Something odd was going on. He was missing a critical piece of the puzzle.

He heard something behind him and as he spun to see what it was, something pressed hard against his back, shoving him into the snow, and for a moment he had visions of a sea lion about to make a snack out of his ass.

"Identify yourself!"

One panic was replaced by another. "Dr. Doug Corkery. I'm the ship's doctor on the Antarctica Quest."

The foot was lifted. "On your knees. Let's see your face."

Corkery warily pushed to his knees then removed his goggles and facemask, squinting at the two figures in front of him, a man and a woman, the man brandishing an axe that could easily cleave a head in two. "Who are you?"

"We're going to ask the questions for now. What are you doing out here?"

Corkery jerked a thumb over his shoulder toward the encampment. "I was following those guys to see what they were up to." His two captors exchanged glances. He pointed at his goggles. "Can I put these back on? I'm freezing here."

The woman nodded. "Go ahead."

He fit his goggles back in place then his facemask.

"Why were you following them?"

Corkery decided it was best to explain fully. "Okay, here's what happened. I've got eight passengers, all Chinese, all young and healthy, on a tour boat where that's rare. Last night, the Russian crew, after curfew, offloaded a bunch of large duffel bags. Today, the eight Chinese passengers left the ship alone, unaccompanied, which is against the rules. My nurse and I decided to follow them to see what was going on. We found them retrieving the offloaded equipment and the bags had guns among other things. My nurse went to try to get help and I followed them here."

The man lowered the axe. "Wait a minute. Are you telling me that these gunmen came from a tour boat?"

"Yes."

The man turned to the woman. "Then it's not the Chinese Special Forces team."

She shook her head. "No, it can't be. What does this mean?"

"I have no idea."

Corkery couldn't take it any longer. "Who are you?"

The woman extended a hand. "I'm Professor Laura Palmer. I'm the head of the expedition here. This is my husband, Professor James Acton. We managed to escape just as the attack began, but we thought it was Chinese Special Forces coming back to seize the operation like they tried yesterday."

Corkery's mouth opened slightly as a connection was made. "Ah, the Chinese military helicopter. Yes, I saw it yesterday."

Acton stepped closer, the axe resting gently by his side, no longer threatening. "Now, just to clarify, these eight guys were always on the ship. They're definitely not part of any Special Forces team that left yesterday by helicopter."

Corkery firmly shook his head. "No, these are passengers. I have their medical files. They were on the ship since the beginning and..." His voice drifted as he made another connection. "And they appeared quite nervous when they saw that helicopter go overhead."

Acton scratched his chin. "Interesting. So then, they're definitely not connected. So why the hell are they here?"

Laura shrugged. "Has to be the same reason. The ship."

Corkery eyed them. "What ship?"

Laura pointed to the left of the camp. "A ship was found in the ice a few weeks ago. We're here to begin the excavation and evaluate the find."

"What kind of ship?"

"We believe it to be a Chinese pirate vessel from the early nineteenth century."

"Really? Could there be gold on it?"

"Anything's possible. Obviously, if they're here, they must think there's something valuable on it."

"Well, people don't go and commit this kind of crime without a reason. They obviously think there's something valuable there."

"Agreed," said Acton. "The question is, what?"

Expedition Site, Antarctica

Zheng Hongli surveyed the scene in front of them. So far, everything had gone according to plan except for two things. One, he hadn't wanted anybody killed until he knew who they were—the dead man could be somebody extremely valuable that could have proven useful. He would admonish his sister for her actions later in private. The second thing that hadn't gone according to plan was the weather, though there was nothing they could do about it since their arrival date was set by others.

Yet this could prove to be a good thing. Nothing could fly in this weather so no rapid rescue could be attempted. And he had a feeling from the banging of the loose cable in their communications tower that nobody had any type of comms. The only question now was whether the work could be done in this weather. He didn't care if the conditions were ideal, and preservation of the wreck was of no importance to him. They were here for one thing, something lost to their family two centuries ago.

The zupu of the Zheng clan.

He stared at his prisoners, all covered head to toe in winter gear just like he and his family were. There was no fooling around in these conditions, and as the wind howled, he shivered. This was brutal, unlike anything he had ever experienced. He wiped his goggles clear. He couldn't see the eyes of anyone he faced and didn't like it. He wanted to see the defiance, the fear, the indifference. It told him what kind of opponent he was facing. Were these all just cowering scientists, or was someone among them going to conspire against them?

He pointed at the body lying in the snow. "If anyone defies us, that will be your fate. Do you understand?"

Everyone turned toward where he was pointing, some of them crying out, the death of one of their comrades revealed to them for the first time. He had seen death before. He had killed before. It was simply part of life in the Triads. There was a time when his family name was revered and feared, but with the loss of the zupu, they had lost the proof to their lineage and a once honorable name that would have commanded seniority within the criminal hierarchy of China, instead relegated them to mere foot soldiers.

It was humiliating, but it was about to end.

When word had reached him of the discovery of his ancestor's ship trapped in the ice of Antarctica, he had immediately acted. Family history told him the zupu had been lost on the Black Dragon. If the vessel were still intact, it could very well still be on board, and there was only one place it could be—the captain's quarters where his ancestor Zheng Bao would have kept it.

Why he had it with him in these waters wasn't known. Bao's sister, the great Zheng Yi Sao, had apparently forbidden the telling of the tale and the story had been lost to history. But now history would be reclaimed, his family's honor restored, the proof of their lineage irrefutable once again.

"Who's in charge here?" Nobody said anything, their loyalty to their leader admirable. He raised his weapon and pointed it at the nearest woman. "Give me the name or she dies."

"Professor Palmer," said someone near the back.

He lowered his weapon. "And this Professor Palmer is too much of a coward to step forward and identify himself?" Nobody said anything, but the group looked at each other as if trying to identify this sad excuse for a leader. He raised his weapon, again pointing it at the woman. "Professor Palmer, if you don't step forward now, she's dead."

Again, nobody came forward.

"Very well." He took aim and the woman collapsed to her knees, covering her head. A man stepped forward, acting as a human shield.

"I don't think she's here."

Hongli stared at him. "What do you mean she's not here?"

"I mean that I don't see her or her husband."

Hongli cursed and jerked a thumb at the cluster of structures. "Search them again. They must be hiding." His fellow clan members sprang into action and within minutes it was confirmed the buildings were all empty—the team lead and her husband were missing. That could mean only one thing.

They had escaped.

Depending on how they were provisioned, they could make it north to the harbor where they would find help and report what was going on, and that couldn't be allowed. He pointed at his sister. "Take three, search the area. We need to find them before they can get help. We'll handle things here."

She nodded curtly then named three of their cousins. They headed off in four different directions which would be unwise anywhere else, but if there was one place they could be sure there weren't weapons to oppose them, it was here. They had found two guns that could best be described as hunting rifles with limited capacity magazines, and even if the entire US military contingent at McMurdo engaged them, they couldn't muster a dozen weapons.

And none were assault rifles like his clan all carried.

He turned his attention back to the others. "If anyone tries to escape, you'll be shot along with two of your comrades. Dissent will not be tolerated."

"Just what the hell do you want?" asked someone, the angry voice tinged with fear.

Hongli had no intention of dealing with the group as a whole. "Since your leader has apparently abandoned you, choose another."

A man raised his hand, stepping forward. "There's no need. The expedition charter says if Professor Palmer and Professor Acton are incapacitated, then I'm in charge."

"And who are you?"

"Professor Parata, University of Otago, New Zealand."

"Very well, come closer."

The man stepped through the crowd and faced him. Parata was close enough to see through the goggles. There was defiance there, but fear as well. This man could be a problem. "There is little time, so I will tell you why we are here. You have found a shipwreck, yes?"

"We believe so."

"And it has been identified as the Black Dragon?"

"Again, we believe so."

"On board that ship is something I want, and you are going to get it for me."

The man stared at him. "What could you possibly want?"

"My family's zupu."

Parata's head tilted to the side. "Your family's what?"

A man stepped forward from the group. "Zupu. It is a Chinese family's genealogy that once held great importance in my country, but now means little to any but those who continue to cling to the old ways."

Hongli beckoned him forward. "And just who are you?"

The man stepped through the crowd. "I am Professor Liu, Peking University."

Hongli regarded him. "The report I read said China wasn't participating."

"Things have changed."

"So it would seem."

Liu stepped closer. "I assume you want us to retrieve your zupu for you?"

"Yes."

"Then you'll need experienced people guiding the work."

222

"Of course."

"Then I propose this. Make me the team lead and my people will direct the others and guarantee your zupu is retrieved if it is still on board."

Grumblings erupted from the crowd, the sentiment indicating they were clearly not in favor of this proposal. There was obvious tension between the Chinese contingent and the rest, which was to be expected. The West never respected his country, and the fact these people didn't like it was exactly why it was a great idea.

He stepped past Parata and stood in front of Liu. "Very well. You are in charge. The work begins immediately."

"But what about the storm?" protested Parata. "We can't work in these conditions. It'll be too dangerous."

Hongli turned slightly, extending his arm, aiming his rifle directly at the man's head. "You'll find it's far more dangerous not to work."

Parata stepped back, raising his hands as one of his comrades put an arm on his shoulder, gently pulling him back into the group.

Liu turned to Hongli. "My colleague is correct. These conditions are already dangerous to work in, and any more delay will only make it worse. May I suggest we get to work immediately?"

"Yes." Hongli raised a finger. "But one thing. I don't want any delays while you attempt to preserve that ship. That ship belongs to my family, and the only thing about this find we care about is the zupu. It should be located in the captain's quarters in a waterproof case."

"If the captain's quarters are intact, you shall have it."

Hongli turned to the group. "Professor Liu is now in charge of you. This is your new reality, so accept it. The faster you work, the sooner this will all be over. Defy us, defy Professor Liu, and you will die."

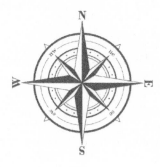

Outside the Expedition Site, Antarctica

Acton peered through Corkery's binoculars. Four of the terrorists, for lack of a better term, had broken off from the main group and headed in opposite directions after a search of the shelters had been completed. "They're definitely looking for us," he said to the others. "Well, obviously not you, Dr. Corkery."

"Call me, Doug. If we're going to be dying together, we might as well be on a first name basis."

Acton chuckled. "We're not dead yet, Doug. We've been in worse than this."

"You have?"

Laura shrugged. "I'm not sure I would say worse, but I would say similar. Certainly never in these temperatures though."

The crowd broke up, most heading for the storage shed. Equipment was brought out and Acton cursed, handing the binoculars over to Laura. "Does it look like they're going to do what I think they're going to do?"

Laura peered through the glasses. "Bloody hell. I think they're going to make them start excavating the wreck."

Corkery grunted. "Well, I guess that confirms why they're here. They want something on board."

"But what?" asked Acton. "Pirate treasure?"

"Isn't that a possibility? I mean, you said it was a pirate ship, so why not pirate gold?"

"It's definitely a possibility," agreed Laura. "But the chances of it still being intact and the chances of there actually being any on board in the first place, are pretty slim. They're taking one hell of a risk with those odds."

"Maybe they know something you don't know."

"Perhaps." Laura handed the binoculars back to Acton and he ignored the group, instead checking on the four that had broken away, one of them slowly heading in their direction. "Whatever it is they're after is irrelevant. Right now, we have to worry about our people. If they're going to put them to work in these conditions, people are going to get hurt. People are going to die."

"What are you thinking?" asked Laura.

He pointed at the one approaching them. "We need answers and we need to thin their numbers."

Corkery's head spun toward him. "Are you nuts? That guy's got a gun."

"I know, and if I can get it, then *we* have a gun."

Laura turned to him. "Are you sure this is the wisest course of action? We should try to get to the harbor and get help."

"That's at least a three-hour walk in good conditions, and that assumes we don't get lost or one of us doesn't get hurt."

"I'm willing to try it," said Corkery. He pointed at the nearby ice field. "I just need to stick to the coastline and I'll reach the harbor."

"I don't think it's wise to go out there alone, Doug."

Corkery grunted. "I don't think it's wise to engage heavily armed terrorists."

Acton chuckled. "No, I suppose it isn't. We don't have a lot of time to decide. He's heading directly for us. He might have seen one of our jackets. In fact, I think we're out of time. If he ever lifts his head, he's going to spot us." He scrambled back from the slight rise they were hiding behind then furiously hacked at the tough snow, breaking through the surface.

"What are you doing?" asked Corkery.

"Making a spider hole. Start digging." He rolled aside then crawled back up the incline. The gunman was still approaching and Acton was beginning to think it was pure luck that he was heading in their direction—their disappearance behind the snowbank hadn't changed the man's demeanor at all. Acton scrambled back down. "Is that big enough for the two of you yet?"

Laura nodded. "It'll be cozy."

"Okay. Get in." Corkery climbed in first then Laura after. Acton covered them over with the snow they had removed then punched his fist through the covering, creating an air hole. "If I don't come back, stay here until things are clear then head to the harbor."

Laura's gloved hand emerged from the hole and gave a thumbs-up. He squeezed it and slowly crawled away, sweeping his arms as he covered his tracks as best he could. He inched up the embankment and spotted the enemy barely ten feet away to the right. Acton gripped his axe, debating on how to do this. If he killed the man with one well-placed blow, it would give him the gun and any other equipment he might have on him, and lower the numbers they were facing by one.

But it wouldn't get them any answers.

Though what answers could this man possibly have that mattered? Even if he told them everything, would any of it change their situation? Would knowing they were after some trinket, or just there for the chance to get gold, change the fate of the others? He didn't see it, though there was another reason to keep him alive.

Leverage and self-preservation.

Killing one of them might result in retaliation, but taking a prisoner might allow them to negotiate. He didn't have much time to make a decision. Experience told him that people that did things like this were either fanatics, willing to die for their cause and even more willing to let someone else die for it, or were often strangers to each other, brought together to do a job, meaning there was no bond therefore negating any perceived leverage.

The more he thought about it, the more the decision became obvious. He had to take the safer of the two options. The reduced visibility, the howling wind, and the thick headgear would be to his advantage.

The decision to attack was taken away from him as the gunman crested the mound of snow Laura and Corkery were hiding under. Acton gripped his axe, the blade outward, then flipped it around. The butt-end was enough to do the job. It could very well kill the man, but it might also just knock him out. Acton crouched low. His target stopped at the crest of the ridge and held his right hand up, shielding his eyes as he peered at the horizon, and Acton took his chance. With the man's arm blocking his view, Acton rose and took the diagonal, closing the gap between his target but also moving behind him as the man looked to his left.

Acton continued his advance when the hand lowered and his target leaned forward. His opponent raised his weapon quickly and Acton cursed as he realized Laura and Corkery's position had been made. Acton flipped the axe back around and raised it over his head, flinging it, praying he hadn't just uselessly thrown away his only weapon. The axe spun through the air and he pushed forward, gaining an extra couple of steps before the sharp blade embedded itself in the man's right shoulder.

He screamed out in agony just as Acton reached him. He shoved him to the ground and pushed his opponent's face into the snow and ice. He grabbed the man's hand still gripping the weapon and broke the finger desperately reaching for the trigger. His opponent cried out again and moments later Laura was at his side. She grabbed the gun and stepped clear with it, aiming it at their prisoner.

"Do you speak English?"

The man only groaned.

Acton shoved the man's face again in the snow then yanked it up. "I said, do you speak English?"

"Yes."

"Do you have any other weapons?"

"Pistol under my jacket, right side, knife left side."

Acton liberated the man of his weapons, tossing them over to Laura as Corkery finally joined them.

"Who the hell are you people?"

"Long story," replied Laura.

Acton continued to search the man for anything useful. He had emergency supplies in a small backpack and some magazines for both weapons, but no radio or any other means of communication. It meant nobody could check on him. They obviously had never anticipated being separated. He pointed at the axe. "Doc, is it okay to pull this out?"

Corkery dropped to his knees, making a careful examination. "It's not going to make much of a difference. Unless we can get this man to a hospital in the next twenty minutes, he's dead."

Acton yanked the axe out and flipped the man over onto his back. He wailed in pain and Acton slapped a hand over the man's mouth. "You're going to be meeting your maker soon, so now is your time to do something right with your life. Why are you here?"

The man glared up at him through his goggles. "Go to hell. I'll never betray my family."

Acton glanced at Laura, the response intriguing. "So, this has something to do with your family." He pointed toward the expedition site. "And I assume something to do with that ship."

Laura stepped a little closer, keeping the rifle aimed at their prisoner. "Are you all family? Are you all descendants of Zheng Yi Sao?"

The man's eyes flared, revealing the truth, and Acton sat back on his haunches, stunned at the explanation. They weren't here because of pirate treasure, they were here because of family honor. "What's on that ship that's so important?"

"I'll never tell you."

"Then tell me this." Acton pressed his knee into the wounded shoulder and the man gasped in agony. "What happens when you find it?" The man said nothing and Acton pressed harder. A cry pierced the wind and Acton eased up.

"Everyone dies."

Approaching the Expedition Site, Antarctica

Mercedes raced across the frozen desolation, leaning forward so the wind screen provided her with some relief. This was far easier and far faster than walking, but she still had to take it slow. Visibility continued to worsen, and every minute or so she would ease off and stand, searching for any sign of Corkery's bright yellow jacket. She was quite certain she had covered half the distance already. If Corkery had made it this far, he might make it the rest of the way if he didn't lose his bearings. The sun overhead was merely a faint glow as the clouds thickened, making things worse.

She still wasn't certain what to do when she got there. She had the flares, and if she fired one in the air, Corkery should see it if he were paying attention. If he were conscious. But so would the Chinese, though Corkery should be closer to her than them. She dropped back down into the seat and gunned it. The sooner she got there, the better, and if he were already this far, she could find him on the way back if she missed him.

She gasped as a thought occurred to her, her hand easing off the throttle for a moment. In her panic, she had forgotten to leave the letter for Roy. In fact, she had even locked the infirmary out of habit. She applied the throttle once again. It was for the best. There was nothing Roy could do to help, and he might just get himself hurt. Their chances of coming out of this safely laid squarely in the hands of Dr. Best, and she just prayed the woman could convince the proper authorities to launch a rescue.

Another thought occurred to her that had the throttle easing again before she cranked it once more. Was an armed rescue even legal in Antarctica? Did the treaties even have a provision for it?

She tensed. Would red tape doom them all?

Antarctic Ocean

February 15, 1810

Zheng's crew of six manned the oars as she stood on the prow of one of the boats that had brought her brother's crew to safety. The moment she witnessed the change in her brother's plight she leaped into action. She had to save him. She had to save him from himself. If he died because of her, she would never forgive herself. They were family. They were blood. They were of the same clan, born into it from the same mother and father, and the dishonor of his death at her hands would negate all the good she had done, all the honor she had accumulated.

She would be nothing but the blood-thirsty pirate whose narcissistic attempt to be remembered against tradition had led to the death of the eldest son of her line.

Her brother's ship foundered ahead, listing heavily forward. From her vantage point, she could see no one on deck. She cusped a hand in front of her mouth. "Brother, are you still with us?" She listened as her men raised the oars for a moment but heard nothing. She waved a hand toward the ship and her men resumed the battle, the ice thick, the water a slurry, the ice ahead having now completely enveloped the hull of her brother's vessel.

"Mistress, port side!" shouted one of her men from behind and she adjusted her gaze, crying in relief at the sight of her brother leaning over the rail.

"Sister, what are you doing? Go back! You'll just get yourself killed!"

She beckoned him. "Then come to us! Save yourself, I beg of you!"

Her brother stared at her, gripping the railing. "Does this mean you forgive me?"

She laughed as the tears flowed. "Of course I forgive you. You're my brother. Do you forgive me?"

It was his turn to laugh. "You never did anything that needed forgiving. You only wanted to be remembered, and I was too jealous. I'm the one who sinned here, not you."

She beckoned to him once again. "Come, join us. Get on the ice before your ship sinks, and we'll save you."

A second man appeared that she recognized as her brother's second-in-command, Qi, and she was pleased to see at least one brave soul had remained behind to provide company to her brother in what could be his final moments. A brief discussion was held between the two men then they both disappeared.

She urged her men to row harder. "We must get as close as we can!"

Netting was thrown over the side of the ship ahead and both men reappeared. Qi climbed over the edge first, scrambling down to the ice pressed hard against the hull. Her brother followed and joined him, both men with wide stances, their arms held out to their sides as they struggled to maintain their balance on the unsteady surface.

A cracking sound was followed by the ship suddenly listing toward her brother and his faithful servant. The large block of ice they were on tilted and both men slid toward the hull.

"No!" she screamed, the voice she heard unrecognizable, the anguish and horror it carried foreign to her. Her heart ached with sorrow, feelings she had only experienced once before when she had received word of her father's death.

And today, as her brother and his servant disappeared below the ice, her heart broke.

And everything changed.

En route to Antarctica

Present Day

Dawson sat in the back of the C17, Bravo Team on one side, the New Zealand SAS team on the other. His team was mostly bunking out, everyone still tired from the mission in the Philippines they had just come off that had involved a lot of hoofing through dense jungle. The Kiwis were fresh, which was good, since they were less than an hour out from insertion and everything had just changed.

They had just received word that armed hostiles from a cruise ship might be involved, which changed the equation entirely. Washington was now busy getting approval for a combat search and rescue operation on the continent that forbade almost all weapons. There was a chance the op could be nixed in the air, though Dawson got a sense from Clancy that Washington might proceed regardless. The Chinese were being kept out of the loop despite the fact they had the closest team that could react to the situation. The powers that be were concerned the Chinese might

237

use it as an opportunity to establish an armed presence on the continent, which could see an arms build-up and the treaty torn asunder.

He finished reassembling his weapon, having given it a good cleaning and re-lubing it with graphite rather than a wet lube that might freeze up in Arctic conditions. The latest weather report was too cold for numbers to matter—exposed skin would freeze in less than a minute. Not to mention exposed airways. He had always said he would go through hell to save a friend.

And today he truly was.

Acton/Palmer Residence

St. Paul, Maryland

Reading sat in his chair, sipping on an ice-cold Diet Coke with a wedge of lemon floating on the surface. With a plastic straw. What a luxury. He absolutely detested paper straws. Unless you inhaled your beverage, there was no way to finish before the tip became a soggy mess. And when he indulged himself at a fast-food restaurant, punching that paper monstrosity through the plastic lid was like fingernails on a chalkboard.

This obsession with reducing plastic waste because of the pollution in the oceans was insane. All one had to do was look at the studies to know that 98% of what was found in the ocean originated in Asia and Africa. This wasn't a Western world problem, this was a Third World creation because they had no proper garbage collection. Hundreds of millions if not billions of people tossed their trash every day into the nearest river that then carried it out into the oceans.

In the West, garbage trucks came to every residence and collected it, and recycling programs redirected the waste to where it should go.

Rather than make miserable the lives of the billion people that weren't causing the problem, why not redirect the money and effort to the Third World and teach them how garbage trucks and landfills worked then move on to recycling programs?

There was a gentle knock at the door, ending his internal rant.

"Yes?"

"Mr. Reading, sir, you have guests."

His eyes narrowed at Rose's announcement. "Guests? Who?"

"Mr. Granger and Miss Trinh."

His eyebrows rose. "Show them in. Have them come up here."

"Yes, sir."

Reading checked himself to make sure he was decent, then ran an eye over his suite, finding it impeccable. Rose had been in here while he last ate and set everything in order once again.

Remarkable woman.

There was another knock at the door.

"Come in."

It opened and he turned to see Mai and Tommy, Mai forcing a smile, Tommy not bothering, merely leaving the concern on his face.

"I hope we're not intruding," said Mai.

Reading wanted to tell them that of course they were, but they were good people and meant well, and were extremely close to his best friends. "Not at all, I could use the company." He gestured toward the couch. "Take a seat."

Rose followed them in. "Can I get you two anything to drink?"

Reading put an end to that nonsense. "They know where the kitchen is."

Mai grinned. "He's right. You're not here to wait on us. You've got more important things to do." She turned to Tommy. "Diet Coke?"

"Yep."

Mai disappeared with Rose as Tommy set up a laptop and two tablets. "I figured if we pooled our efforts, maybe we could figure out more about what's going on."

"Good thinking."

Tommy turned to him. "What's the latest you've heard?"

"Not much. My partner contacted me a little while ago. Apparently, there's an unconfirmed report of armed Chinese passengers from a tour boat spotted heading toward the expedition site."

Tommy's eyes bulged. "You're kidding me." He cursed. "After everything I've done for them, they still keep me out of the loop."

Reading regarded the young man. "Who?"

"Dylan and Chris. It's like they don't trust me."

Reading chuckled. "It's not that they don't trust you, son, it's that they could lose their jobs if they told you everything they know. You don't have the security clearances, and all the information I have is coming from my end of things, not theirs. They're not telling me anything either. Don't take it personally, just be thankful you have people in your life like them."

Mai entered the room carrying a tray with a pitcher of ice water, another of what Reading assumed was Diet Coke, and three glasses.

The entire tray shook and she grinned. "While this may look impressive, Rose carried it all the way to the door."

Rose giggled from the hallway. "If you had said nothing, they would've never known!"

Mai laughed but said nothing as she bit her lip, determined to deliver the tray to the table with nothing spilled. She put it down and stepped back, her hands raised. "Nailed it!"

There was clapping from the hallway that faded as Rose headed back downstairs. Mai poured the drinks, topping off Reading's Diet Coke, and giving him a fresh glass of water. "Let me know if you need anything, Mr. Reading, and I'll get it for you."

Reading smiled at her. "I think after all we've been through you can call me Hugh."

She shook her head. "After everything we've been through, we should be calling you, Sir Hugh. They should have knighted you for what you did for us." Her eyes darted to his chest and his scars throbbed.

Reading gestured toward Tommy's setup. "Can you reach Leroux on that through Dylan's secure network?"

Tommy nodded. "Yes, sir."

"Then send him a message letting him know that we're aware of the armed Chinese tourists, and ask if he has an ETA on when help could arrive. Make sure he knows it's me who wants the information. Maybe he'll be a little more forthcoming with his elders."

Operations Center 2, CIA Headquarters
Langley, Virginia

Leroux sat at his workstation in the center of the impressive operations center located under CIA headquarters in Langley, Virginia. He brought up the message from Tommy Granger and read it, smiling slightly at Tommy's insistence that the questions were coming from Hugh Reading and not him. He tossed them a bone and replied with two simple characters,

1H

He hit send then stared at the massive displays wrapping across the front of the room. One portion showed a map of the region with all the relative points plotted. McMurdo, the expedition site, the harbor where the tour boat was docked and the initial report of the Chinese had come from, the current location of the Chinese ship with the Special Forces team, and a blip approaching the coastline where Bravo Team's C17 was located, less than an hour out.

Another display showed the storm blanketing the entire region, the conditions continuing to worsen, no reprieve expected for two days. It would be nearly impossible to conduct an op in this weather.

The drop zone was indicated on the map. It was roughly a fifteen-minute snowmobile ride from the encampment. With visibility so low, there was little risk of their insertion being spotted by the enemy. McMurdo was sending two snowcats, one with equipment, one a mobile hospital. They had left the station hours ago and should be in position by the time Delta arrived. It was a risky move, but this was a unique situation.

Never before had armed terrorists taken action on the southern continent.

The question they were all dying to get answered was why, why were they doing this? He didn't believe this had anything to do with pirate treasure. There was something else going on, but until they got boots on the ground, they couldn't even know *if* something was going on. It was frustrating. Their satellite coverage was useless, they couldn't put a drone in even if they wanted to, and they had no communication with the expedition site at all.

These were the types of operations that drove him nuts. Whoever said ignorance was bliss clearly never worked in intelligence. With everything they knew so far, which was minimal, they were looking at another hour at least before the next bit of intel might arrive.

This one was going to peg his stress level.

Outside the Expedition Site, Antarctica

Laura squeezed Acton's hand. He had killed a lot of people over the years, all bad, all trying to kill him or someone he loved, as had she, but it never got easier, especially when it was something so close up. He couldn't recall ever killing a man with an axe who then bled out slowly in front of him for twenty minutes, but at least they had their answers.

Once their prisoner had admitted that the entire expedition was doomed, the flood gates had opened and he had told them everything about why they were here. He spilled about the zupu, about the Russian crew's involvement, about the bribes paid to have eight tourists medically refused to create the berths for the last-minute substitutions, about the family honor and dishonor, about the fact they were descendants of the great female pirate Zheng Yi Sao.

Corkery's nurse, Mercedes, if all went according to plan, would have already called for help, but they couldn't count on that. Any number of things could have gone wrong. She might not have found the other tour group, the man who owned the phone might have refused to let her use

245

it, she might not have been able to make the call due to the weather. Any number of things could have gone wrong.

Laura peered out at the storm, growing in intensity. "What do we do now? There's no way we can reach the harbor."

Acton agreed. "It's getting too bad. I think we're going to have to either tough it out until the storm passes, or try to retake the camp."

Corkery stared at him, wide-eyed. "Are you nuts? There are three of us. We've got two guns. There are seven of them and God knows how many guns they have."

Acton shook his head, pointing at the camp. "There may be seven of them, but three of them are still searching for us in the wrong direction. That leaves four, split between the expedition site and our people heading to the excavation site. This is our best shot at saving our people."

"But surely we've got time for a better plan. The ship is buried in the ice, isn't it?"

"Yes and no. It was buried in the ice, but when the crevasse opened, it exposed a large part of the hull. The photos we saw suggest the ship was likely carried with the ice and then forced up on the shore as part of the ice pack. Depending on the state of the ship before it was forced above the water line, the interior could be free of ice, and if it is, all they need to do is break through the hull and they could have access to any part of the ship that was never flooded."

Corkery sat back on his haunches. "So basically what you're saying is they could have what they want, this zupu thing, in a matter of minutes?"

"Yes. And then like our dead man said, they intend to kill everyone to hide their crime."

"But surely they can't think they'll get away with it."

"Think about it. As far as they're concerned, nobody knows this is happening. By the time the storm clears, they'll have returned to the ship. The crew will swear up and down that they were always on it. That assumes they're ever questioned. And this is a crime family, used to evading authorities. Also remember this is about family honor. They might not care at all whether they live or die as long as their family honor is restored with the zupu."

Corkery growled. "This is insane."

A strange whistling sound behind them had everyone turning. Acton shielded his eyes and pointed at what had to be a flare, slowly falling from the sky. "Now, who the hell could that be?"

Laura shook her head. "More bad guys? Maybe they got lost so they sent up a flare so their partners in crime could find them."

"Maybe it's a rescue team?" suggested Corkery.

Acton dismissed the idea. "No, they'd have GPS. And they wouldn't fire a flare like that unless they were in incredible trouble. Merely signaling that they're there or that they're somehow lost would put lives at risk. And besides, it hasn't been long enough for them to get here. They wouldn't come just because of the storm. Storms are normal. And even if Mercedes got through to your friend, there's no way they could have mounted an operation this quickly. No, this is somebody else, either more bad guys, like you said, or someone else that needs help"

Corkery grabbed him by the arm, shaking it. "It could be Mercedes!"

Acton regarded him. "Was that part of the plan?"

247

"No, but she's an incredibly brave woman. The plan was for me to see where they were going and then return. If she made it back to the ship and saw I wasn't there, what little I know of her makes me think she'd be foolish enough to come and find me."

"But could she have made it back so quickly?"

Corkery shook his head. "I can't see how, but there's somebody out there who either needs help or might be able to help us. I think we need to check it out."

Laura readied her pistol. "It could be more bad guys."

Acton smacked his assault rifle. "Then we better take them out while we can."

Approaching the Expedition Site, Antarctica

Mercedes stood on the seat of her snowmobile as she scanned the horizon in all directions, seeing nothing. She was sure Corkery couldn't have gone much farther than this on foot, though it was possible—she had been slowing them down with her shorter stride and Corkery was a fit man. But she had never taken him to be foolish, and to have gone this far was exactly that.

She debated firing a second flare just in case he had missed the first, but held back. She only had so many, and the Chinese could see the flares just as easily as Corkery, and they had eight sets of eyes to his one. But he was also a brave man. No one continued to follow armed men unless they were filled with courage. Or stupidity. Her opinion of this man continued to grow. He wasn't stupid. He was courageous, and she smiled as her head on a swivel came to a stop.

He *was* courageous. And he was walking directly toward her, his bright yellow jacket unmistakable. She waved at him, both arms high above her head, but through the worsening storm, all she could make out was his form. The bright yellow, while a great idea in good conditions, was proving terrible in a whiteout. He continued to approach and it was evident he had seen her. She sat back down and gunned the idling engine, sending her racing toward him—if he had seen the flare, then the Chinese might have as well.

Time was now of the essence.

She rapidly closed the distance between them, her hammering heart continuing to pound as more of his figure was revealed, removing all doubt that it was indeed him and not just some other soul lost in the storm wearing the same color gear. She eased off on the throttle and came to a halt, and as she climbed off the machine, two figures stepped out from behind him, one carrying a machine gun, the other a handgun, both pointed directly at her.

And she screamed.

Corkery rushed forward and grabbed her, waving off the other two. "It's Mercedes! It's Mercedes! Put the damn guns down!"

The weapons lowered and he held her tight. She latched on to him as she continued to sob in both relief and fear. He gently pushed her away, still holding her by the shoulders. "You're crazy, you know that?"

She pulled away her goggles and wiped her eyes with her gloves. "You're the crazy one. Why didn't you turn back?"

"Because our passengers kept going and I had to know where they went."

"Was it the shipwreck?"

Corkery's eyes widened as he stared at her in disbelief. "How could you possibly know that?"

"Google."

He laughed. "You're right. They're after something on board an old Chinese pirate ship." He stepped back and held out a hand to the smaller person holding the handgun. "This is the expedition leader, Professor Laura Palmer, and this is her husband, Professor James Acton. They managed to escape just before the camp was taken prisoner."

"Is everyone okay?"

Laura shook her head. "One of my people is dead, and it looks like they intend to force the rest to work in the storm. We managed to take one of them out, and before he died, he admitted that their intention is to kill everyone once they have what they want."

Mercedes held her hand to her chest the entire time. People were dead, and more were going to die. This was everything they had feared and more. "What are we going to do?" She pointed at the snowmobile. "I came here to get Dr. Corkery. There's not enough room for all of us on this."

Acton shook his head. "I have no intention of leaving."

Laura took his hand. "Nor do I."

Corkery turned to her. "Did you reach Katherine?"

Mercedes nodded. "Yes, I told her everything you said to say, and she said she would make sure help was sent. And then when I found out about the pirate ship, I called her back and told her that's where I thought everything was happening, so she knows everything and will hopefully get word to the right people."

Acton patted her on the shoulder. "That's excellent work."

Laura gave her a thumbs-up. "Extremely brave of you." She turned to her husband. "It probably means McMurdo either knows or will know soon. But even if they do, it's a minimum three hours for them to get here by snowcat in ideal conditions. This storm has to add some time to that."

Acton grunted. "Not to mention the fact they still only have peashooters. All they'd be doing is sending in cannon fodder. There's no way they can mount a rescue operation. Nobody's prepared for this."

Corkery rubbed his hands together, stomping his feet. "Surely, they must have some sort of plan for a scenario like this."

Laura shook her head. "No, I read the Antarctic Treaty. The only weapons allowed are restricted in number and type. I think McMurdo actually only has about a dozen weapons, and they're all meant for protection against wildlife, not heavily armed criminals. If there's going to be an armed response, it's likely to come from New Zealand, and depending on the type of plane, it's anywhere from five to nine hours to get here, not to mention the fact I doubt they would land in this weather. I'm afraid the only response is thousands of miles away."

Acton cleared his throat. "Actually, that's not true."

Everyone turned to him. "What do you mean?"

"There's a Chinese Special Forces team sitting just off the coast, more than capable of rescuing our people."

Laura's jaw dropped. "You're right. But how do we even let them know there's a problem?"

En route to the Excavation Site, Antarctica

Ortega and McAlister hauled a skid loaded with supplies in silence. Everyone was terrified. There was no denying that. He had met Ericksen on several occasions. Ericksen was a great guy, a family man down here doing what he loved to help pay for his kids' college. This shouldn't be happening. Not here. He came to Antarctica to get away from the craziness of the streets back home, and now here he was, in the thick of it.

He glared at one of the Chinese scientists walking along with them. Their betrayal enraged him even more than the death of Ericksen. He was quite certain everyone here was going to die. They had already shown no hesitation in killing poor Ericksen, and by forcing everyone to work in these conditions, they were putting all their lives at risk. But more significantly, they had told them all who they were. They were the Zheng family, here to get their zupu. Surely, they couldn't leave anyone alive knowing this.

His biggest concern was not for himself, but for McAlister. He kept his eyes peeled for any opportunity to escape. Professors Acton and Palmer were out there somewhere, and if they could find them and join forces, maybe they could do something together. What that might be, he wasn't sure. It would still be fists against guns, but with this weather, it would be fairly easy to sneak up on someone.

Professor Liu walked up beside him and he was tempted to punch the man in the throat and stomp his head until his traitorous life was extinguished. Instead, he was shocked by what the man said.

"Don't say anything. In our shelter is an emergency radio beacon. It's at the bottom of my pack with my name on it. I'm going to send you back to get my spare gloves from my pack, and use your friend here as leverage to make sure you return. That should have them letting you go alone. Find the transmitter. It's a bright yellow box. Open it up, turn the key, then press the big red button. Make sure you keep it hidden in the structure. Don't bring it with you. Understood?"

"Yes," said Ortega, his entire body shaking with the revelation that Liu hadn't betrayed them at all, but in fact was attempting to save them.

And he shook even harder with the responsibility that had just been thrust upon his shoulders.

Outside the Expedition Site, Antarctica

The wind howled with a ferocious gust, knocking Mercedes to the ground and Laura to her knees. Acton helped Laura up and Corkery did the same with Mercedes, and they all huddled together. "There's no way we can travel in this. We're going to have to ride it out," said Acton.

Mercedes pointed at the gear she had brought, still loaded on the back of the snowmobile. "I brought emergency supplies. I've got a tent, a portable heater, food, fuel for the heater, shovels, anything I could think of that I could grab without being noticed."

Corkery gave her a one-armed hug. "That's my girl." He turned to Laura. "What do you think, expedition leader?"

"How big is that tent?"

Mercedes glanced at the gear. "It'll only fit two, I'm afraid."

Acton dismissed the concern. "Not a problem. It's more important as a windbreak. It's the fuel and heater you brought that are key." He pointed at the snowmobile. "We're going to have to relocate. Someone else might have seen that flare."

"How far?" asked Laura.

"Not much." He pointed toward a snow ridge. "Let's just head over there. It's maybe a hundred yards. If we get on the opposite side of that ridge, nobody will see us. Mercedes, why don't you take Laura over there, and Doug and I will follow on foot. Get those shovels out and start digging out something big enough for the four of us."

"Yes, sir." Mercedes climbed on the snowmobile and Laura straddled it behind her. Moments later, they were heading toward the embankment while Acton watched the landscape behind them, searching for anyone who might have spotted the flare or heard the engine of the snowmobile.

"I don't see anything, do you?" asked Corkery.

Acton shoved the man to the ground and hit the deck, pointing just to their left at a shadowy figure coming toward them. "Something tells me that's not a penguin."

Corkery cursed. "Or a sea lion after our ass."

Acton gave the man a look. "What?"

Corkery chuckled. "Ask me later." He indicated the new arrival. "What are we going to do?"

"We have to take him out. No choice."

"But won't they miss him?"

"They will eventually, but he's far enough from the camp I doubt they'd even hear the shot."

Corkery stared at him in horror. "You mean you're going to shoot him?"

Acton prepped his weapon. "What? You want me to use the axe again?"

"No, I guess not. I guess I'm just not that used to taking lives. My job has always been to save them."

"That's exactly what we're doing here. We're saving lives. Right now, ours and those two ladies back there that we care about, but eventually maybe the entire expedition. Are you okay with this?"

Corkery reluctantly nodded. "I guess you have to do what you have to do. Better him than us."

"Exactly." Acton lined up the shot and waited, letting the target get closer. With the high winds, he was concerned about his aim. Every foot he could take off the shot improved his odds of hitting him. He only wanted to fire a single round. If someone did hear it, it would be harder for them to pinpoint the direction.

His heart hammered. This wasn't how he usually did things. Usually, he was firing in the heat of the moment, bullets ripping past him from an enemy hell-bent on killing him. Here, he had an unsuspecting victim, though a murderer nonetheless. He peered through the scope mounted to the Chinese assault rifle and confirmed that the target walking toward him had the same weapon gripped in his hand.

There was no doubt this was one of the hostiles.

The man stopped and raised his weapon, apparently having spotted at least one of them. Acton squeezed the trigger and the man dropped. Acton sprang to his feet and ran as quickly as he could, praying he had taken the man out with a clean shot. He reached his target and ripped the gun away from him. He flipped him over and checked for any signs of life. There were none. A clean kill.

He stripped the man of anything useful, handing the assault rifle to Corkery and pocketing the handgun and extra magazines. He stripped the jacket off the man then buried him in the snow, an uncomfortable Corkery assisting. Acton scanned the horizon for any other hostiles but found it clear. "Okay, let's go join the others and come up with a plan for what to do next."

"You're going to kill more of them?"

Acton turned to Corkery. "Doug, I'm going to kill every damn last one of them if I have to."

Excavation Site, Antarctica

Evans glanced over at Min, the cute little Chinese number he had zoned in on the moment their people had arrived. She was shy but seemed to enjoy his sense of humor, if her giggling was any indication. She probably wasn't accustomed to this kind of attention, and he got the distinct impression she was enjoying it.

But she shook her head slightly.

He didn't acknowledge her warning, but the fact she had given it rather than rebuking him verbally suggested to him that she wasn't necessarily a willing participant in her boss' betrayal of the team. At the moment, all their hopes were on Palmer and Acton getting help. How they had managed to escape when no one else had, he had no clue. They must have been outside for some reason when the attack happened. A process of elimination had identified Ericksen as the victim, and he had been in their shelter.

He had no problem with Laura Palmer. He had been in the wrong, but he always played the odds. He hit on everyone he could, and yes, the vast majority rejected him. But there was that small minority that didn't. It meant he rarely left a bar alone. He was determined to have sex in Antarctica so he could complete his goal of having done it on every continent on this planet.

And if they ever started sex tours in space, he was on the first rocket.

He had a problem. He knew it, but he didn't care. What harm was there in having lots of consensual sex with willing partners? He never forced anyone. He always backed off when they were clearly not interested. It wasn't like he was smoking or drinking himself to death or gambling away his life savings. He was just having fun, which was why Acton humiliating him had gone too far, though the fact most of the room had laughed at him, a room that barely knew him, perhaps suggested he was coming on a little too strong. One of these days, maybe he'd meet the right woman, perhaps settle down, have a family. But there was plenty of time left for that.

He glanced over at the Chinese vixen buried under layers of clothing behind a facemask and goggles. He had no idea what she really looked like, but he didn't care. She was within reach, no matter how unattainable.

They reached the pegged-off crevasse discovered accidentally by the two unqualified members of their team. It was how many things were discovered in this business—by complete accident. And if it weren't for them, this ship could have been buried here for another millennium.

The traitor, Liu, turned to the group. "Who has the most climbing experience?"

Evans frowned but raised his hand. It was why he was on the expedition. He had years of experience on the ice, much of it in

Greenland, the environment there quite similar to that here. "I do," he said, someone else nearby also raising their hand.

"Me too."

"All right, you two get over here and start rigging your equipment. I want a hole punched in that hull within an hour. The sooner we get this done, the sooner we let you go."

Evans stepped toward the edge, glancing over at Min, and he could see the concern in her eyes. The woman did care. He turned and pointed to the skid Ortega was dragging. "Bring me that bag on the top. Let's get this over and done with."

Outside the Expedition Site, Antarctica

The crack of a shot from a rifle had Laura poking her head up to see what was going on. She could barely see James and Corkery in the distance heading toward something that she couldn't make out. The fact they were both alive and not running away suggested whatever danger there had been was over. There was little she could do to help, so rather than get in the way, she continued the work she and Mercedes were responsible for.

The snow was thick, deep, and hard, but the shovels that the young nurse had wisely brought were making quick work of it. Laura crawled inside and continued to hack away, widening the cavern that just might save their lives. Being inside and out of the wind was already cutting the chill.

"Do you think this is going to work?" asked Mercedes behind her as she scooped out the snow that Laura shoveled from the walls.

"It's a technique used for thousands of years, so I don't see why not."

"When do you think the others will be back?"

262

Laura stabbed the shovel blade into the snow upside down then pushed the handle up, breaking off another chunk. "Pretty soon. I'm guessing something happened out there that they're dealing with, and when they're done, they'll be back."

"I hope they're all right."

Laura smiled slightly. "You mean you hope Dr. Corkery is all right."

"Your husband too."

Laura chuckled. "I think he's sweet on you."

"Your husband?"

Laura outright laughed. "No, Doug."

"Oh no, we barely know each other."

Laura stopped and turned to look at her. "I saw that hug. He cares about you."

"Just as a friend."

"Do you like him?"

Mercedes shrugged and resumed her work, Laura doing the same as they continued the conversation. "He's nice, but I doubt I'm his type."

"Yeah, you're right. Most men don't like young, beautiful, courageous, funny, skilled women."

Mercedes paused her work. "Is that what you think of me?"

"I barely know you, but like I said, I saw that hug."

"Hello!" called James from outside, and Laura breathed a sigh of relief, twisting around.

"In here!"

James poked his head in. "Hey, babe, sorry we took so long. We ran into another unruly passenger."

263

"Is everybody okay?"

"Well, he's not, but Doug and I are fine."

Mercedes scrambled out of the cavern and Laura smiled slightly at the sounds of the reunion outside, hands slapping on jackets indicating a healthy hug was underway. Relationships forged under fire rarely worked out, but hers and James had, so why couldn't others?

James looked about. "Looks like this is almost there." He grabbed Mercedes' shovel. "Let's get this done. It's getting really bad out there. Pretty soon you won't see a foot in front of your face."

She returned to work, joined by her husband, her thoughts drifting to her team and what they must be going through working in these unbearable conditions.

En route to Antarctica

Dawson peered at the laptop screen, the latest satellite imagery useless. The storm continued to grow in intensity. They were going in blind. Literally.

Squadron Leader Dunn looked at him from across the airframe. "Still no joy?"

Dawson shook his head. "Nothing. All we've got is a general layout from some shots taken a couple of days ago and then the planned layout that Professor Palmer had approved. We know where the structures should be, but who the hell knows?"

Dunn leaned forward and tapped his earpiece. "My CO has just informed me that if the weather gets any worse, they're scrubbing your jump."

"Balls to that!" cried Niner.

Dawson raised his hand slightly, settling Niner down. "No decision has been made yet, so let's just calm down. We knew this could be a possibility." He turned his attention back to Dunn and tapped his laptop.

265

"Every indication is that this storm is getting worse. When do you expect your CO to make the decision?"

"Top of the hour. That's when McMurdo is supposed to do the next update on the storm. If it's worse than last hour, they'll scrub it."

Dawson checked his watch. "That'll be only minutes before the drop. While this is a joint op under your command, this plane is operated by the American military."

Dunn smirked. "Sergeant Major, as far as I'm concerned, I'm not in command until our boots are on the ground. Anything you choose to do between now and then is up to you and your own CO."

Dawson smiled slightly. "I always like working with you Kiwis. You're so easygoing."

"Until you get us on the rugby pitch. Then we'll make you wish you had never been born."

Operations Center 2, CIA Headquarters
Langley, Virginia

Leroux sat at his station, his arms folded, a finger tapping as he stared at what might as well be white noise. His team was essentially useless. They couldn't see anything beyond dots on a screen. Delta was half an hour away from insertion and he had just received word that the Kiwis were looking to pull the plug on the drop as it was now deemed too dangerous.

And they were right. It was.

The weather had gotten worse than anyone had anticipated, and the only thing keeping anyone in was the personal connection to the professors. But having six Delta operators dying to save people who might already be dead or might not even be in danger, was calculus he didn't want to do. If it were up to him, he'd abort, and unfortunately, his recommendation would possibly be what was used to decide what happened to the American side of the operation.

"What do you think?" he asked Sonya Tong, and she turned her chair to face him.

"I think we should abort, but knowing Bravo Team, if they get those orders, they'll ignore them. They're willing to take the risk."

"Is there any sign of a break in that storm?"

She shook her head. "I just got off the phone with the Met people and they said there's none. This thing's going to hang around for at least two days."

Leroux cursed. "If only it wasn't so damn far away from everything, we might have been able to insert them by sea. What would you recommend if you were in my shoes?"

Tong smiled at him. "Just like you can ruin my weekend because of your position, I can bow out of this decision because of mine."

He laughed. "Okay, I guess I deserved that one." He chewed his cheek for a moment, debating what to do. The Delta Team would want to go in. He had no doubt about that, no matter what the safety concerns. It was a dangerous drop, but they did dangerous things all the time. Friends were involved, but that shouldn't enter the equation. What should were the dozens of innocents that might be held hostage at this moment. The fact there had been no type of ransom demand suggested the hostiles were there for something they believed to be on board the shipwreck. The question was, what would they do when they retrieved it? Would they walk away, leaving everybody alive, or would they kill all the witnesses?

There was no way to know.

But if they were to err on the side of caution, he had to assume they either intended to kill everyone or leave them to die, which could be as simple as sabotaging all their generators and leaving them to freeze to death before help could arrive. And there was one fact that needed to be remembered here—the hostiles likely had no idea they were on to them.

And that fact was critical.

The hostiles had no reason to rush.

The door hissed open and their boss, National Clandestine Service Chief Leif Morrison entered. He glanced at the screens, showing the whiteout conditions, and cursed. "Okay, Pentagon wants our recommendation. Go, no go?"

Leroux rose and the entire room fell silent. This was the most challenging part of the job. This was where he could be sending people to their deaths or saving dozens. "Sir, the dangerous part is the jump. Once they're on the ground, they're just in inhospitable conditions. They're trained for that, they expect that, and they knew that from the beginning. We all did. The only variable here is the storm, which has made the jump more difficult, though not exponentially so. On a difficulty level, it's not like we went from a two to a ten, we've gone from an eight to a ten. If Delta feels they can safely do the jump, then I say let them. Let's get them on the ground and deal with the consequences. Hopefully we'll have enough that make it through unscathed to put up a fight."

Morrison turned to Tong. "What do you think?"

She grinned. "Way above my pay grade."

Morrison laughed. "Good answer." He headed for the doors. "I'll pass on the CIA's official recommendation." He glanced over his shoulder at Leroux. "One that I agree with, by the way."

Leroux bowed his head slightly. "Thank you, sir." The door closed and Leroux sat back down.

Randy Child, their tech wunderkind, spun in his chair behind him. "Man, it must be nice to have brass balls."

Leroux chuckled. "Just remember, like reputations, they can tarnish as well."

Outside the Expedition Site, Antarctica

Acton sat with the others, huddled around the heater taking the edge off the cold, their own body heat doing more to warm the area than anything. They had managed to dig out a cavern big enough to comfortably hold all four of them and set up the tent at the entrance. They had the floor lined with the jackets of the dead men and the guns sitting out in the tent where they wouldn't accumulate any condensation from their breath.

A pot sat on top of the flame, snow melting inside it. It was easy to forget that dehydration was a serious issue in these conditions, and they would all have to continue to take that into account. But as he sat there, getting comfortable, his facemask lowered and his goggles up on his forehead, he thought of the other expedition team members and the hell they were going through.

And it racked him with guilt.

Laura reached out and squeezed his forearm. "What's wrong?"

He shrugged. "You know me, I don't like just sitting by, especially when people could be dying."

271

"Me neither. But I don't see that we have much choice. If we go out in this, we'll never find the shelter again."

"We only have to come back if we don't win."

Corkery stared at them wide-eyed. "You two are a real piece of work, you know that? Listen to yourselves. The two of you are going to go out there and fight them to the death, aren't you?"

Acton held up a hand. "There's something you need to understand. My wife and I are both Special Forces trained."

Corkery's eyes narrowed. "You were in the Special Forces?"

Acton laughed. "No, but we were trained by former Special Forces. We know how to shoot, we know hand-to-hand combat, and we've seen a lot of action over the years."

"Action? But you're archaeology professors!"

Laura grinned. "A charmed life. But my husband's right. We are trained for this, and it's been our experience that quite often people like this are merely armed thugs who barely know how to hold their weapons, let alone hit a target."

Corkery stared at her then turned to Mercedes. "Can you believe this?"

Mercedes appeared equally shocked, but Acton got a sense she wanted to join in.

Corkery took a breath, calming himself. "Listen, I understand your desire to help, especially if you have these skills you claim to have. But don't you risk triggering the massacre you're trying to prevent? You've managed to kill two of them so far, and you assume you got away with it because either nobody's noticed they're missing or they assume they're still out looking for you. Remember, we don't know what's going on out there. You can't just shoot anything that moves. People might have escaped, or other innocent people like Mercedes might be here for some reason. You have to be awfully sure before you take that shot. The best thing you can do right now is save yourselves and hope that the authorities get here soon. And think about it. If they do arrive and they see the two of you brandishing weapons, whose side do you think they're going to assume you're on? You're liable to get yourself shot by the good guys."

Corkery was making sense, but what he was forgetting was that it was hours before any help could arrive. If the Zheng family were indeed after their zupu, held in the captain's quarters of the vessel, they could have it in a matter of minutes depending on the condition of the ship's interior.

Then the massacre would ensue.

Acton shook his head. "Listen, Doug, I understand your concern, but those are our people out there, and once that zupu is recovered, they're going to kill them all long before any help can arrive. Now, you two are perfectly safe in here. We'll leave the handguns with you so you can defend yourselves if necessary. But if you hear somebody, yell, 'identify yourself!' If you don't like what you hear, shoot them. Hopefully, it'll be us coming back with good news, but most likely it will be a rescue team."

"They're never going to find us in this," said Corkery.

"They might not find you, but you've got enough supplies to last a few days until the storm breaks. But I wouldn't worry about that."

Mercedes' eyes narrowed. "What do you mean?"

Acton smiled, pointing outside. "That snowmobile you stole has a GPS tracker on it. All vehicles in Antarctica do to aid in search and rescue operations. When the good guys arrive, they're going to be coming right here, maybe first."

Mercedes smiled for a brief instant before it turned to fear. "Could those gangsters track it?"

Acton shook his head. "I doubt it. They'd have to have the proper equipment and these guys weren't even carrying radios. I don't think they anticipated the storm."

Laura leaned forward and squeezed Mercedes' hand. "Don't worry about us. You two are going to be perfectly safe, and we're just going to see what we can do. We're not going to do anything stupid."

Corkery grunted. "Umm, I think the moment you leave this shelter you've just broken that commitment."

Acton geared up for what awaited them outside. "Don't worry, Doug, we rarely get shot and almost never die. We'll be okay."

Corkery stared at him. "Almost never die? You mean you've died?"

Laura put on her own outerwear. "No. Well, I guess he technically died, but he was only out a couple of minutes."

Acton grinned. "I don't know what my record is. Nobody's ever really timing these things when they happen."

Corkery's head thrust forward, his jaw dropping. "You mean this has happened more than once?"

Acton shrugged as he fit his goggles in place. "After the first couple, why bother keeping count? I'll start to get nervous when I get close to nine."

"You two are certifiable."

Laura patted Corkery on the shoulder. "Don't worry, Doug, we've been called far worse." She patted Mercedes' cheek. "But not by far better." She jerked a thumb at Corkery. "You've got a keeper here."

Mercedes flushed and turned away, and Acton laughed. "You kids have fun. Mom and Dad have to go kill the bad guys."

Excavation Site, Antarctica

Ortega stared over the edge of the crevasse as Evans hacked away at the hull with an axe. It had been difficult work at first, but once the Welshman had gotten into a rhythm of shorter swings that didn't have the axe head constantly hitting the ice wall behind him, he began to make progress.

The last time Ortega had been here had been terrifying. Falling thirty feet in a snowcat was no Disney ride, but after witnessing the excitement when the powers that be realized what they had found, he had been caught up in it as well. A piece of history, a piece of humanity lost to the ages, found in the most impossible of places, and his name would be associated with it forever.

But now he wished they had never found it.

He had a sickening sense their captors didn't plan to let them go. He wasn't sure what it was that had him convinced of this. They had killed Ericksen in cold blood as they arrived. Clearly, they had no problems with killing—they had to be Chinese criminals. He couldn't remember what they were called, Yakuza, Triad—all he knew was that those gangs were known for their brutality. Bloods versus Crips was senseless violence. Yakuza and Triad? Their violence was purposeful.

With the storm raging and their comms down, these bastards could kill them all then get back to wherever they came from before anyone knew something had happened. Even if Professor Palmer managed to get help, it could be days away. Their only real hope was either that ship being filled brim to brim with frozen water that they would have to hack through, or the Chinese Special Forces that weren't that far away actually responding.

He just prayed the professor sent him on his errand soon so that he could activate that emergency beacon.

Evans shouted from below. "I'm through!"

Liu stepped up to the edge. "How does it look?"

Evans stared up, frowning. "It's clear. No ice."

Ortega closed his eyes. This was all going to be over soon. Too soon.

Liu slapped him on the shoulder. "I need you to get me something in my shelter."

Over Antarctica

The mission had been split in mid-deployment. The initial mission had been to counteract any moves the Chinese Special Forces might make by merely stationing a force that could quickly respond to any Chinese aggression. But after receiving the report about the armed passengers while in the air, the powers that be had reworked things. There were now two targets. The Russian ship that had equipped the hostiles, and the expedition site. It had been decided that Squadron Leader Dunn's SAS team would take the ship, and Bravo Team would deal with whatever was happening at the expedition site.

Dawson checked Jimmy's gear and Jimmy returned the favor as everyone prepped for the highly dangerous jump. The Kiwi CO had relented when Clancy had insisted his team was capable of and willing to make the jump. They could land safely near McMurdo but it would put them too far from their destination. Even if they went by snowmobile from McMurdo, it would take too long, and traveling the unfamiliar landscape in these conditions would be more dangerous than the jump.

Dunn stepped over, extending a hand. "Good luck, Sergeant Major." He squatted slightly. "Just remember, bend the knees, bend the knees."

Dawson chuckled. "I'll try to remember that, sir." He held up his M4. "And don't forget, you're dealing with Russians. Just remember, shoot first, shoot first."

Dunn roared, smacking Dawson on the shoulder. "You Yanks crack me up." He stepped back then let his gaze fall on all six operators. "Good hunting, Bravo Team. We'll see you all on the other side."

The warning light flashed at the rear of the plane and the cargo deck lowered. Niner yelped. "Holy shit! That's cold." He pointed at the floor, his finger following something. "I think I just lost one of my nuts."

Atlas grunted. "Me too." He turned to the Kiwis. "If you find them, hang on to them for us."

One of them smirked. "How will we know the difference?"

Atlas grinned. "His will be the marble, mine will be the medicine ball."

Outside the Expedition Site, Antarctica

Acton took a knee not ten paces from their shelter. He looked behind them but could barely see the snowmobile. He stared up at the sky but he couldn't find the sun. The clouds were too thick now. He stuck the butt of the rifle in the snow then stepped back, noting the direction the faint shadow was cast. He pointed in the opposite direction. "That's where the sun is. It should basically be in the same direction for the next hour or so. If we fall back or we get separated, locate the sun, then bear twenty degrees to the right. Got it?"

"Got it."

He pointed ahead and slightly to the left. "The site should be in this direction. How do you want to tackle this?"

"I say we head straight forward. Every hundred paces we stop and check to see what we see. If we spot anyone, we take them out as soon as we've confirmed they're hostile."

"Sounds good. You ready?"

"Aren't I always?"

Acton laughed and grabbed her by the back of the head, pressing his forehead against hers. "I love you so much."

She reached up and squeezed the back of his head, pulling him tight. "I love you too. Now let's go save my people."

Expedition Site, Antarctica

The two guards standing in the center of the camp turned toward him and Ortega raised a hand, waving, forcing as friendly and as calm a voice as he could. "Professor Liu sent me to get something from his shelter. I'll just be a minute."

They both nodded and resumed their conversation. The conditions were brutal now. From where he stood, he couldn't even see the communications antenna, but he could hear a loose cable banging away. How any rescue team could get here was beyond him, but that wasn't his responsibility. He had been given a task, a task that might save all their lives, and standing here debating whether he could reach the communications gear unseen was pointless.

He headed to the Chinese structure and opened the door, stepping inside. He closed the door behind him and breathed a relieved sigh. The heater was still going, the generator still chugging on the other side of the wall, and just being out of the wind and whipping snow provided tremendous relief. He raised his goggles and pulled down his facemask, filling his lungs with the warm air.

But luxuries would have to wait. He had a job to do.

Six backpacks were neatly lined up against the wall, the owners' names all stitched on the packs in Chinese characters with English translations underneath. He spotted Liu's and grabbed it, tossing it onto the lone table in the room. He opened the top of the pack and started pulling out the gear, then almost cried out in jubilation when he found the emergency beacon at the bottom, exactly as the professor had said. He flipped open the protective cover, turned the key already in the panel, and pressed the button to activate it.

All the characters on it were in Chinese so he had no way of knowing whether it was functioning properly. He had to assume that green meant good and red meant bad, but with this being communist China, who the hell knew? With red being their color, it could run the opposite of the rest of the world.

He snapped the lid shut and shoved the device back into the bottom of the backpack. He pushed everything back inside in the order he had removed them, setting aside a pair of gloves. He zipped up the backpack and returned it to its position against the wall.

His job was done. If he died now, he would die knowing he had helped the others, especially McAlister. He took a moment to clear the ice and snow off his gear while standing near the heater. He desperately wanted to stay, just for five minutes—he had never been so cold in his life. The 300 Club couldn't compare to what they were going through.

Temperature differential was a stunt. Working out in it for over an hour was suicide.

But McAlister was being held at gunpoint to guarantee his return, and he didn't know how long the guard holding her hostage would consider reasonable. He zipped up his jacket again, fit his goggles and facemask back in place, then grabbed Liu's spare set of gloves. He stepped back into the cold, closed the door, and waved the gloves in the air at the two guards before heading back toward the excavation site. He hooked on to the safety line they had rigged that led to the site, then followed it, praying the Chinese Special Forces team picked up the signal and that they would save them.

Assuming he had activated the beacon properly.

Operations Center 2, CIA Headquarters

Langley, Virginia

"We've got a new signal in the area."

Leroux stared at the display as Tong updated the map. A new pulsating dot appeared where the expedition site was. "What do we think it is?"

"It's an emergency beacon. Chinese."

Leroux pursed his lips. "That might have been useful an hour ago."

"At least it's proof of life," said Tong.

Child stopped spinning in his chair. "How do you figure?"

"Somebody had to activate it, and I can't see it being the hostiles."

Leroux shook his head. "I wouldn't be so sure. We don't know what their exit plan was. It could have been on foot, but now with the storm, they might think they need rescuing themselves. We don't know who that signal was intended for. It could be their coconspirators on the ship. The only people who are going to be able to tell us who that beacon belongs to are the Chinese. If they recognize the identifier as one of theirs, then they might take action."

Child held up his hand and Leroux rolled his eyes. "Yes?"

"Do we actually want the Chinese to take action now?"

"What do you mean?"

Child pointed at the screen. "Delta's inserting now, and the Kiwis are going to be on the ground in the next few minutes. Do we really want the Chinese getting into the mix? Bravo Team could end up having to fight on two fronts."

"You're right, but if we can make this a joint operation, we know the Chinese have at least a dozen Special Forces on site, and we're only sending in six against eight. I'd prefer to be going in better than even at over two to one than worse than even." Leroux fit his earpiece back in place. "Get me Control. I want to see if they've had any word from the Chinese now that that beacon is broadcasting."

They weren't Control here, they were merely observers—there was no way in hell the international community would agree to the CIA running the op. They were relegated to the back seat, only allowed to feed intel into the beast, not act on it.

And he didn't like it.

Over Antarctica

Dawson stared at the vast whiteness below. This was nuts. It was worse than a night dive. At least then you could have headgear with night vision letting you see the ground below, but here, all of that was useless. All he had was his altimeter, rapidly ticking down to what they prayed was an accurate ground level.

They had jumped at as low an altitude as they safely could. There was no point in freefalling and picking up speed, possibly drifting off course with the winds. They needed to be as accurate as possible and hit their LZ, otherwise they could end up adding hours until they were in position to engage. The GPS on his heads-up display showed they were good so far.

His altimeter beeped at the preprogrammed altitude and he pulled his chute, announcing it to the team. "This is Zero-One, deploying chute, over." He stared up and could just make out four good corners of his canopy. He grabbed the toggles as the wind buffeted him. He counted in his head as the others announced their chute deployments. "This is Zero-

One. Good chute, over." The others confirmed their own and he breathed a sigh of relief. With these wind speeds, their lines could easily become twisted, but the fact they had six successful deployments dramatically reduced the risk of someone dying.

"Bravo Team, watch your altimeters and keep your knees bent. These ice fields can vary in altitude by hundreds of feet. The LZ is supposed to be flat, but who the hell knows." The string of acknowledgments came in then Niner's voice broke in over the comms.

"I'm just staying above my man Atlas so I've got something big and cushy to hit."

Atlas growled a reply. "If you land on me, little man, I'm going to punch you so hard, you'll skid all the way to McMurdo."

Dawson could almost hear Spock's eyebrow cocking. "Might I suggest you punch him in the direction of the expedition site? He could finish the job before we get there."

Dawson chuckled as the chatter continued, his altimeter still counting down toward zero. They were dropping far slower than a few moments ago when they were in freefall, but one of the things about jumping was you flared your chute at the last moment by pulling down on the toggles. It helped kill your speed drastically, and if you timed it just right, you could land on your feet and walk away from the jump. But if the ground came up suddenly, giving you no time to flare, you could shove your legs through your hips and shatter a whole lot more than your ego.

He was fifty feet from the surface. If the altimeter was to be believed, he had to take the chance. He couldn't wait to confirm sight of the ground. "Zero-One, flaring at fifty feet." He yanked down on both toggles, partially collapsing the chute above him. With his speed momentarily killed, he bent his knees rather than risk a walkaway landing—this would be a standard Parachute Landing Fall. He hit the ground hard and without warning, but instinctively rolled, absorbing the shock, and immediately knew he was fine. "Zero-One on the ground safe. Flared at fifty feet, over."

"Flaring," called Atlas followed quickly by the others in the order they had jumped. Dawson rose to a knee, hauling in his chute. He bundled it up and shoved it into the snow for later retrieval. Everything brought onto the continent came off the continent.

He wondered who would be tasked to retrieve all the bullet casings.

"One-One safely on the ground," reported Niner.

"Zero-Seven safely on the ground," announced Atlas, the others soon following.

Dawson activated the strobe beacon on his gear then slowly did a 360. More beacons flashed around him and they all converged in a huddle. "Everybody good? No twisted ankles, no broken asses?"

Thumbs-up all around.

Dawson checked his tactical computer. "GPS says we're right on target." He took a bearing then pointed to his left. "The welcome wagon from McMurdo should be in this direction. We'll make contact and get our snowmobiles and get this over with. I want to get off this damn continent as fast as I can. My fur-lined cup that Red was sending me never got a chance to arrive."

"Should have used Amazon Prime," said Atlas.

"Yeah," agreed Niner. "Same-day delivery in some cases."

"I'll keep it in mind for next time." Dawson headed toward where the snowcat should be, and just prayed they could find it in the storm. He had seen all kinds of weather, but he'd never actually experienced a blizzard, and it had him wishing for the heat and sands of the Middle East he'd never complain about again.

Outside the Expedition Site, Antarctica

Laura peered through her scope, struggling with her tactical breathing, made difficult by the biting cold and the fact her husband was lying in the snow playing possum while what they assumed was a hostile approached. They had spotted something moving in a brief break in the wind gusts and whoever it was had spotted them as well. A quick plan had been hatched and James had laid down in the snow while she crawled off to get in position for a shot.

The figure continued to approach, clearly seeing James, but gave no indication that they had seen her. She waited for the signal. They couldn't risk killing one of their own who might have escaped or someone sent to rescue them. The target was holding something and to her it appeared to be a weapon exactly like her own. But she watched, waiting for the signal.

James' thumb raised.

She squeezed the trigger and the target whipped around, dropping to the ground. James immediately jumped up and grabbed the target's weapon, stepping back and aiming at the unmoving form. Laura leaped to her feet and rushed forward, keeping her gun trained on her target.

"Got him?"

She nodded. "I've got him."

James tossed his weapon aside so there would be no chance of it being taken from him, then he moved in, confirming the kill. "He's dead." He tore off the facemask and goggles. "Chinese. I don't recognize him as part of Liu's team, so it looks like we got a third bad guy here. Good work."

She took the compliment with a nod, but she didn't feel good about it. She hadn't been put on this earth to kill, yet she had killed more than almost any civilian on the face of the planet. And she'd never get used to it. She just had to keep reminding herself that these were bad people. They had killed one of her team already and maybe more, and they intended to kill everybody she had vowed to protect as the leader of this expedition.

James stuffed a pistol and several magazines into his pockets then buried the man in the snow before joining her. "That's three down, and I'm willing to bet all three of them are part of the four that were sent out to probably look for us. The chance of finding the fourth one in this is pretty slim unless they saw the flare too. I suggest we head to the site and see what we see."

She agreed, and as they continued toward the camp, she glanced over her shoulder and said a silent prayer for the life she had taken, and for her soul she feared she was slowly losing.

Rendezvous Point, Antarctica

Dawson pointed directly ahead. A harsh white light could be seen spinning like a lighthouse, cutting however slightly through the heavy snow. "That has to be our welcome wagon." They pushed forward as quickly as they could, the terrain horrendous, some of it slippery ice, some of it crackling snow that ate up their feet with every step. It was slow going, but once they reached the snowcat, snowmobiles awaited them.

The beacon changed and focused in their direction, and he could make out a figure standing in front of it, waving at their own still-lit beacons. They weren't hiding here—they were nowhere near any of the hostiles. They were still in the survival phase of the mission. It took five minutes but felt like thirty-five before they were huddled inside a temporary haven set up by the McMurdo staff, heavy tarps used to create a shelter tied to the snowcat.

A woman extended her hand. "I'm Julie Pyne. Which one of you is Sergeant Major White?"

Dawson shook the hand. "I am, ma'am. Glad we were able to find you in this mess."

"Me too. I'd hate to have come out here and frozen my ample ass off for nothing."

Dawson laughed. "Well, we appreciate it, ma'am, and we're not going to take a lot of your time. You've got our equipment?"

She jerked a thumb at the attached trailer. "Six snowmobiles, fully fueled with standard safety kit. You sure you want to do this?"

"Not much choice, ma'am."

An engine roared to life and one of the McMurdo crew backed a snowmobile off the trailer and into the snow.

"Well, it's your funeral." She cursed. "Sorry. I guess I could have chosen a better word."

Niner held up a finger, leaning forward. "I would've said party."

A second engine fired up and Dawson brought things back on track. "Any advice?"

"Yeah. Check your balls. And by that, I don't mean to see if they're there, I mean set them aside. Those machines can go fast, but speed is your enemy here. You could come up on a crevasse in a heartbeat and they'll never find the body. If you see something dark in front of you, stop and check. It could be the shadow caused by an opening. You just never know. You don't have far to go so you don't have to go fast. These machines will just make it nice and easy for you."

Dawson extended a hand. "Thanks for the advice. Beers are on me if we get out of this alive."

Pyne laughed and shook Dawson's hand hard. "Sweetheart, I'm a straight-up JD woman, and I take the whole bottle."

Excavation Site, Antarctica

Evans was exhausted from the effort but he kept going. He could have asked for relief, but he didn't bother. He had set a slow, methodical pace that so far had kept their captors happy. As long as he continued to show progress, they didn't seem to care how long it took, and the way he figured it, every extra minute he bought them improved their chances of rescue. If Palmer and her husband had been captured, their captors absolutely would have made a show out of it.

And so far, there had been nothing.

It meant they had escaped. It would take at least several hours for them to get somewhere to call for help and probably worse in these conditions. But it was hope, however faint. Unfortunately, he was reaching the end of how far he could delay. He had made the small opening initially confirming the void on the other side was clear of ice, then he had methodically widened the hole so that it was large enough for a man to fit in. He had dragged it out for well over an hour, but unfortunately, he was almost finished.

The final piece of wood snapped away and he sighed, tossing it inside the void rather than down the crevasse where it would be lost forever. Every timber, every splinter was a piece of history that he was destroying, and it broke his heart. He leaned his back against the wall of the crevasse, every muscle in his body aching. He forced himself to take long, slow breaths, steadying his hammering heart, the exhaustion overwhelming.

But they had made it this far without anyone getting hurt, and as long as he could tough it out, he intended to keep it that way.

"What's going on down there?" asked Liu, and Evans silently cursed the traitorous bastard, having guaranteed his people wouldn't suffer or put their lives at risk by betraying all of them.

"I'm about to make entry," he replied. "Once I'm inside, we might not be able to hear each other so don't panic. I could be a while."

"Understood. Take all the time you need."

Evans' eyes narrowed slightly at the tone. He got the sense that Liu was actually encouraging him to take his time. He had to be imagining it, but was he? "Thanks. Safety first." He holstered his hatchet and stuck a foot inside the opening, bending over and poking his head in, uncertain as to what he would find.

He played his headlamp around and sighed in relief at what appeared to be an intact floor, not two feet below the opening he had cut. "Give me some more slack!" he yelled, and the ropes were played out a bit, held by those above in the howling wind. He grabbed either side of the opening and pulled himself through, planting a foot tentatively on the centuries-old floor. He gently applied pressure then shifted more of his weight. There was a creak but the floor held. He brought his other foot through then stood.

It continued to hold.

He disconnected himself from the harness but kept the safety line attached. He poked his head outside the hole. "I'm inside the ship. Give me lots of slack on the safety line. I'll tug three times if I need help."

"Copy that!" acknowledged Parata from above.

Evans stepped back inside and carefully examined his surroundings. The plans for the Admiral Gardner had been part of the briefing notes, but until this moment, they couldn't be sure that the Black Dragon was once the proud ship of the East India Company lost to pirates in the South China Sea so long ago. He recognized the layout and the fit and finish were clearly not Chinese. This was a British vessel, and he wondered if any Welshman had ever crewed it in its lifetime.

He got his bearings. The captain's quarters should be to his right, and the fact it was on an incline could be good news. The fear, even before the expedition had begun, was always that the ship could be filled with ice from stem to stern, and they would have to meticulously chip and melt their way to anything of interest.

That was proving not to be the case, at least not on this deck in this portion of the ship. That would have been fantastic news for the expedition, but it was terrible news for this hostage situation. He could have their zupu in minutes, potentially sealing the fate of the entire expedition.

He didn't believe for a second that these people intended to leave them alive.

Expedition Site, Antarctica

Acton opened the rear door to the supply shed and Laura entered, her weapon raised. "Clear!" she hissed. He followed her inside, closing the door behind them, immediately confirming his wife's findings. They were alone, for how long who knew, but they had managed to enter the camp with nobody noticing, no doubt due to the near whiteout conditions.

The advantage of this building was that all safety lines led here. They could go out the front door and hitch on to any line that would take them to any structure, including the excavation site. The only thing they would have to worry about would be the hostiles spotting them, but three of them were dead leaving only five. They hadn't spotted anybody on their approach, which suggested most if not all the expedition members were at the excavation site. He figured there would be at least two guards on them, which meant at most three in and around the camp. If they could spot them first, they could easily take them out.

The trick was being first.

The only advantage they had was that he couldn't imagine the Triad thinking they would come back. Only fools would.

They both gathered around the heater, brushing off the snow and breaking off the ice that had accumulated on their way here. "What do you think we should do?" asked Laura.

He held up his shaking hands. "There's no way I can take a shot like this. I have to warm up."

She held up hands that shook even harder. "I feel your pain."

He laughed. "Okay. We're going to have to do this in turns. Someone has to keep a watch at all times." He pointed at the heater. "You warm up first, I'll keep watch." He pointed at a camp stove. "Let's get that lit and some coffee going. We need to warm our innards. Just make sure whatever kettle you use doesn't whistle."

En route to the Expedition Site, Antarctica

Dawson peered ahead uselessly. Someone might as well be holding a white sheet in front of his face. They were making good time, all things considered, but the lack of visibility had them traveling far slower than he would like. A briefing from the snowcat operator indicated that when she traveled the route this morning, there were no surprises. But things could change in a heartbeat, which was exactly how the shipwreck had been found in the first place, so he was taking point. If anyone was getting hurt or killed, it would be him.

They didn't have much farther to go, and he was starting to think they might just make it there unscathed. He slowed then came to a halt, the rest of the team flanking him. He checked his tactical computer and saw that their initial target, the stolen snowmobile, was just ahead. He activated his comms so everyone could hear him clearly rather than competing with the wind. He pointed just ahead and to the left. "The tracker says the stolen snowmobile is two hundred meters in that direction. Since we can't see five feet in front of our faces, we have to be very careful about crossfire. I want everybody to spread out ten feet apart and keep the man on your left and right in sight until we reach the target signal. If you lose sight of anyone, call it out and we all stop and reacquire.

"And remember, it's been storming all day, so when we do reach the signal, that snowmobile could be buried. First person who spots it stops and calls it out. When we find it, we sweep the area. Remember, we're looking for a friendly, so let's try to not blow her away. Let's go." He dropped back into his seat, adjusted his heading, then gunned the motor. The distance to the GPS tracker rapidly closed and he peered into the swirling snow, still eerily lit by the midnight sun.

"Got something," came Niner's voice over the comms. Dawson eased off the throttle and checked right to see Niner at a complete stop, waving. Dawson climbed off his machine and readied his M4 as the others did the same. He joined Niner as he used his forearm to clear off a snowmobile. "This has gotta be it. I don't see anybody though," he said, as he purposely stomped his feet while making a loop around the vehicle.

Atlas shoved him aside. "Get out of the way, little man," said the massive Atlas as he made his own stomping loop. "Watching you is like watching a cherub tip-toe on a cloud."

"BD, your nine o'clock."

Dawson looked to his left to see what Spock was talking about. He caught a glimpse of something bright red in the snow. With hand signals, he indicated for the team to spread out and they advanced on whatever was half-buried nearby. As the amount of snow between his retinas and the object reduced with the closing distance, it became obvious it was a tent. He indicated for Atlas, Niner, Spock, and Jimmy to watch their sixes as he and Wings approached. He lowered his facemask and immediately regretted it, quickly putting it back in place. "United States Army! Is there anyone in there?" He heard no response though couldn't be certain if anyone inside would even hear him, and there was no way to know if anyone was even alive—this tent would provide almost no protection against the cold.

He advanced, not sure what they were about to find. A frozen corpse, a shivering woman, or a hostile with a gun taking shelter from the storm.

Things could be about to get dicey.

Outside the Expedition Site, Antarctica

Corkery stared into Mercedes' eyes, brushing a tress of hair aside. The professors hadn't been gone long, but by removing two sources of body heat, things had become chilly again. Mercedes had suggested sharing body heat, and from a medical standpoint, he readily agreed. They had both unzipped their jackets then huddled together, their bodies pressed against each other, and it was the most intimate thing he had experienced in years. As he smiled at her, he could imagine far worse ways to die than in the arms of a wonderful woman like this.

He moved his hand away but she grabbed it, pressing it against her cheek as she closed her eyes. "Part of me hopes they never come back." Her eyes shot wide. "Oh, that sounded terrible, didn't it? That's not what I meant."

He laughed. "I know what you meant. And I agree."

"You do?" She pulled her mittens off one hand and placed her cold hand against his face. "What are you going to do when we get out of this?"

He savored the growing warmth of her hand and ran his thumb over her cheek. "Well, first, I'm going to the hottest place I can think of, where I can lie on a beach and soak up the sun."

"That sounds nice. And will there be somebody lying beside you on this beach?"

His thumb ran over her lips. "I'd like there to be."

She smiled as her lips gently kissed his thumb. "I'd like to volunteer."

He smiled. "I was hoping you would."

She closed her eyes and he leaned in. Their lips met and his heart pounded with the excitement that always came with the first kiss. It was something that could never be recaptured, never be relived, never be experienced again unless the relationship about to begin ended in heartbreak. As they held each other tight, forgetting the dangers they still faced, he thanked whatever angel that had flapped their wings to bring them together.

He couldn't imagine a more perfect moment.

Somebody shouted from outside and he stopped. Mercedes continued her assault on his mouth, forcing him to hold up a hand. "I thought I heard something."

She cocked an ear. "I don't hear anything."

"I could have sworn I heard somebody shouting. It could be the professors looking for us."

Mercedes groaned but quickly made herself presentable. He tucked his various layers back into place, her hands having torn at him furiously, and they both giggled as they realized the ridiculousness of it all while they scrambled like teenagers, hoping not to get caught.

"United States Army! Is anyone in there?"

Corkery nearly pissed his pants, the voice immediately outside their tent. "Yes, we're in here!"

"Identify yourselves!"

"I'm Dr. Doug Corkery, ship's doctor of the Antarctica Quest. I'm here with my nurse, Mercedes Garcia!"

"Are you armed?"

"Yes, sir. We have two handguns."

"Are you dressed for the weather conditions?"

"Yes, sir."

"Okay, Doctor, I want you to come out first, unzip the tent, and then ma'am, you come out after him. Leave the weapons behind."

Corkery glanced at Mercedes. "Are you ready?"

She fit her goggles in place and lifted her facemask. "Yes."

He reached out and took her hand. "You know what this means, don't you?"

She shook her head. "What?"

"It means we're saved, and that beach vacation is ours."

She lunged forward and hugged him hard, saying nothing. He embraced her, wrapping his arms completely around her tiny frame. He knew this was probably nothing, that it might last only days, perhaps a few months. When all the stress and emotions of these circumstances were forgotten, they could find they had nothing in common beyond the trauma.

But right here, right now, she was the most important thing in his world.

He gently pushed her away. "Let's go meet our saviors."

She smiled. "Let's go."

He poked his head out. "I'm coming out now!" He crawled out of the cavern that had saved their lives and into the tent. He unzipped the outer flap and was greeted by the muzzles of two rifles. "Don't shoot! Don't shoot!" he said, holding up one hand. "I'm unarmed!"

"Come out all the way, sir."

Corkery crawled through and into the harsh wind. He pushed to his feet and held his hands high. One man kept a weapon trained on him as the other patted him down, though how effective a pat down that could be through all the thick layers of clothing, he couldn't say.

"Now your friend."

Corkery took a knee by the entrance. "Mercedes, it's safe."

She appeared a moment later and he took her hand, helping her to her feet as she too was patted down. A man who seemed to be the leader motioned for one of his men to go inside. Corkery could count six of them now. One of them plunged through the tent then reemerged a few moments later holding up their confiscated handguns. "Nice little cubbyhole they've dug in there, Sergeant Major. Emergency heater, food, and water. Very cozy."

"Are you two injured?" asked the sergeant major.

Corkery shook his head. "No, sir. We're all right."

"Do you think you can tough it out a little while longer?"

"I think so, but isn't the storm supposed to last another couple of days?"

"It is, but we'll have transport out of here once we've figured out what's going on."

"Oh, I can tell you what's going on."

"You can?"

"Yes."

The man pointed. "Get back inside, I'll join you." He turned to the others. "Keep an eye out. We have no idea if we're alone out here."

Expedition Site, Antarctica

A pot of hot coffee poured into both of them had done wonders, especially when combined with the warmth radiating from the heater. Unfortunately, this was the largest structure at the expedition site, and one heater wasn't enough. It merely took the edge off.

Acton finished filling an empty water bottle and twisted the cap in place. He put it on the floor near the door. "I hope nobody thinks that's apple juice."

Laura chuckled. "Let's hope if someone does, it's one of our uninvited Chinese guests." Her head darted away from the window and she pressed against the wall. She held a finger to her lips and Acton took a quick step to his left, hiding behind a large shelving unit as a shadow passed in front of the window.

He eyed his weapon sitting against the opposite wall and cursed. Using hand signals, he indicated for Laura to duck down and move under the window so she'd have a better shot at anyone coming through the door. Where she was positioned right now, she'd have no room to

309

maneuver if they came through fast. She nodded, crouching down and scurrying past the window before popping back up, aiming her assault rifle at the door.

Acton drew his knife and approached the door at a crouch. Someone fumbled with the handle then the door opened. Acton reached forward and grabbed the person by the chest, yanking them inside and tossing them onto the floor. He raised the blade high, ready to plunge it in the person's heart, when he noticed they were unarmed and not wearing the same gear the other hostiles had been wearing.

He tore away their facemask and goggles, revealing a terrified McAlister. His shoulders slumped in relief as he lowered the knife. "It's McAlister," he said, and Laura lowered her weapon, closing the door behind them. He rose then helped McAlister to her feet. "What are you doing? Did you escape?"

She shook her head. "No, they sent me to get some packing materials. Apparently, they're about to find whatever it is they're here for."

"The zupu?"

Her eyes widened. "Yes. How did you know?"

Laura returned to the window. "We interrogated one of them before he died."

McAlister's eyes bulged. "Died?"

Acton nodded. "We've killed three of them so far. How many are there?"

"There were eight of them. They sent four out to look for you. As far as I know, now there are two at the dig site and two here. Oh, and don't forget the Chinese team. They betrayed us. Professor Liu is now in charge."

Acton cursed. "Damn Chinese. They were in on it from the beginning."

Laura shook her head. "I doubt that. If they were, that Special Forces team would've just come in and shot anybody they needed to." She turned to McAlister. "Do any of the Chinese team have weapons?"

McAlister shook her head. "No."

Laura waved her hand. "There you go. If they were really in on it, they'd be armed too. He's probably just taking advantage of the fact they're Chinese, trying to play for better treatment of his own team."

Acton growled. "Well, they'll all die in the end, along with our people."

McAlister gasped. "What do you mean?"

"I mean, as soon as they have the artifact, they intend to kill everyone."

"But they said they'd let us go!"

"If they said you were dead regardless, you'd hardly cooperate. Our prisoner said that the intention is to kill all of you."

"Oh my God, what are we going to do? Ortega is at the site now and Evans is inside the ship. He could have that zupu thing any minute."

"Evans?"

"Yes. He's been amazing. He's been down there the entire time. He refused to switch off with anybody."

Acton's head bobbed with respect. "Way to go Evans. Maybe I misjudged him."

"What are we going to do? They're expecting me back, and they said if anybody tries to escape, they'll kill two of the others."

Laura shook her head. "They're killing everyone anyway. You said there were two here and two at the dig?"

"Yes."

"Where are the two here?"

"I don't know. I didn't see them when I came in. And there's another one still out there, isn't there? You said you killed three, but I know four left."

Laura glanced out the window again then cursed as she dropped to a knee.

"What?"

"Two of them are coming this way and they've got their weapons raised, aimed directly at this building."

"They're looking for me. I should have been out by now."

Laura pointed at McAlister. "Get the stuff you were supposed to get then do whatever they say. Don't worry. We're coming for you." She headed for the rear exit and Acton didn't need to ask why they were leaving without a fight. It was obvious. If these two were smart, one would come in while the other covered. The first sound of an altercation and the partner would open fire on this thinly skinned building.

Killing everyone inside.

They ducked outside the rear door and Acton gently closed it as the front door opened. A man shouted, but through the wind he couldn't hear what was said. McAlister cried out as she responded in a panic, but there were no sounds of violence.

Laura clipped on one of the guide wires leading to their shelter and he did the same while saying a silent prayer that they hadn't just condemned poor McAlister to death.

Outside the Expedition Site, Antarctica

Dawson shook his head, shocked but not surprised. "So, you're telling me that the professors have already killed two of the enemy."

"Yes, sir." Corkery threw up his hands. "I've never seen anything like it. The first one, Professor Acton used an axe on him."

Dawson's eyes bulged slightly. "Holy shit. I think that's a new one even for the Doc. And how long ago did they leave?"

"Not long. Not even half an hour. Maybe fifteen minutes."

"And you're sure there were only eight hostiles."

"Certainly only eight that came in the group I saw. I have no idea if anybody was already there. If they were, they certainly hadn't revealed themselves. And I don't know if anybody came later, but I doubt it in this weather, but then again"—Corkery shrugged, waving a hand at Dawson—"you guys did."

Dawson looked about him. "Okay, it looks like you two are well situated here. We've got your GPS location thanks to the snowmobile. I'll update my people to tell them exactly where you are in relation to that. I can't guarantee when we're coming to actually pull you out. Could be a few hours, worst-case scenario could be a couple of days, but someone will come get you, that I guarantee. Your safest bet is to just stay in here. Keep warm, keep hydrated, keep yourselves fed. Are there any supplies you're short on? We've got some emergency supplies with us."

They both shook their heads. "No, Mercedes brought everything we need, so we should be good. Don't worry about us. Just go save the others. They could be killing the hostages any minute now."

Excavation Site, Antarctica

Evans braced himself against the walls of the corridor leading down the center of the ship. The captain's quarters should be at the far end, and so far, he had only encountered slick surfaces—no obstacles had impeded him yet. He was still taking his time, going far slower than need be, yet what was the point? Whether he retrieved the zupu in ten minutes rather than eight, everyone was still dying before the hour was out.

He stared at the door just ahead of him, the woodwork over the top clearly indicating this was the captain's quarters of a once-proud ship. A thought occurred to him that had him pausing. What would happen if he encountered a wall of ice on the other side of that door? It could take hours if not days to get through it, yet the chances of encountering that wall of ice were next to nothing.

But a fake wall of ice could take even longer.

The question was, if he announced that his way was blocked by ice, would his captors take his word for it, or would they investigate themselves to confirm his story? He got a sense that they wouldn't, but Liu would.

He cursed. "That traitorous bastard."

If the Chinese team wasn't cooperating with the gunmen, he might pull off the subterfuge, but Liu would just send one of his own in to take a look. The lie would be discovered, and they would probably execute him for his treachery. Yet he was going to die anyway. He reached out and yanked open the door revealing the captain's quarters, perfectly preserved for over 200 years. As he played his light over the room, his mouth agape, his head slowly shaking in awe, he couldn't help but wonder what tragedy had befallen this crew. Had anybody survived? He hadn't seen any bodies yet, but if the crew had evacuated, it couldn't have been in an orderly fashion. If the zupu were indeed as important as it appeared to be, it would have been taken with the captain. His eyes narrowed. Perhaps the captain *had* taken it with him and died in the effort.

He stepped into the room, carefully surveying the small space, his light coming to rest on a small chest sitting on a desk in the corner. It had to be it. His heart hammered as he made his way in front of it. He examined the chest, a combination of wood, metal, leather, and gold. He wasn't certain if it was watertight, but from the looks of the cabin, no water had ever entered here. If the zupu was indeed inside, perhaps leaving the case untouched might be best.

Yet he had to know.

He unhooked the latch and lifted the lid then directed his light inside. He wasn't sure what he was looking at. It appeared to be a large stack of folded pages with Chinese lettering. He couldn't be certain if it was the zupu, yet he had to believe it was. He had no idea how brittle the pages might be so he didn't dare reach in to examine it further. He instead closed the lid and relatched it, then sat on the edge of the bunk the captains of this ship once slept in, and debated what to do.

He was convinced their captors were going to kill them all, and every minute he delayed was a minute purchased for their possible rescuers. Yet the math never worked out. Rescue was at a minimum hours away, and there was no way he could buy them that much time. Not without attempting the lie. If it worked, if the lie somehow worked, it could buy them all the time they needed.

He had to take the chance, even if it could mean his life.

Operations Center 2, CIA Headquarters
Langley, Virginia

Leroux stared at the screen, his eyes burning. The monitored communications had revealed far more than anything they could see on the displays. Bravo Team had located the ship's doctor and nurse and they were safe. The more remarkable revelation was that the professors had escaped a mass hostage-taking. The hostiles, part of the Chinese Triad, were searching for a long-lost family heirloom called the zupu. Tong had already explained what a zupu was and its significance to Chinese families that believed in the old ways. Reports that the professors had already taken out two hostiles were impressive and not unexpected when it came to those two, and he wouldn't be surprised if they had cleaned up the entire situation by the time Bravo Team arrived.

Another dot appeared on the map. He rose. "What the hell is that?"

Tong stared at it then attacked her keyboard. "I don't know. It's another GPS transponder."

"Do we have anything in that area?"

She shook her head. "No. All of our people are accounted for. Bravo Team is heading into the expedition site, the doctor and nurse are in their shelter, and the New Zealanders are about to hit the ship. There shouldn't be anybody there."

"Yet there is." He pointed. "And it's moving toward the expedition site."

Child spun in his chair. "Bring up the flight path of the Chinese helicopter."

Leroux turned toward him. "What? Why?"

"Trust me."

Leroux nodded at Tong and she tapped at her keyboard. The flight path the Chinese helicopter had taken was displayed and Leroux smiled slightly. It intersected their new signal. "Well, I'll be damned."

Tong peered at it. "There's no way they're flying in this."

Child shook his head. "Of course not. They never left. They flew out then the chopper landed, dropped them off probably with a bunch of safety gear so they could set up camp for a few days, just in case they got orders from Beijing to take the camp before the weather cleared."

Leroux smiled. "That's one hell of a theory."

"You don't believe me?"

Leroux shook his head. "Oh, I believe you. You just might be running the show one day."

"God help us all!" yelled one of their senior analysts Marc Therrien from the back.

Child spun, a bird thrust high in the air. "You'll all be my bitches!"

Leroux laughed then turned to Tong. "Contact Control. Make sure they know about that signal and our theory on what it is. Last thing we need is a firefight between our guys and them."

Expedition Site, Antarctica

Acton entered their shelter, closing the door behind him. He peered through all the windows to see if anyone had spotted them and saw nothing, the other structures barely visible. "We should be good in here for a few minutes." He grabbed the satellite phone he had left sitting on the table and tried to turn it on. It was dead, likely from the cold. He sat it on top of the heater, still going this entire time, then returned to his position at the window as Laura warmed up.

"It's too bad the bloody radio isn't working."

Acton agreed. "Nothing we can do about that now, but I'd recommend in the future any type of expedition like this have two communications masts in case one fails."

"Agreed. If you remember, I recommended a backup system but the powers that be overruled me due to budgetary concerns."

"We should have offered to pay."

She frowned. "I didn't want anyone thinking I got the job because of my money."

322

"The way you've managed things so far I think should remove any doubt about that." He gestured toward the phone. "Check it out."

She picked it up and tried to turn it on then shook her head, returning it to the heater. "Not yet." She rose. "Well, we can't stick around waiting for it to heat up and possibly still be dead when it does. They still plan to kill our people, and if they're about to find the zupu, we need to act fast." She rubbed her hands together then put her gloves back on. "Your turn."

She replaced him as lookout and he huddled around the heater. The relief was almost instantaneous and he would kill to stand there for the next hour relishing in the warmth, but instead he just ran his hands in front of the elements. He needed his fingers working so he could take the shots that would be needed.

As soon as the tingling went away and the circulation had been restored, he nodded at Laura. "Okay, I'm ready." He zipped up all of his gear as she did the same. He peered out the window and could still see little. He turned to Laura. "So, boss, what do you think?"

"We know there are two in the camp. If they believed McAlister and let her go back to the excavation site, they're probably still here, maybe even inside the supply hut. I think our safest kills are them, but we'll have to be careful. Just because we can't see them doesn't mean they can't see us."

Acton agreed. "Then let's go." He opened the door and stepped outside, his weapon raised as he scanned from left to right. He couldn't see anybody, but that didn't mean they weren't there. He hooked on to the safety line that would take him back to the supply hut as Laura closed the door behind them and hooked on herself.

He turned to her and put his mouth to her ear. "Stay ten feet behind me just in case."

She gave a thumbs-up then he set out, covering the distance as quickly as he could, checking all directions for any sign of the enemy, though focusing mostly on the cable ahead and the storage shed at the far end of it. Something moved just ahead and he stopped, aiming his weapon at the shadowy figure. He had to be careful. It could be McAlister or another member of the team. There was no way to be sure until they got closer.

Then it was gone, probably a phantom created by the storm.

He heard something behind him but he ignored it. It had to be Laura. Suddenly an incredible pain in the back of his head overwhelmed him as he was struck by something. He collapsed in the snow as his world turned dark.

Laura peered through the heavy snow, swearing she had heard something. She raised her weapon but kept her finger off the trigger, not wanting to risk killing her own husband. Something was on the ground just ahead and she gasped, rushing forward. "James! Are you all right?"

She didn't see any obvious signs of trauma, no blood in the snow, yet something had to have happened to him. She rolled him over and he groaned. She breathed a sigh of relief that he was still alive. "Are you all right? What happened?"

He said nothing but her question was answered when the muzzle of a gun pressed into her back.

"Drop your weapon."

Her shoulders slumped and she tossed the gun onto the ground.

"Professors Palmer and Acton, I presume?"

"Yes."

It was a woman's voice, and it had Laura debating whether she should attempt to execute some of her self-defense moves and disarm the woman who foolishly still held the muzzle against her back. If she were wearing a loose shirt, she'd attempt it, but in this heavy gear, she wasn't even certain she could twist around to deflect then grab the gun. She was more likely to get caught up in her layers of clothing and get herself shot in the back.

Their rescue attempt was over.

Dawson and the others rapidly advanced, their M4s held high. Corkery had shown him the jacket confiscated from one of the hostiles and was assured they were all wearing the same outfits. Corkery was also fairly confident, though not 100% certain, that all of the expedition staff were wearing brightly colored jackets. Dawson was more confident of that fact than the inexperienced Corkery.

There was no way anyone on the expedition was wearing any clothing that might blend with their surroundings.

And that was why when he spotted two brightly colored figures, one lying in the snow, the other on their knees, and someone in gray camo holding a weapon on them, he fired twice then rushed forward, still covering his downed target as the rest of the team spread out.

"US Army! Identify yourselves!"

The figure on their knees turned. "BD, is that you?"

He breathed a relieved sigh at Laura's voice and took a knee beside her as he checked to make sure he had a good kill. "Yes, Professor. Are you okay?"

"I am, but something happened to James. I'm not sure what. I didn't see it happen."

Dawson turned. "Niner, take a look."

Niner, their most experienced medic, dropped to his knees beside Acton and began checking him over. The man groaned, which was a good sign. "Hey, Doc, what happened to you?" asked Niner as he gently slapped Acton on the cheek.

Acton swatted Niner's hand away. "Somebody hit me in the head."

"So, you weren't shot?"

"Not unless they did it after they knocked me out."

Laura piped in with an obvious fact. "I think I would've heard a shot."

Acton rubbed the back of his head and winced. "I think I'll be okay." He looked at the now dead figure. "So, you got him?"

"Got her," corrected Laura.

Dawson frowned at the revelation it was a woman. He hated killing women but would never hesitate in situations like this. Having boobs didn't mean you avoided burials.

Acton pushed to his knees, hunching over as he attempted to recover from the assault. "The two that were at the supply hut were definitely men. They're still out there."

Dawson tapped his goggles and pointed out into the storm and his team redirected their attention. He turned to Laura. "Can you confirm eight hostiles?"

"Not visually, but according to a doctor we ran into, he said it was eight people that had left his ship."

"We've confirmed that. And we found them, they're safe."

"Oh, thank God," said Laura, a hand pressed against her heart. "We took out three." She pointed at the woman lying in the snow. "That makes four. Did you take out any others before this?"

Dawson shook his head. "No."

"So, we still have four remaining."

"Any idea where they might be?"

Laura pointed ahead, along the guideline she was still clipped to. "We saw two at a storage shed with one of our people not even fifteen minutes ago, and then two are supposed to be at the excavation site."

Dawson got his bearings and pointed in the general direction. "That way?"

"Yes."

"I haven't seen anybody except you guys. Do you know where your people are?"

"They're using them as slave labor to recover an artifact, so I'm assuming they're all at the excavation site. According to my team member that we just encountered, they're about to recover it, and according to the prisoner we interrogated, once it's recovered, they're killing everyone. We don't have any time to waste."

Dawson pursed his lips for a moment as he stared into the billowing snow. He grabbed the safety line and shook it. "Does one of these lead to the dig site?"

"Yes."

"Then that's where we'll head. We could spend the next hour searching for the two guys that are here in this snow. We know where your people are. They're our top priority. We'll clean up later. Let's go save your people, Professor, before it's too late."

Excavation Site, Antarctica

Evans' worst nightmare had come true. Within moments of him shouting up that he needed equipment to pick through the ice he had found blocking the captain's quarters, Professor Liu had immediately thrown a monkey wrench into the plan.

"I'm coming down to see for myself."

As Liu was lowered, Evans debated what to do. He still had the axe. He could use it to cut the man's line and send him down into the crevasse that ended far below and pretend it was an accident, or he could kill the traitor as soon as he got him inside the ship. The only other alternative was to let him live, discover the lie, and report it.

It was the gamble Evans had been willing to take, but now that he had lost the bet, he found none of his options appealing. He wasn't a killer. He had never even been hunting and preferred to trap insects in his house rather than squash them.

Liu reached the hole and Evans' axe remained holstered. He just couldn't do it. He pulled the man inside and pointed toward the captain's quarters at the far end of the corridor they were in. "Down there."

Liu said nothing, and instead walked up the incline and opened the door, stepping inside the room. Evans held back as Liu remained silent. He reemerged, walked past Evans, then stuck his head out the hole. "Send down two of my people with pickaxes. We've got a lot of work to do."

"Yes, Professor!" shouted someone from above as Evans' jaw dropped.

Liu turned to face him. "Not everything is as it seems, Professor."

Expedition Site, Antarctica

Dawson took point as he rushed toward the storage shed, the safety line rubbing against his winter combat gear. There was no sign of the other two guards, but it would be foolish not to check the shed where they had last been seen. He spotted it just ahead and indicated for Niner and Atlas to take the rear as he and Spock took the front while everyone else covered their sixes.

He yanked open the door and Spock surged forward as Niner and Atlas made entry at the rear. Dawson followed, clearing his arc then reconfirming the rest of the building was empty.

"Clear!" announced Spock, everyone else doing the same.

The four of them huddled around the heater when Niner broke away for a moment, picking something up. He held it out to Atlas. "Apple juice?"

Atlas reached for it then stopped. "That's someone's piss, asshole!"

Niner laughed. "I almost got you. You *never* would have lived that down. It would have been told at your retirement party. Hell, I'd have told it when I gave your eulogy."

Atlas eyeballed him. "What the hell makes you think you're delivering my eulogy?"

"I'm your best friend."

"Best friends don't try to get their friends to drink someone else's piss."

Dawson chuckled. "Niner, put the stranger's piss down. You don't know how good an aim he had. You could be getting that all over your gloves."

Niner shuddered then returned the bottle to where he found it. "So, what now?"

"We've got four hostiles still out there. Two at the dig site. Two presumed to be here. However, there's no way they didn't hear those shots. If I'm two guys stuck in the middle of a storm where I can't see shit, and I hear gunshots where no gunshots should have ever happened, I'm either immediately investigating or I'm getting the hell out of Dodge and joining my buddies at the dig site. The fact we haven't encountered anybody is telling me they bugged out. Besides, we don't have time to waste looking for them."

Niner fit his goggles back in place. "Pirate treasure. Can't wait! Can I search the ship? I promise, I'll share whatever I find."

Atlas turned to Dawson. "Please, BD, let him go play under the ice while I play with the C4."

Dawson chuckled as he fit his goggles in place. "If you both play nice, I'll consider it."

Excavation Site, Antarctica

Evans extended a hand and pulled in one of Liu's people, and was delighted to find it was Min. He pulled down his facemask and smiled at her, but she again slightly shook her head. And that's when he saw the fear in her eyes, evident even through the goggles she wore. He brought her all the way in, and when the second member of Liu's team lowered into position, he understood the fear, for this was no team member at all.

They were wearing the light gray camouflage of their captors.

His bluff had been called.

He reached for his hatchet as he ushered Min behind him. He raised it, prepared to take a swing, when a pistol appeared, aimed directly at him.

"Everybody stand back. And drop that axe, Professor."

Evans' shoulders slumped as the hatchet clattered on the floor. The three of them stepped back as Hongli struggled to get through the hole alone. Evans was tempted to rush forward and overwhelm him, but he

334

was terrified of what the man's comrades might do to the others if their leader were killed.

So he held his ground.

Hongli finally made it inside and pointed his gun directly at Evans. "Where is it?"

"Where is what?"

"The captain's quarters."

Evans pointed down the corridor. Hongli yanked down his facemask and moved his goggles aside. "It's down there, up this *incline?*"

"Yes."

"And you expect me to believe that this room, which is higher than where we're standing, is filled with ice?"

"Yes."

Hongli turned to Liu. "And this is your story as well?"

"Yes."

"Then you must think me a fool."

"Not at all. Just because the ship is at this angle now doesn't mean it always was. And it's not safe here. You should go back to the surface and let my people deal with it. It's just going to be a little more time, that's all. You'll get your zupu, I promise."

Hongli chuckled. "The arrogance is stunning. You academics think you're better than everyone, especially those of you from Beijing. I can tell from your accent, you were probably born and bred there, a faithful member of the Communist Party since the moment you could join, slowly working your way up into a position of prominence in your field.

And you thought you could fool me, the simple commoner from the provinces. Fool! I knew you weren't cooperating with us."

Liu's head sagged into his chest and he clasped his hands in front of him as he stared at the floor. "I beg your forgiveness, sir. What I did, I did in an attempt to save my team. I had hoped by aligning myself with you, you would spare them the dangerous labor. Then I feared once we found the zupu, you would kill us all, so I attempted to trick you into delaying our deaths."

Hongli regarded him for a moment. "Thank you for your honesty, Professor. It's refreshing." He squeezed the trigger twice, both rounds slamming into Liu's chest. The man gasped in shock then collapsed to his knees as Min screamed.

"You bastard!" Evans lunged for the gun but Hongli sidestepped him then pistol-whipped him, sending him to the floor in a blinding pain, rendering him momentarily useless. As he rolled onto his back, Min roared in rage, charging Hongli, and managed to get her hands on his arm. Evans forced himself to his knees and spotted the hatchet nearby as Hongli and Min struggled for the weapon. He crawled along the floor, reaching out for the handle when Min yelped as if something had gone wrong.

As Evans grabbed the hatchet, two shots rang out as he swung. Min collapsed beside him as the axe blade buried itself in Hongli's shin. He roared in agony then two more shots rang out, Evans' body jerking with each impact. An odd warmth flowed over his stomach and chest, and it took him a moment to realize it was his own blood. The axe handle was torn from his hand and he heard another scream as Hongli ripped the blade out of his leg.

Evans felt a hand on his face, and as the life drained from him, he struggled to focus on what was right in front of him the entire time. Min's tears flowed as she suffered beside him, and he reached out with his last ounce of strength and cupped the side of her face as his world went dark.

And he allowed himself to think that in the end, he had finally found the woman he would spend the rest of his life with.

Hongli leaned against the wall, his leg throbbing in agony. Blood was soaking his snowsuit and he had to act quickly. He unzipped Evans' jacket and yanked off the man's belt. He cinched it around his leg, just above the wound, and tightened it with a roar.

"Hongli, are you all right?" shouted his cousin from above.

"No, the bastard hit me with his axe. Just give me a minute." He tested his leg. It didn't feel broken, though it hurt like a mother, but this was almost over. Using the walls to support himself, he slowly made his way to the captain's quarters, and when he finally reached them, gasping for breath, he gripped the handle then opened the door.

This was it.

This was the moment of truth.

The next few minutes could free his family from the centuries of humiliation it had suffered with the loss of their proud history. He stepped inside the quarters and inhaled deeply, disappointed in how plain it smelled. He had hoped to catch a sense of his ancestor Bao, but all he smelled was the cold.

He spotted the chest sitting on a desk nearby and his heart hammered in excitement. He shuffled over to it, undid the latch, and flipped it open. Tears filled his eyes at the sight of the zupu sitting untouched for over two hundred years. This was it. He had done it. He had fulfilled the promise he had made the moment he had heard about the discovery of the ship. But more importantly, he had fulfilled the promise he had made to his eldest brother as he died in his arms.

He would raise the family station so that none of them would ever again be sacrificed on the orders of another clan.

He closed the lid and relatched it, placing a hand on top. When they got home, two centuries of kin would be added. And now with tradition allowing women to be recorded, the first entry he would make would be for the greatest ancestor of them all.

Zheng Yi Sao.

Approaching Excavation Site, Antarctica

Dawson held up a fist. "Anyone else hear that?"

A string of negatives came in over his comms. He could have sworn he heard two gunshots. Two more faint thuds repeated themselves.

"I heard *that*," said Niner.

"I *felt* that," said Atlas. "Are they coming from underground?"

Another two thuds.

Dawson cursed. "If those are gunshots, then they're killing the hostages. Let's move!"

They pressed forward as hard as they could, the wind battling them the entire way, the snow-covered ground swallowing them up with each step. The excavation site wasn't far, only a few hundred yards, but these conditions were making it seem like miles.

"Check left, ten o'clock from the line," snapped Spock over the comms.

Everyone took a knee, the professors without comms following suit, and adjusted their aim to Spock's indicated bearing. Dawson squinted but could see nothing. "What am I looking for?"

"I thought I saw something. I don't know."

"I can barely see shit in this."

"Well, I thought I saw something moving."

"Does anybody else see anything?"

Another round of negatives.

"Okay, Spock, Jimmy, you two hang back and cover our sixes. If you don't see anything in sixty seconds, rejoin us."

"Roger that," replied the two men.

Dawson rose and they continued toward the excavation site. They didn't have time to waste chasing ghosts. Someone shouted ahead and another voice joined in.

Niner came in over the comms. "Umm, BD, remember when I made mention of a party? That sounds a hell of a lot like a celebration to me."

Dawson cursed for Niner was right, and if someone was celebrating, it likely meant the zupu had been found and the hostages were about to die.

Excavation Site, Antarctica

Hongli stood triumphantly on the ice, his leg throbbing from the axe wound, but he didn't care. They had the zupu. The mission had been accomplished. This ordeal was almost over.

"Brother!" shouted his youngest sibling, Lingyun. "Something's happened! Our sister is dead!"

Hongli tensed, beckoning Lingyun closer as the crowd of prisoners made a path. "What's happened?"

"I heard two gunshots. I went to look and I found our sister dead in the snow."

"Did you see who did it?"

Lingyun shook his head. "No, I'm lucky I even found her."

"How long ago was this?"

"Not even ten minutes."

Hongli cursed. It had to be one of the escaped professors. A pit formed in his stomach as an explanation for why none of the search team had returned yet occurred to him. Could they have all been taken out by these professors? He refused to believe that. These were teachers. What did they know of killing? Yet his sister was dead. Somebody had killed her. If it were the professors, then they were armed. If they had fired a gun, it suggested they had either taken it from his sister or they already had one, perhaps taken from one of his other relatives out on the hunt. It meant they both could be armed. Two against four in this brutal climate.

They had to get out of here, and they had to get out of here now.

He gripped his brother's shoulder. "There will be time to mourn later. For now"—he pointed at the chest sitting at his feet—"we have what we came for."

Lingyun's eyes brightened. "You found it? You found the zupu?"

"Yes. Now it's time to finish the job." He raised his weapon, switching to English. "Everybody line up at the edge, backs facing us! It's time for us to leave! We got what we came for!"

He watched as they slowly moved when a stabbing pain shot up through his leg. There was no way he was walking out of here. He grabbed one of the prisoners as they scurried by. "Are you strong?" The man nodded. "Good. Pick another strong man."

The man vehemently shook his head. "Don't make me do that."

"Pick another strong man, or I shoot you and two of your friends."

"I'm strong," said one of the prisoners, stepping forward. "No need for him to choose."

Hongli didn't have time to argue. The professors were out there somewhere with guns. He pointed at the pile of supplies. "Is there a stretcher in there?"

"Yes. We brought a full med kit, including a stretcher."

"Good. Get it."

"Brother!" shouted Lingyun, and Hongli's heart leaped into his throat at the fear the cry contained.

The professors were here.

Dawson surged forward with the others, everyone spread out as they reached the cluster of civilians. There was little point in shouting orders in the howling winds—it could merely trigger the massacre. He grabbed the first person he encountered and shoved them to the ground, holding a finger to his lips. "Stay down," he said, and the man nodded. They continued forward, the six of them including the professors getting everyone they encountered on the ground and out of the line of fire. Somebody shouted something and Dawson cursed.

They had been discovered.

"United States Army! Everyone down!" he shouted, the others repeating it. Those still on their feet spun toward them, confused. Dawson fired a round over their heads. Screams erupted, but it had the desired effect as those in the line of fire dropped.

A shot rang out to his right as Niner engaged a target. Dawson continued forward as quickly as he could when a weapon opened up on full auto. Another shot immediately on his right from Atlas silenced the weapon, but Dawson feared the damage could have already been done.

Laura's team wasn't getting out of this unscathed.

Ortega stood frozen, uncertain as to what to do when a shot rang out. He couldn't tell who had fired it, but it was clear what was happening here. Everyone was being lined up along the crevasse where they would be shot in the backs and their bodies would fall hundreds of feet below the surface, likely never to be recovered. That shot either represented the first of his team being killed, or it was the professors recognizing what was about to happen and engaging.

It meant he had to act now.

More gunfire rang out. This wasn't a single shot. It was somebody firing fully automatic. There was no way the professors would do that in a rescue operation. It was too risky. It had to mean the massacre had begun. He spun to where he thought McAlister was but couldn't make her out in the storm. He had to do something, something to even the odds.

The Chinese bastard in charge of this raised his weapon and Ortega saw red. He rushed toward him, grabbing the rifle at both ends and shoved the wounded man toward the crevasse. The gun fired but Ortega didn't let go. He just roared with rage and fear as he pushed the man responsible for so much pain and so much misery toward the gaping maw in the earth that should have never revealed the history it had hidden.

The gun continued to rattle off rounds as Ortega pushed the bastard the final few feet, and as he reached the edge, he stared the man in his eyes and saw fear. And he smiled, letting go, taking tremendous satisfaction in the scream that quickly faded away.

A shot rang out and he gasped, collapsing forward, toward the edge of the abyss, as his world was overcome with searing pain.

McAlister screamed as Ortega tumbled toward the edge. She rushed toward the man that had killed him when another shot rang out from behind her and the target of her anger dropped into a heap at her feet. She rushed toward where Ortega had fallen, but so many people were on the ground now, she couldn't tell what was going on. Were they dead? Were they alive? Who was who?

She reached the edge and found someone lying prone on the ground, their arm in the crevasse.

"Help me! I don't know how long I can hold him!"

She peered over the edge and gasped. Ortega was hanging in the air, held only by this man's hand. She flipped over onto her back. "We need help over here! Now!"

She rolled back onto her stomach and struggled to reach Ortega's wrist but couldn't. Her arms were too short. She scurried back and instead held the man by the legs as people rushed over, the gunfire having quietened. Suddenly a massive shadow loomed over her and she stared up to see a man in winter combat gear standing over her.

"Excuse me, miss." The voice was impossibly deep.

She scrambled out of the way then he dropped onto his stomach, reached over, and moments later Ortega was out of the crevasse and lying on his back.

The big man turned. "Medic!"

A man half his size rushed over, skidding to a stop on his knees, and he quickly went to work on Ortega's wound.

"Is he going to be all right?"

The big man gently held her back. "I guarantee you this guy's the best medic on the continent. If anybody can save him, he can."

Another man walked over. "Zero-Seven, I need you on perimeter watch just in case we've got the count wrong."

"Who are you people?" she asked.

The small man working on Ortega glanced over his shoulder. "We're the cavalry, ma'am."

The big man grunted. "Yeah, like they had tiny Korean cavalry."

The small man flipped a bird then went back to work as the big man gave her a pat and headed off to execute his orders.

And she cried out in relief as Ortega groaned.

Acton and Laura were swarmed by the expedition team members, hugging them, shaking their hands, slapping them on the back as if they had single-handedly saved them. "You're safe now," said Acton, shaking Baroni's hand. "But keep down, okay? Everybody stay down. We need to secure the scene."

Somebody pointed at one of the Chinese members in their red gear. "You should shoot them too, those traitorous bastards!"

Another person stood. "Yeah, Liu sold us all out! As soon as you guys escaped, he made himself team lead and cooperated with those sonsabitches. They're all in on it!"

Acton surveyed the crowd and saw only four of the suits, all slowly clustering together, their hands slightly raised. If they had indeed betrayed the group, he understood their fear, but this couldn't descend into mob rule.

Laura stepped forward, her hands raised, palm out. "Everybody just calm down. There'll be plenty of time to figure out who's to blame here. And if they're involved, I guarantee you they'll be brought to justice."

"Bullshit! This is Antarctica and they're Chinese. Their government will just take them and probably give them a medal."

"Wait!"

Everybody turned toward the shout but nobody could figure out where it came from.

Niner held up an arm. "That'll be my patient."

Acton and Laura walked over and she gasped, taking a knee when they recognized it was Ortega. Niner continued to work and Ortega reached up, grabbing Laura by the jacket.

"He didn't betray us. He just played along. He had me activate an emergency beacon in his shelter. They're innocent."

Atlas shouted from behind them. "We've got a situation here!"

Dawson spun toward Atlas' warning then rushed toward his position as the others joined him through the swirling snow. He spotted figures moving toward them, all armed, all in winter combat gear. He raised his weapon as did the others. "United States Army! Identify yourselves!" he shouted, but they continued to advance, their weapons trained on him and the others. "Identify yourselves or we will be forced to open fire!"

One of them held up a hand. "I am Major Chen, Chinese People's Liberation Army. We are here on a rescue mission."

Laura rushed past them, her hands up, and she placed herself between the two opposing forces. "Everybody calm down. Major Chen, these are friendlies. All the hostage takers are dead. Please lower your weapons."

Dawson aimed his M4 directly at Chen's chest, the man in his arc.

Laura turned to him. "Please, BD, order your men to lower your weapons. We're all friends here."

Dawson wasn't so sure about that, but he eased up. "Bravo Team, lower your weapons." He kept his at the ready, pointing at a 45-degree angle which would give him enough time to react should it become necessary.

Chen snapped out an order and his men did the same. Everyone was still prepared to fight, but with the weapons lowered, Dawson took a chance. "Stand down, Bravo Team." Dawson slung his M4 and the others did the same, the disengagement move copied by the Chinese a moment later.

Dawson stepped forward. "Professor Palmer, perhaps introductions are in order?"

She smiled but lowered her voice as she leaned in. "And what name will we be using today, Sergeant Major?"

National Science Foundation Chalet

McMurdo Station, Antarctica

Acton sat on a couch in the NSF Chalet. Laura sat beside him as they both stared at his phone. "So, you fools are staying there?" asked Reading, shaking his head at them in the video call.

Acton shrugged. "Well, there's no reason to leave now. We've proven we've got an intact ship and God knows we paid a high enough price for its secrets."

"It's just making the news now, but the details are sketchy. How many are dead?"

"Well, the eight Chinese gang members are all dead. We lost two members of the Chinese expedition and two members of my team," said Laura, her voice cracking.

Acton took over. "Three Russian crewmembers died as well when the New Zealanders took the ship where this all started, plus we have five wounded on our team, one serious."

349

Acton's chest tightened as he thought back on the several hours of hell. This had been different. The kills this time were personal. He had killed a man with an axe. He had shot a man who wasn't attacking, and Laura had done the same. They all deserved to die for what they had done and for what they planned to do, but it didn't make the killings any easier. This would haunt them for a while.

Tommy and Mai poked their faces in front of the camera for a brief moment, waving. "So glad to hear you two are all right," said Mai. "Is there anything we can do?"

Laura laughed. "I think you've all done enough. BD says one of the reasons they were sent in early was because you guys let them know we were involved."

Acton chuckled. "Yeah, that probably scared the shit out of the Pentagon, so they figured they better send in Delta before we made a mess of things."

Laura smiled at him. "Well, that saved hours on the flight time, which saved all of our lives."

The door opened and Corkery entered the room with Mercedes. Acton turned the phone toward himself. "Gotta let you go. But thanks again for all your help, guys. We'll talk to you tomorrow."

Goodbyes were exchanged then Acton ended the call as they both rose. Corkery and Mercedes had assisted in treating the wounded until they could reach McMurdo on the snowcat. Ortega was the most critical, and they were all awaiting word on his surgery.

"How's our patient, Doc?" asked Acton.

"He'll make a full recovery, ironically because I wasn't at my post."

Mercedes chuckled, patting his chest. Acton noted her other hand was firmly gripping the doctor's. Acton decided to have a little fun. "Sooo, what did you two do while we were gone?"

They both blushed. Corkery merely smirked. "A gentleman never tells."

Acton laughed and Laura gave Mercedes a hug. "Told you."

Dawson entered and beckoned them over. "Excuse us," said Laura, and they joined their friend, away from everyone else.

"I just heard the kid's going to be fine?"

Acton nodded. "Apparently so. Full recovery."

"That's good. We got lucky on this one. It could have been far worse."

"It could have been."

"I read your statements. What you two did was incredible."

Neither of them said anything, for it didn't feel like something they should take credit for. Dawson picked up on this and lowered his voice slightly.

"Listen, you two did what you had to do. You were fighting not only to save your own lives, but the lives of dozens of people that you were responsible for. There should be no guilt there. None whatsoever. That being said, the next few weeks are going to be tough. Talk about it. Don't try to hide what you did. Talk among yourselves. Tell your friends what you had to do. Share the pain, share the suffering, share the nightmares, because if you don't, the suffering could go on a lot longer." He put a hand on each of their shoulders. "If you need to talk, I'm available day or night." He smirked. "Assuming I'm in country."

Acton shook the man's hand. "Thanks, BD. That means a lot. And you're right, it'll be tough, but we'll get over it. We all did the right thing. We lost good people, though."

Laura agreed. "Unexpectedly good people."

Acton chuckled. "Yeah, who would have thought our horny Welshman would turn out to be the hero?"

Dawson's eyes narrowed. "Horny Welshman?"

Laura giggled. "We'll explain it to you later. Let's just say within ten minutes of being on the ground, he propositioned me, asking me to join the Three-Hundred Club."

Dawson gave her a look. "Three-Hundred Club? Niner just invited Atlas to join that. What is it?"

Acton roared. "No way! If I tell you, you'll just try to stop it, and I have to see this!"

Guangdong, Qing China
April 20, 1810

Zheng had returned a broken woman. But other than the month-long voyage home, she had no time to mourn her loss. Her empire was in chaos. The infighting among the six fleets had grown during her two-month absence and weakened the entire organization to the point where the authorities gained ground against them. If her brother had survived, perhaps she would have had the heart to fight.

But she didn't.

She had already been questioning the life she had chosen, and had decided before she arrived it was time for a change. The chaos had merely provided her with an opportunity she otherwise wouldn't have had. She struck a deal, and today, that deal was about to be finalized.

"You understand the consequences should you violate the terms?"

She eyed the emperor's representative. "I'm fully aware, as I am the one who set the terms."

"Just to reiterate, should you ever commit a crime again, you shall be executed."

She wagged her finger. "No, my dear. That is not the agreement."

The man stared at her puzzled. "What do you mean? The document clearly states—"

She interrupted him. "The document clearly states that if I commit a crime of piracy or a crime on the seas, then I shall be executed. As long as my feet remain on land and anything I do has no connection to the water, I'm free to do as I please."

The man frowned. "What are you saying?"

She dipped her pen into the ink well and signed her name to the document, the emperor's seal already in place. "It means, my dear, I'm free to do whatever I want, wherever I want, as long as it has no connection to my former life." She pushed the now official document across her desk. "No one said it had to be legal."

Something crashed below and a roar from scores of men erupted followed by laughter. A moment later there was a rap at the door.

"Come!"

The door opened, and Yingshi poked his head inside, his eyes bulging. "Mistress, things are getting a little out of hand. I believe an appearance by you will settle things down."

She gave a curt nod. "I'll be there momentarily."

Yingshi closed the door behind him and the emperor's representative stared at her, his mouth agape. "You own this establishment?"

She smiled. "Obviously. Why else would I insist we meet here at a brothel, one of the most notorious in Guangdong, I might add."

The clearly flustered man stumbled out of his chair and reached forward, grabbing the signed document. "You never had any intention of retiring, did you?"

She smiled at him. "Trust me, my dear, managing a bawdyhouse like this is retirement compared to managing fifty-thousand men and hundreds of vessels as the head of the Guangdong Pirate Confederacy." She rose and smirked at the man. "Before you leave, perhaps you'd enjoy the company of one of my girls. On the house, of course."

The man's eyes bulged and he quickly shook his head. "No, no, that would be…" He didn't finish the sentence as he bolted from the room, followed by her cackling laugh.

This new life was going to be fun.

And definitely something her family wouldn't want recorded in the now lost zupu that lay forever at the bottom of the ocean surrounding the icy continent of Antarctica.

THE END

ACKNOWLEDGMENTS

Zheng Yi Sao was a real person, though with some significant differences from the character I built off her. For those of you in the know, Zheng Yi Sao literally means "Wife of Zheng Yi," or, perhaps, "Mrs. Zheng" with Yi the given name of her husband.

Yes, in real life, she married into the Zheng family, took over her husband's "pirate business" when he died, and made it into what it ultimately became. And a fun (if not disturbing) fact is that Bao was actually the adopted son of her late husband.

They later married.

A little too odd even for me, so I twisted things again to my own ends and made them actual siblings by birth.

And in the "it's a small world" category, I mentioned to my doctor that I'd be writing a book about Antarctica and he revealed he had been there.

As a ship's doctor.

Last minute.

And his predecessor had to deal with a sea lion attack, as described, and yes, a retired vascular surgeon helped save the man's life.

My doctor?

Corkery.

Yes, many of the crazy things you read in these pages are taken from real life.

As usual, there are people to thank. My dad for all the research, Sherrie Menn for some Chinese cultural info, Brent Richards for some weapons info, and, as always, my wife, my daughter, my late mother who will always be an angel on my shoulder as I write, as well as my friends for their continued support, and my fantastic proofreading team!

Also, a special thanks to the following members of my Facebook page who helped name some of the characters: Barbara Garnier, Michael Broughton, Kanja Wilson Weldy, Scott Buck, Andy Brown, John Haynes, and Dee Denton.

To those who have not already done so, please visit my website at www.jrobertkennedy.com, then sign up for the Insider's Club to be notified of new book releases. Your email address will never be shared or sold.

Thank you once again for reading.

Made in United States
Orlando, FL
01 August 2022